RUBY AND THE BLUE SKY

RUBY AND THE BLUE SKY

....

A NOVEL BY

KATHERINE DEWAR

Ruru Press

First published by Ruru Press, 2016

ISBN: 978-0-473-34550-1 (Trade paperback)

Printed and bound on-demand, to reduce environmental impacts, by CreateSpace.

Set in Hattori and Rosarivo.

Ruru Press:
Europe: 13 Hayes Road, Allport CS Suite NZ4001807, Southall, Middlesex, UK, UB2 5NS
NZ: CMB 110, New Lynn RD2, Auckland, Aotearoa 0646

For Nita and Gavin Dewar, who have always told me I could.

"I'm a fountain of blood. In the shape of a girl."

– Björk

God said to them, "Be fruitful and multiply, and fill the earth, and subdue it; and rule over the fish of the sea and over the birds of the sky and over every living thing that moves on the earth."

– Genesis 1:28 (NASB)

Curled here in her chair, where I have always felt safe, I'm going to write it down. I'm going to do it the old school way, with one of Mum's leaky biros. I have to do it now, before any of it starts to heal, while I can still get its shape and sharpness right. When I get to the end, when I reach today, then I'll start the packing up.

The recent stuff is just too raw, even for me, and I've made a fortune from angry confession. I'll get there but I need to work up to it. It's one thing to express yourself in glimpses of the present - snatches of life as it happens, pasted into songs or status updates. This is different. I need to retrace my steps and try to understand. I need to start at the beginning.

I think it kicked off when Stellar skinned up, in the loos, Grammy night, back in Feb. Weed has always made me cocky and delusional. There might have been warning signs earlier - I'd picked scarlet lippy and taken my knitting. Knitting at the Grammys marks you as a rebel, but I was more concerned about finishing the spangly mittens for Clara, Stellar's little girl, than in embellishing my image.

Of course it really began long before that night, in the garden, with Mum lifting me to see the eggs in the blackbird's nest - the start of the best science trick I will ever witness, and the beginning of my awe.

So I had the stoned buzz and the upbringing, but what made it inevitable were the winners thanking God. Everyone did it, except for the Scientologists who hadn't the guts to thank the Aliens. But every other singer, writer and guitarist was on stage by divine intervention, if you believed their acceptance speeches, not because of the hard work, talent and pure bloody luck that had actually got them there. If God was real maybe there would be something in the success of his followers. But he isn't. Christian, Muslim or Jewish, God's a figment of vindictive men's imagination.

As I listened to Britney get her lifetime achievement award and thank God for the 20th time, my irritation spawned the evil idea. It's the kind I dream up all the time but usually stitch into songs or throw away. It was an impulse, a splatter of rebellion, and of course, had The Carnival Owls not won that night, it would have come to nothing.

But we did win - Best Song for *Peanut Heart* - so I found myself on stage with the power of the mic, wearing vintage McQueen and wrestling boots, still clutching my knitting. I should have just said 'thank you', like everybody else. But the hit of winning hadn't landed yet - I was still snarled in cocky and delusional –

so somewhere between the shock of hearing my name over the PA and reaching the stage I decided to do what Grandad had always told me and spoke my mind.

"I want to thank my mum and my music teachers and my band," I said. "I'm not going to thank any God tonight because I don't believe in any. I do believe in the splendour of our tiny planet and if we all spent less time praying or shopping and more time looking out for it, we might actually have a future."

I wasn't any more pissed off and wasted than most other 27 year olds, mouthing off round the world that weekend, except I had the mic and a global feed to millions. Looking back it was a small way to start - just words. But words have always had power, especially when you say the unexpected.

There was this huge silence after I'd spoken, like everyone held their breath. I'd stepped on a landmine of reality in the air kiss fakery of the night. Everything slowed, as if the mine would explode the wedding cake world we hid in, with our mwah-mwah fame, while the flood riots surged in Miami and Perth's whole thirsty population got shipped to New Zealand.

Well I told my truth and nothing exploded. The applause kicked in. Turns out the world is made of guts and carbon, not icing sugar, after all.

I grinned my way back to my seat and into the hugs Stellar and Sam wrapped around me. Even Fate seemed briefly excited and our drummer's the least impressable girl I know.

By the time 'Best Metal Performance' was announced, my cocky was wearing off. I thumbed a text to Sinead but hit delete instead of send. If I was going to warn her, I should have done it before I opened my mouth so she could get a press release out. It was too late. She'd be watching live and composing some sarcastic Glaswegian message for me. I sent Mum a smiley-face then turned off my phone. The speeches and clapping lapped around me as I finished Clara's second mitten, my mind flickering between a growing glee at our win – not bad for a too skinny, too pale girl from Chapel A! – and a grim paranoia I'd blown our bookings for the next six months.

But no one rushed over to tell us we'd never work again. No one snubbed us or pitied me for my inevitable damnation. The music biz applies a glossy Christianity with their mascara, all love thy neighbour and none of the patriarchal fire and brimstone – like they pick the nutty bits out of their muesli and only eat the fruit.

Out on the red carpet for the winners' photos, I made Fate and Sam stand with me while the paps snapped us. Even though technically Best Song is for the writer, it's those two I compose for. Feed your band mates tunes and your friends love and the world keeps turning. So we all posed together with the phony gilded gramophone they'd given me because the real trophy isn't engraved yet. Stellar held my bag and took a scatter of pics of our own.

There was a squall of questions I didn't catch from some indie bloggers, beyond the velvet rope, but security blocked them. I made sure we all smiled for the cute photographer from NME, who always makes me look better than I do, and then the flashbulbs turned from us to grab Kanye getting onto his new, electric Harley.

It was time to party.

Plenty of bands, especially in Britain, bitch about the Grammys. Of course they're industry bollocks and way too mainstream to reward anything experimental, but it's rock and roll not rocket science. I try to see the funny side. Besides I don't ever snub a chance to wear a funky frock.

So, when I'd got the nomination, I had rallied The Carnival Owls. We had decided, over beers at The Adelphi, to tag a swagger of US dates in front of our North West Europe tour. We would hit the awards, then fly straight to Berlin for the gigs we'd already booked for later in Feb, and play our way home to Leeds. Sinead had reckoned we'd get better ticket sales in the States before the Awards, on the back of a nomination than after them, following a loss - you can always count on her for a bit of optimism.

Once we'd set the dates, I nagged Stellar till she agreed to stow Clara with her Dad for the weekend and come as my plus one, found the perfect frock on old-glam.com, said 'yes' to everything Sinead suggested, spent a weekend planting pear trees at Meanwood School with Mum, to offset my flying guilt, packed way too big a bag, and there we were.

We'd played five gigs in five days at a string of 5,000 seater clubs down the West Coast from Seattle to San Fran, stirring up a swarm of hot reviews that buzzed ahead of us so the last three nights sold out. By the time Stellar had escaped her flight and the body scan to meet us in LA I was ready to celebrate, even before we won.

With the cameras done with us, I let the security guy prise the fake trophy off me, bundled up my underskirts and we hopped in the next waiting car.

Maybe the red carpet questions should have alerted me, or the drunken accolades at the after-party, all 'Ruby, I loved what you said,' which annoyed me because, by that time, I was over it - I wanted everyone talking about *Peanut Heart* not my speech - but it was only coming down, back at the hotel, that I really began to understand what I'd done.

Stellar and I were having our little nightcap smoke, wrapped in our duvets on the windowsill of my room at the Ritz on the 19th floor, with all the galaxies of the city spread around, and the hint of morning leaking into the sky. I told her I was sad my speech had got more people talking than winning Best Song. She screwed up her face like we were doing slammers and she'd just bitten the lemon slice.

"Shit no," she said, "What you said up there was way more important than some music award. I've always thought *Dead Heat* was better than *Peanut Heart*, anyway."

"Well thank you!" I told her, passing back the spliff.

"No, I mean there's so much bullshit and it's important it gets challenged, that's all. You just stirred people up saying something new."

"Well, not exactly," I told her. "People have been saying the same thing since the sixties at least. Probably way before."

"Not on stage at the Grammys they haven't, not broadcast live to 30 million."

"But why make a deal about what I believe in and not about the rest of the winners?" I asked her, like some petulant media virgin after a bad interview.

"Well," she said, doing the cross-eyed thing she does when she's inhaling for a serious hit. I waited while she held the smoke in her lungs, till she rolled her eyes right up and exhaled the faint puff of residue. "It rang true. I reckon loads of people find their soul in nature, not in any kind of church. And everyone's fed up with the religious nuts on both sides blowing each other up and taking kids out with them. But most of us just keep it to ourselves. You set it out there. You've got people talking."

My phone bleeped then with a message from Sinead to say we'd leave any media comment till morning. She thought it might die down. I could have told her then she was wrong but I turned my phone off again and took the spliff back from Stellar instead.

When I fought my way to the edge of the bed to answer my wake-up call I turned my phone back on. Sinead had left me a message. I was front page. Everywhere. Maybe, she said, the publicity would outweigh the cancelled jobs. Maybe.

I didn't read anything. I got up and peed and cleaned off last night's face paint, added a little happy lippy then went back to bed. I did a bit of breathing then switched my phone to live-video and started the feed.

"Hey people, how you doing? Had a pretty crazy time last night. Picked up my glitzy gramophone but not everyone rated my speech. I'm guessing what I said's been posted a million times so I won't repeat it. But I do want to know what you think. Was I out of line? Or was it fair enough? Let me know, alright? Be happy."

Two clicks and the stream ran from my site, to the four main vid-channels and to my HeadSpace page. I made tea, never the same with UHT milk, and hugged the cup while the clicks ricocheted through my followers. Twenty minutes later the 'views' had gone ballistic.

When Sinead rang she told me the calls had started at 5am London-time and she'd logged 64 requests for interviews.

"Shit," I said.

"Oh and the Mail's got a red carpet pic of you with pentacles up and down your arms on the front page. 'Pagan's prize spell', it says."

I ask you.

I got Sinead to hold while I ordered more tea, from room service, so it would come in a pot and I'd get some decent milk, and then we made a plan. Actually we made five plans and rejected them all. Too coy or too cowardly. I kept thinking about Mum and her panic the bees are dying because of spraying and the coral reefs are stuffed because the oceans are too hot.

"I just want to stand by what I said," I told her. "That's all."

"You want to be the next eco-celeb, like DiCaprio with his climate schmoozing and his private jet?"

"I don't have a jet."

"Well, that's a start."

"No, I just mean it shouldn't be that big a deal, just saying what I believe in. It's ok for Cruise to believe in Aliens and Madonna to try and sign half Marylebone up to Kaballah, but a bit of good old fashioned planet hugging and I'm a traitor to humanity? What about all those girls who buy my songs. If I back off now who else will make it ok to say 'I worship nature'?"

"Are you sure?"

The trick with any haters is to never, ever let them win. You have to pretend you don't care when they say every track you release is worse than your last and that your voice reminds them of a strangled cow. You have to get out of bed, hide the savage posts on your Headspace page, and make your music anyway.

My hardest to ignore was Nicole, who'd been a best mate since Infants. When she told me I should get a degree, in case the band 'didn't work out', as if music was a loser boyfriend I could ditch for a better prospect, I was flattened for a week. Mum only got me out of my room by telling me the girl was jealous. She said I was rare and lucky, knowing what I loved to do.

"There's a price for everything, Ruby," she had said. "Some people will hate you for your music when they don't have anything they care about that much. Only you can decide if that's a price you're willing to pay." She left me then, to go and fix the trellis for her broad beans. Put like that, it was clear. I unfriended Nicole. These days, I grit the teeth behind my grin and stare the haters down.

"Yes, I'm sure," I told Sinead. "We'll do a press conference. Today. Just put it out there that I don't believe in God but I do believe in the planet and shut the paparazzi up. It'll be a one minute wonder, you'll see."

"And what if it isn't Ruby? What if they don't let it drop?"

"Fuck, don't fuss. It will. Besides, what's the worst that can happen? All publicity is good publicity, right?"

"No," she said, "it isn't. I'll make the conference for four at the Accor. They've just got an award for some green nonsense."

Sinead isn't a greenie. She thinks people have enough worries in their lives, without stressing about climate change and plastic in the ocean.

We did the presser at four and the Accor was brilliant – they gave all the journos organic muffins and Fair Trade coffee. C4 news had me live to air and I blathered about how there was enough wonder in primroses and moonlight for me to never need anything else to believe in. I said we had heaven right here if we'd stop smearing tarmac over it and pumping it full of exhaust fumes.

When I rang Mum from the airport, her face shone out of the screen at me. I asked her to turn away from the light, it was making her glow. She told me the glow was pride. I might be on eggshells with everyone else but at least I'd made Mum happy.

The Owls flew straight to Berlin that night, waving goodbye to Stellar and to Fate's drum kit in the numb white corridor between Arrivals and Transit. Fate was sulking because we wouldn't have a bus in Europe and you can't take drums on a train the way you can a laptop and guitars. Sinead's production team had drums lined up for us at every venue along with the lights and PAs and roadies. We'd spurned her offer of wardrobe and makeup, choreographer and fitness coach, nutritionist and lion tamer, or whatever other entourage members you're meant to drag along once you're a four album, Grammy winning band.

I'd pushed for us to go by train because I needed to get some new songs down and public transport is an endless well of inspiration. Besides, I like travelling with just a rucksack, my two hard cases and a bag of pedals and leads. It reminds me of starting out and catching the train from Leeds to Manchester to play at The Band on the Wall and go dancing. Back then no one knew us and we wanted everyone to stare. Now we wear hats and sunglasses, even in winter. If we're lucky, people think we're just another last season X-Factor band and pay us no attention. I like to people-watch.

Fate said touring with sticks but no skins was like touring naked. I was grouchy from too much weed and not enough sleep so I bit back when I should have shut up. We rehashed the old 'you're jealous cos I'm the singer' routine while we waited for the train into the city and Sam snoozed beneath his fringe, standing propped against the wall, hugging his laptop to his chest, his chin on the case.

When she wasn't deprived of her drums or grumpy from not performing, Fate was generous in every way - height, curves and kindness. She's been the sort of blonde that comes with instructions and polythene gloves since I met her at Sinead's party and dragged her up to Leeds to meet Sam, birthing The Carnival Owls in an all-night session of vodka-fuelled jamming.

She stood, smouldering like a black Valkyrie on the platform, wrapped in the army fatigues she'd cut and stitched tight and her riding boots, like two angry exclamation marks, at the bottom. The shades and shape of the khaki tops and pants changed every day but the style and silhouette stayed the same. Even on stage. Her one concession to performing; two parallel bars of hot pink war paint against each dark cheek bone.

"And you're pissed cos my speech got the media pick up, not *Peanut Heart*," I poked at her, needling her with my own gripe.

"What you say's your own business," she shrugged, tapping the rhythm for *Tenderlust* on her duffel bag with her fingers.

"It's not," I told her, hoping Sam was less asleep than he looked, that he was just staying out of our squabble but would hear what I had to say. "Anything I say is band business. You know it. I know it. I should have checked first. I'm sorry."

"I don't give a fuck," she said. "Religion's just bullshit. You live, you die, that's it." For Fate the world is binary. It's on or it's off. It's black or it's white. It's a beat or it's silence. There isn't any in between. "I just want my sodding drums."

She glared at me with such stormy melodrama it made us both laugh and then the train came and the refreshment car had vodka and by the time we reached Hauptbanhof we were happy again.

I knew the fans had changed as soon as we hit the stage that first night. They looked the same - more colourful girls than there were muso boys - and packed in tight, as usual, right up to the dress circle. We'd sold out weeks before. And they smelled the same - sweet and electrical, a cocktail of booze and adrenalin, perfume and pheromones. But they sounded different. I hadn't heard it in the dressing room, but standing in front of them it was obvious. Even the beat of it was different. The ocean roar of their voices wasn't calling 'Owls', it was calling my name.

Fate kicked us straight into *Peanut Heart*, the way we'd planned, to get it out of the way so it didn't haunt the set. I've always hated the game of keeping your hit to the encore or worse, leaving it out. The whole house was on their feet by the second chorus and the gig just got better from there.

The US dates had limbered us up, fingers, muscles and voices flexed, raggedy changeovers smoothed to relay-team perfection. The tighter you can perform to the plan, the more confident you can be to deviate from it.

Fate builds stone barricades when she drums so Sam and I can charge around between them and still get where we're going. We play our best like that, when we let go, ride each other's endorphin giddiness, and trust the crowd's indulgence to catch us if we fall. Their arms were high in Columbiahalle that night and they would have held us but we didn't stumble.

After the show, the ones that came backstage, they didn't want my autograph. They wanted to talk. They wanted to keep in touch. They wanted to come along.

When Bishop Hamilton summoned me, I was typing his condemnation of the students who had protested the segregated stairway for the campus newsletter. While others might turn away in idleness, the Bishop knows how easily sin starts and strikes it down before it takes a hold. He had written "should the male and female students share there stairway ...". Most of my work as his assistant was easy, like this, fixing 'there' with 'their'. I never graduated from high school but my English teacher was kind and I paid attention to her class. When the Bishop's summons came I made the change quickly and hurried up the long hall to his rooms. Lateness disappoints him.

I knocked and pushed the heavy wood of his door open, a prayer in my heart that the Lord and the Bishop would find a way for me to prove my worthiness. I will have been with The Bishop 12 years this Fall and yet still he keeps me close to him, as if he does not trust me. He has an entire staff here at the College who could easily accomplish the small tasks I do for him. I know in my heart I can do more and yet I must be patient and turn from pride, as my daddy would have said.

The Bishop is a tall man, though not so tall as my daddy. He is standing by the door to the garden and I cross to stand beside him, letting the same late, pale sun wash over me.

He bids me kneel and as I do it takes me down into the shadow. When I look up at him he is alight like an angel, his face tawny and hair golden. He does not look at me.

"You are grown impatient of your time with me, my son," he says. My neck is growing stiff and it is lonely to look at someone when they do not look back so I follow his gaze out of the window while I wait to see if he wants me to reply. Mostly the Bishop prefers to do the talking. "God is testing you with this time," he says, "as he tested Jesus in the desert. Will you weary of the task you are set?"

He moves, sudden as the wind, and takes hold of my face, turning me to look at him. "Will you weary?" he asks again, eyes wide with the question and the air of his words catching in my breath.

"Never Father," I tell him, "I will serve you here until I am old and bent and will never tire of it."

He looks into me for a moment longer, then laughs gently and lets me go.

"I believe you would," he says, crossing to his desk. Seated, he takes the fine ink pen he uses for important mail, the kind he writes by hand and doesn't let me retype, even though his grammar is lacking and writing poor, despite the pen. While he writes he tells me I may not stay. That I must go, leave him and leave America and prove myself in ways more worthy of the Lord.

He comes back to where I kneel and places his hand on my head. His signet ring is hard against my skull. "May God be with you," he says and hands me the slip of paper.

My prayer was answered. I am to go. I have a name in London, the Pastor of our Church there who will receive me. I am to be trained. At last I have a mission sufficient to make my daddy proud.

Some of the new fans did come along, tagging after us to Amsterdam and hanging outside the shows till we relented and put them on the guest list. Twins from Dusseldorf, each with a matching recyclable symbol tattooed on the opposite cheekbone, Francois, a postman from Paris who really should have been called Pierre (I'm a sucker for alliteration), a shiny flouro chick who wanted to be our backing singer and would ambush me from behind corners, belting out our lyrics. I was kinder to her than I should have been because she'd escaped the Crimea before Putin grabbed it and we both loved Pussy Riot. They were into our tunes, the way our fans had always been, but they wanted us to be the soundtrack to their revolution, not just to their lives. Their talk was full of corruption and catastrophe - they ate fear and swigged change at every meal and argued over which corporations were most evil and asked me what I thought.

The after-parties ran longer into the night and in Barcelona I fell asleep on a purple leather couch in the Guru bar, as the plotting of rebellion in broken English ebbed around me.

Michael was there when I woke up, tapping away at his tablet. I watched him for a moment, the bony curves of his face washed slightly blue by his screen, all swoops circling large eyes, like a Gaudi building.

"You're going to have to take control," he said, looking up from his screen. "The talk is getting danger-ous. People are watching."

"Hello," I said, stretching, sliding vertical and clocking Sam and Francois at the bar just a few metres away. Fate and the other eco-groupies, as she'd started calling our flock of followers, seemed to have gone and the barman was disemboweling the till.

"Michael," he told me, leaning over to shake my hand, "Michael Bell." I told him it was nice to meet him but had to wipe my hand on my jeans before I shook be-cause my palm was sticky with what I guessed was the remains of the one last Jägermeister I'd intended to drink.

I got up to leave but he caught my arm, gently, just a touch to make me look at him. "I'm serious," he said. "All this talk, it can get people into trouble. You don't know these people. You don't know who might have sent them. It's dangerous, Ruby, for them and for you."

His accent was English, somewhere solid and central - Derby I learned, later. There was nothing melodramatic in his tone and his face was as calm as his voice but I marked him down as paranoid.

"Thank you, Michael," I said, taking care to sound clear and considered despite my fuggy mouth and urge to pee. "I hope you liked the show."

I found my bag in the cleft of the sofa and Sam spotted me moving, downed the last of his beer and slid some euros over the counter, thanking the barman in slightly slurry Spanish.

"Your music isn't really my thing," said Michael, tucking his tablet into a canvas satchel and lifting a holdall from beside his chair, "but you need me, so I'm here."

"We're a band," I said, "all we need is our gear and somewhere to plug in." I managed a flamboyant shrug and made it over to Sam, who scooped an arm around me, steady as scaffolding.

"You'll see," Michael said, so seriously it made me laugh and he followed Sam, Francois and me into the dregs of the night.

When I made it down to breakfast he nodded at me, all cosy in his cardigan, from behind a teapot and some Spanish newspaper. I swore gently and went to sit with Fate, my back to him, and focused on feeding omelette and toast, gently, to my hangover.

He never told me where he'd spent the night, if he'd couch surfed the city like most of the other tag-alongs or booked somewhere nearby, and he sat in a train carriage apart from our other waifs, cocooned by his headphones and tablet.

"What's with Michael?" I moaned to Fate, as I cast off the last stitches of the purple scarf I'd made Francois. She was painting camouflage stripes of black and green down her fingernails and the hazy chemical smell hung over the table between us.

"Attention seeking?" she said, turning her hand to check her edges. "Fancies you? Nutter maybe? Who cares, they're all the same, running away to join the circus."

"Yeah maybe," I said, but I wasn't sure. I watched the muddy edge of rural Spain stream past the window. I was supposed to be writing - eaves-dropping the crumbs of words that, spliced with a melody, might coalesce into a song or people watching to find a lyric in a life. On the crest of a fallow hill a line of turbines, graceful as swans, turned in the wind. Fate switched to clear polish top coat. Sam's face flickered with the emotional lurches of the latest Halo battle unfolding in his hands.

We were nearing the outskirts of Madrid. Tonight we'd play our last set of the tour and tomorrow head for home. The beginning of the end always makes me melancholy, like the damp drop into autumn, snagged on the cusp between the bright abstraction of playing and travelling every day and the snug reality of rest and home. Underneath the rock star, there's a hibernating human. I wanted to tour for ever. I was missing my mum.

The end of a tour means change, and the end of this tour stank of it. I'd ridden the novelty of the eco-groupies as casually as I'd ridden the trains - scribbled snatches of the twins' chattering duet into my notebook and shagged Francois merrily three times, my limit for groupies or they decide they're boyfriends. (It's a rule I gave myself when we spent a fortnight gigging in pubs across London. I took a gynae nurse and her Rasta-poet boyfriend to bed, separately, on different nights, as I fancied. By the second Sunday they were both plotting to ditch the other for me. I left them at war on the pavement outside the Lexington and fled back to Leeds, in the van, with Fate and Sam.)

Anyway, I'd sashayed my way through those dates in Europe as if it were perfectly normal to have a crew of angry agitators tagging along. They had made Sam and Fate weary with their incessant analysis and arguments and they had distracted me from writing, but they made Michael nervous.

We'd only spoken that once but every time I saw him I remembered what he'd said. And then there were the posts Sinead was deleting before I saw them - gaps and stumbles in the comment threads of our HeadSpace and Witter pages, where something had been said. When I messaged her she dismissed it as cranks and told me to ignore them. I had an idea of some of the themes from the more loosely moderated music forums. My planet Earth speech had run hot, shared and satirised, set to music, reassembled intercut with oil spills and flooded cities, played behind a catwalk show and projected as a word cloud on a wall in San Francisco 30 storeys high.

But beyond the riffing on my content ran a furious barrage of distortion. No one denies God and escapes the wrath of his divided devotees. Most people manage to offend one faith at a time. I'd upset the three biggies all at once in 15 seconds.

I've never been much of one for doing things by halves.

I blame the red hair. When you're blessed with ginger genes from both sides, it's your destiny to be labelled tempestuous at first glance. It's a shame to disappoint. I had enough of that from Dad.

Mum could sense me in overdrive at 50 paces. "Here comes a storm," she'd say when I used to blow in from school, fired up by some raging idea that needed executing right then and there. It's a Hole lyric. The full couplet goes "Here comes a storm in the form of a girl," so I guess it's appropriate. Mum was a late-Eighties teen so, for me as a kid, home was always awash with urgent guitars and the grazed female vocals of Courtney Love and Kristen Hirsch, Tanya Donnelly and Björk.

When things get under my skin I pick at them, so I left Fate to her nails and trundled down the train to Michael.

"It's just a tour," I told him, launching myself into the seat opposite. He took his headphones off and smiled as if I'd popped round for tea exactly on time. He was annoying right from the start.

"Well yes and no," he said. "You're playing, doing your Owls thing, but everyone's really just waiting to see what you'll do next."

"My 'Owls thing' is my life," I told him. "You may not appreciate our sounds but millions do and that's what pays the bills. We're a band, we tour and then we sleep and then we write and then we record and then we tour again. Sometimes there's interviews. Anyone expecting anything else is going to have an epic wait."

He asked me why I was encouraging them and glanced down the train to Francois, the twins and the gaggle of others tagging along today. Of course I denied I had but he just rolled his eyes in their architectural sockets and waited me out.

"They worry about the things that worry me," I told him, leaning back, my legs right out under the far seat, so he wouldn't think I was too caught up in it all. "At home I chew over this stuff with Mum but usually, on tour, it just festers. It's been fun after the shows to talk about how things can be different. That's all." I might even have shrugged.

"So has it given you a plan?"

I laughed. "I'm not after a plan. I've got a tour to finish, a home to go to and an album to make. Besides, mostly they just want to blow things up."

He told me he'd noticed. He told me they were undisciplined and that made them dangerous. He told me flippant talk could get people locked up, and sometimes even killed.

"Yes," I said, "you told me in the bar. And if they're not genuinely, dangerously fanatical then you think someone spooky sent them and we're all being watched by the CIA." It was my turn to eye roll. I should have stayed in my seat and got Fate to paint my nails.

"It's more likely to be Interpol, here," he said, deadpan. "I've checked for bugs when I can but I haven't got the proper gear for it really." He started to laugh but then looked anxious and said we needed an expert.

"You are serious," I said, not a question, more that I'd realised for the first time and needed to make it real. If I'm honest I'd started feeling clammy and slightly frayed.

"You've seen the posts. Religious nuts have carried bombs on their belts since 9/11. But the state security and the corporate machines, they're the stealthy ones, the ones you won't see coming till you're banged up or worse."

I huffed and sighed for a while, as if he was exaggerating, but the clammy fraying feeling meant he was right. I told him, after Madrid, we'd all go home. I spent the rest of the journey through the choked beige suburbs of the city wondering what else I'd thought might happen.

I waited for our eco-groupies on the platform at Madrid, letting Sam and Fate unload our gear. "The tour's over," I said, "After tonight we all go home."

"I have no home," flouro Marina flounced and I thought she might start to sing and turn the whole farewell into some dark, Slavic musical.

Francois actually stuck his lip out so I tied the scarf around his neck and he managed a wounded grin instead. The recyclable twins had both started to cry.

The station was freezing. I wanted a beer and a bath before the show. I wanted to tell them all to just fuck off and leave me alone.

At 16 I would have, but in a band you learn how to bundle outbursts into songs or the crew implodes. Plenty have, but not The Owls. Besides, I had a peace offering - Fate and Sam had agreed everyone could watch the last gig from the wings if it meant they would be safe from haranguing all the way back to Leeds. I told them and hugged them all and said we'd see them backstage.

We soared that night, roaring our way to the end of the set and ripping two encores apart. We were outrageously good. Afterwards, we sent our entourage off into the night, fibbing glibly about the train we were catching in the morning, and took a taxi back to the station. Sinead had booked us the sleeper to Paris.

We drank champagne with croissants in a grimy café at Gare Du Nord and Sam read snippets of the reviews to us, translating the Spanish as he went. The media agreed - we were 'Fantástico!' I think we all slept on the Eurostar and Mum met us at Leeds. I hugged her so long even Sam and Fate looked embarrassed and they're used to it. When you've only got one parent you've got to make the most of them and we'd been away three weeks all up.

Mum insisted in squishing us all in her Honda around our bags and my guitars, like we were teens after a scout hall set, which made us giggly. Finally we'd dropped them home and lugged in my gear and I was here in her house, tucked into her kitchen table with its piles of seed catalogues and wildlife books, newsletters and torn out clippings, hugging my mug of tea, Furball purring away on my lap. I had named the poor mog when I was 8 and already wilful. He was fluffy and round, both more significant than Mum's patient advice that, technically, a fur ball was something slimy he'd cough up one day. By the time he produced his first, the name had stuck.

I watched her cook veggie lasagne for me, and drank her wine and patted my cat and nothing else mattered.

While we ate, I told her about the gigs in the States. She got tearful about my Grammy and the speech and so I made her laugh hamming up the Europe dates, promising her of course I'd used a condom with Francois and showing the pic I'd sneaked of him, pretty and sleeping, on my phone. I glossed past Michael because I couldn't think of anything to say about him that wouldn't worry her. I stayed the night, Furball snoring by my feet, in my old room which doubles these days as a seed potato store.

P astor Brian is younger than I expected. He wears a cream suit the same colour as Momma's best sweater and has grown his prairie grass hair long to the sides and the back, past his collar.

He does not sit forward in his seat, like a man of action, but drapes himself back in his chair as if he is comfortable with the world just the way it is. His smile is slow and he shrugs and waves his arm as if he is lounging on a veranda drinking iced tea with old ladies.

I want to shake him.

I cannot understand how the Bishop trusts such a complacent man to build our church here. I am hungry for my training to begin and yet again I must wait. London has cold fingers she sticks between my ribs.

Mum was out by the time I got up, the next morning, her stereo blasting Belly's *Someone To Die For* to the open doors. Of course, I found her in her garden. The still air offered a tang of spring and a thrush belted out an audacious solo from the lilac. Mum was kneeling in her beekeeper suit on the path between the empty beds, turned away from me, head bent forward. I thought she was doing something with the hive. Only when I got close did I hear the heaving sobs of grief.

I called and ran to her, gathering her up in a bundle of muslin, turning her to me, a handful of bees drifting into the air as she moved. I pulled the hat and veil from her head and held her face into my neck till her crying eased.

"I've tried so hard," she told me, when she could speak. "Planted everything I could think of to keep them healthy. Left them heaps of honey over winter. I even used acid on the bloody mites. But they're dying again Ruby, these," she waved at the two hives under the bare fruit trees, "and the ones out at Alwoodly and Roundhay.

41

I don't know what it is. I don't know what to do. It's like they've given up."

When I'd been little we'd watched The Hitchhikers Guide to the Galaxy together, the Eighties version she'd seen as a kid. Holding her there in the garden, the thrush singing and the scatter of dead bees on the ground around us, I remembered it. I'd cried when the dolphins left, even though it was meant to be funny. Mum's bees weren't leaving for a better planet. I don't think they wanted to leave us at all.

"If we can't save the bees, Ruby, it really is all over."

I knew the story. She'd told me a thousand times how pesticides wreck their nerves. Without bees, no pollination and bye bye crops that become brekkie, lunch or dinner. Mum wasn't really one for conspiracy theories but she did think Monsanto saw bees as competition and wanted them gone.

I didn't know if Monsanto was to blame. I wasn't sure it mattered much. It was just one more strand unravelling in the world, like a knitting disaster on a mammoth scale. The runs spread in every direction, faster than we could catch them. It was too big to think about so I made us tea. To distract her I talked some more about the eco-groupies (except Michael) and remembering there are people everywhere gnawing at the same things cheered her up a bit. She even flickered a small smile at the selfie I'd grabbed with the recyclable twins.

"I am so proud of you Ruby," she said, "Standing up for what's right. So many people are too scared to use their power, but not my girl."

"Mum!" I said, then stopped. I could see her fragility like hairline cracks in the glaze of her skin, as if the faintest jolt would shatter her. There are times when it's a daughter's job to just agree. Later, I'd tell her the speech was just a moment, nothing more, that all the swelling noise about what I'd said would fade into the background hum of gossip column history.

We went back out and swept up the dead bees, burying them where the dahlias grow, in their swathes of sunset colours. Then she plied me with so many jars of pickled veg and jam I had to catch a cab home with my gear and my guitars. There's a limit to what even I can manage on a bus.

Home is Flat 170 on the top floor of Clarence House. When the developers carved up this stretch of crumpled warehouses, between the canal and the River Aire, it was meant to become the Canary Wharf of the North. The GFC back in '08 left the canal side boulevards and concrete boxes they'd built for apartment living, gastro pubs and fashion stores empty. Not even a Gok Wan 'passion for fashion' opening extravaganza could save Leeds Dock. I remember a Rock Couture and @Larocca opened but closed within months. You might think anywhere with such pretentious pre-crash names was bound to fail, but it wasn't just the swanky places that copped it. The whole Dock is like a steel and glass monument to 120% mortgages and a purse-full of unpaid Platinum, with Clarence House an 18-storey tombstone at the far end. People aren't stupid. They know failure can be catching and they stayed away. There's always a drift of tourists, drawn by the Armouries, mooching about with an ice cream, looking at the canal boats, but Leeds people don't come more than once. You only need to see The Tower of London loot once in a lifetime, or maybe twice if your parents take you and then you bring your kids. I went with Stellar and her parents because Mum said it was too militaristic. When Clara's a bit bigger we'll take her too - there's some serious bling besides the swords and shotguns.

Over 10 years later, some of the 1,000 apartments along the wharf have still never been lived in. They're called the Jinxed Pads and not even the squatters will take them. It's weird here but I like it. Besides, the Adelphi pub is only three blocks away and the two best guitar shops in the city are just across the river.

Clarence House was the last tower block to go up in Leeds. It's as if the developers got vertigo and haven't dared risk such heights again. It took me two trips up the lift, which was graciously running, but finally I'd tipped the cabbie and lugged everything inside and found myself properly on my own for the first time since we left for the States. I just left everything in a pile inside the door and went straight to the window, hand to the glass. From there you can see right over Leeds, past the ring road, to the hills. I loved it - the sense of countryside all round our soup bowl of a city and the feeling on my face of the last drops of sunlight squeezed from the day when the clouds clear in the evening. I'm not much of a morning girl so facing the sunrise would be wasted on me. I'm usually up before dusk.

There were hours before sunset - a whole day with no travelling and no gig at the end of it. I stuffed all my clothes in the washer, except the McQueen - not even I'm that cavalier - piled the jars and bottles in the fridge and treated myself to twenty minutes noodling on Elsie, coaxing my old acoustic back into tune after the weeks of neglect.

I found my way to D Minor and experimented with a lament for the bees but it came out trite and I couldn't imagine it consoling Mum. A mass shift to bee-friendly farms and organic gardens might cheer her up but that would be about all. Francois had been into organics too. He'd started to explain the link between healthy organic soil and slowing down climate change but I distracted him with my tongue.

I thrashed Elsie through *Killer Heels* but it didn't help. Songs weren't going to save the bees or stop us washing away in the swollen seas of our consumption.

For years all I'd needed was music - to make it and have it heard. I mean really heard, so you could see you'd touched your finger to someone's heart, by the light in their eyes or the escape in their face as they listened, head back, fist in the air. Or in the street, when they come up to you and mumble how they loved your album and you can hear in their voice they really mean it. It was all I lived for.

But the world is full of forgotten music and faded stars. It's all very well inspiring fans to oblivion with three-minute rock wonders but I wasn't sure I could just keep strumming blithely while Rome, and the rest of our pretty planet, burned.

I've tried doing the 'save the world' stuff in my lyrics. I can't help it. It matters to me so it leaks into songs. People sing along to them while they drive their SUV, eating a Big Mac.

Maybe one in 10,000 might follow the emotional breadcrumbs in the music and understand what you're trying to say but most people don't even get the words right in the two lines of lyrics they think they know.

Music just isn't that great a way to change the world. But it is good for Grandad. I snuggled Elsie into her case, extracted my bike from my bedroom and squeezed the three of us down the lift.

They had him up in the dayroom which I hate because it becomes obvious he's as doolally as the rest of them. When he's in his own room, I can pretend it's just Grandad being eccentric. He grinned when he saw me which is always a relief. Two of the old ladies remembered me too and fluttered frail hands to say hello. Everyone was sitting in a horseshoe of beige vinyl chairs around the huge TV. The room smelt of old skin and regret. I leant Elsie against the wall, well away from the walking frames, and pulled one of the hard plastic visitor seats up next to Grandad. I tried to position myself in the way of the TV but the screen was bigger than me and I could tell he was watching Emmerdale over my shoulder.

I asked him how he'd been and a couple of the other useless questions. It always takes me a few minutes to settle into the two modes of conversation that work for him - reminiscing about things we did together when I was little or getting him to tell me things from when he was young. The here and now just leads to confusion.

I learned a long time ago not to tell him I'd brought Elsie or he takes me literally and thinks I've brought his mum to see him. I never knew her but she played the piano at City Varieties for years and I credit her with the music genes.

We rambled on a bit about what he had for lunch and then the nurse came in. "Will you play for them?" she asked me. Of course I did.

The nurse turned the TV off and I moved my chair to the middle of the room and one of them started clapping before I'd played a note. It was a room of baby boomers so I played to the crowd - *Brown Sugar, Yellow Submarine, Piece Of My Heart, Those Were The Days* then *Imagine*, which always makes me cry. Watery eyes are normal there so no one noticed. Everyone sang along. The tea trolley arrived and I couldn't compete so

I zipped Elsie away and took a cuppa over to Diane and Kaye, the ladies who remembered me, then took Grandad his coffee. They only serve filter and he's been an espresso man since we went to Pizza Express for his 60th so he moaned. I promised him a takeaway next time I went and swore to myself not to forget. He does enough of that for both of us. Just as I was about to leave, he tightened his grip on my hand and focused his stray, blue eyes hard through his glasses into mine.

"I saw you on the telly," he said.

"Was I singing Grandad?" I asked him, assuming he'd caught one of our videos.

"At the Oscars," he said.

"Grammys," I said, gently, but he wasn't listening, chasing his thought fast before it escaped him.

"Fine fucking speech," he said. "Fine fucking speech."

Someone turned the TV back on and I lost him again. Outside it was misting down and I cycled and cried my way home.

As I coasted past Armley Mills, down onto the tow path, my phone chirped. When we played Japan I was inspired by the suited cyclists texting with one hand and holding a brolley in the other. I tried for a while and the grazes taught me I need at least one hand on the handle bars. I managed to fish my phone out of the top pocket of my parka without taking a dive into the canal and found a text from Stellar inviting me for cake. I hadn't had any lunch or seen her since LA, so I swung onto Viaduct Road and up to her Burley Lodge bedsit.

Clara was wearing the mittens I'd made. Stellar told me, over her shoulder while she poured boiling water into the teapot, that she'd worn them day and night. After the first four days she'd had to smuggle them off Clara's hands while she slept to wash and dry them free of marmite and snot.

"They're overdue another soak," she said bringing over our mugs. Clara glared at her and clenched both little fists, like a boxing fairy. It made me laugh so she did it again making more and more aggro expressions and then we got into a 'you're funny' – 'no YOU'RE funny' contest which Clara won spangly hands down because, at 2½, she is even more stubborn than I'll ever be.

"So, how's the post tour come-down?" Stellar asked when we'd got Clara settled in front of *Sarah & Duck*.

"Early days," I told her, wondering if I had the strength to give voice to all the churning in my chest. She poured me more tea and waited. "It's always good to be home and of course I'm itching to get back out there already. I'm used to that see-saw thing, but this time there's this other pull too. Like neither of them is, you know? Enough?"

"Since your speech?"

"Yeah. When we were touring, I could just keep my head down and play. We had a bunch of greenie-fans tagging along, who talked A LOT, but there was still a set every night, so it was normal really. Now I'm home my speech is the one thing Grandad made sense about just now, my HeadSpace page is full of questions about it I haven't answered and even Mum's blasted bees are dying. It's like the whole world is telling me to become some frigging activist. But what I need to do is sit down and write songs, which is all I know, anyway."

I grimaced at her and slurped my tea. We watched Duck caper for a couple of minutes.

"Well, you did stir things up, even if you didn't know what you were doing."

"Or plan it!"

"True. But you said what's in people's heads. You got them talking. That's powerful, babe."

She slid off the sofa and peeked in Clara's nappy, "Poo!"

"Poo!" Clara yelled back gleefully, struggling to her feet just as Stellar scooped her up, magicked a nappy and a towel from nowhere and changed her. While her Mum brandished baby wipes, Clara stole the remote and channel surfed her way from *Sarah & Duck*, through golf, a man selling anti-static dusters, a re-run of *Hollyoaks* and settled on a wildlife show. A lone polar bear walked through the snow, casting its huge head carefully from side to side like Grandad when he's lost his glasses.

"Sorry," Stellar said, bundling the old nappy into a ball with one hand and sitting Clara up with the other. "It's her latest obsession, after dinosaurs."

"Attenborough?" I asked her. I'd heard they'd made a new show with a hologram of him beamed into exotic locations as even he'd finally got too old to travel.

"No, it's the live feed," she said, from the sink. "You know, the last polar bear."

"I didn't know she was on TV," I said as the grief of the thing settled in an icy drift round my lungs. Stellar was putting plates away so I hugged a cushion instead, determined not to cry again. I'd heard it on the radio news just before we flew to the States.

There were meant to be six, enough to keep the species going after the scattering in zoos all succumbed to the mosquito virus two years back. Tear-stained vets had filled our newsfeeds as they injected horse vaccines that proved, in the end, not to work on bears.

They rounded up a last half-dozen when they realised the wild ones the virus hadn't killed really were all drowning. It hadn't looked good from the start. Within days, one of the captured males had fought the other to death. A few months later, he went demented and killed two of his intended mates before they put him down.

The PR spin promised baby bears from frozen sperm but, as we had waited at Manchester Airport, KMAH cut from streaming the Estrons into my ears to tell me another female had died, from an infection. So that left us just Gerda, padding round her geodesic fridge, looking and looking for the way out.

"It takes her 32 hours to go right round," Stellar said. She'd come to stand behind the sofa, her hand on my shoulder. I put my hand up over hers. "I watched her do a full circuit last week, when this one had a fever and neither of us could sleep. When she reaches the bit where there's a rock outcrop, she just turns back and goes around the other way."

There weren't any words in response to that so we both had more cake. Clara started to droop, lulled by Gerda's endless, lonely padding so Stellar tucked her into their bed for a nap. "She'll need her own bed soon," she said, back next to me on the sofa, "and it won't be long before she's asking questions about that bear. Fuck knows what I'll say."

We held hands and watched two of the Dr Who episodes I'd missed while I was gone.

I bought celery and tomato juice at the shop on Swinegate and got home just as the sun started to drop over the Pennines. I made Bloody Mary properly, with Tabasco as well as Worcestershire sauce and settled down in the Egg chair I treated myself to when our first album went Gold. It was that perfect pause between afternoon and evening, the first street lights flickering on in the darkest streets and the hills awash with the day's swansong. I swizzled my celery round and round and my head buzzed with dying bees and snow bear footfalls and Grandad cursing me with praise, like the chorus line in some wretched Gilbert & Sullivan. I knew it was just synchronicity. When you're looking for signs the world gives them to you. Like when your period's a few days late every woman you see is pregnant. They aren't, it's just you notice them.

I chewed on the celery, with its vodka tang, while I looked at the situation from every side, the way Grandad taught me to do when I'm writing a song. You've got to step back and look at all the angles, he'd said. Even when it's personal, you still need perspective to fix it.

From the outside looking in, it felt like it does when I'm improvising on stage. I've done a lot of that at smaller gigs, just for fun, because an idea comes and the crowd are up for it or at private functions, when they'll pay a premium for you to make them something new on the fly. There's a moment, when your fingers are experimenting, when you have to decide to let the notes you just played drop away or build into something new. You've got to trust your gut if they're worthwhile or some derivative dross you half-heard on the radio. This decision was the same - either I was going to let my speech fade away or I was going to build on it, like the first notes in a new song, and see where it took me. You never really know how an improv will go till it's over. The only way to find out is to play it.

Right then, doing something to build on my speech felt easier than telling Mum I wouldn't be doing anything at all.

I rang Sinead before I changed my mind.

"But you don't have to actually do anything yourself, gorgeous. We can just set up a Trust and put some charity types into an office to do whatever you like."

I told her that wasn't enough. "I need to be hands on, somehow" I said. "I want to be. I need something besides gigs and interviews."

She muttered darkly about the building list of interview requests but I pushed us back on track.

"Alrighty!" she sighed. "I'll hook you up with Greenpeace. Or Oxfam. If they did Nicky Hilton they'll do you. There'll be briefings so you don't make a tit of yourself and then they fly you into places when they want TV cameras there." I could hear her fingers summoning phone numbers from her laptop. The whole celeb do-gooder machine would chug into action at her command.

"No. I don't need you to do anything. This isn't band business. This is me. I'll work it out. I just wanted you to know."

The line went quiet and I could imagine her wincing at my foolishness.

"Ok, ok. I'll butt out," she sighed, when she'd been silent long enough to ensure I was squirming. "Just let me know when you stuff up and need rescuing."

She rang off and I threw my cushion at the window. It's less wasteful than hurling TVs.

I swigged my vodka. The ice had melted. Sinead was right. I might well stuff it up. I didn't have a clue what

I was doing, or even where to start. But I knew someone who did.

Michael had made me take his number, just in case. I stood, pressing my forehead into the cold window, the whole twilight city glimmering like a grey glitter ball beneath me. I pressed his name and it rang three times.

"Hello Ruby," he said.

It transpired Michael had followed us up to Leeds. I almost backed out, for fear he really was a psycho, but he wouldn't have been the first I'd met for coffee so I went ahead.

The Gallery Cafe was thick with the smell of roasting and the noise of aspiring artists chewing what they hoped were enough toasted teacakes to earn their pictures a space on the wall. He had another cardigan, a heavy grey knit, shrugged around him and his hair was newly cut back into its tidy pudding bowl. There was something about the way he touched it, self-consciously, when he saw me that made me think he was probably gay. In my work you encounter the full spectrum of sexual and gender orientations, frequently inside the same complex human, and I slide into the bi-zone myself, given the right temptation, so my radar's pretty good. It meant I could cross off one of Fate's speculations - he wasn't after my body. Now I just had to work out what he did want, and if I wanted the same.

There wasn't any small talk. I didn't ask why he came to Leeds. I just told him, straight up, "If *Imagine* didn't change anything, my songs never will. But maybe there is something I can do, with the fame."

"You can," he said. "You can reach people. You can make them care."

We talked about how the organisations he'd worked for had all used climate calculations, percentages and acronyms to fight for change and failed. People can't be brave or make sacrifices for statistics, and drowning animals or children just make them sad.

"If we want people to act, they have to feel powerful, Ruby. They have to be inspired. That's what your speech did; it jolted them awake. Hell it jolted me awake. I'd started to give up. I was even looking at call centre jobs. All those years of petitions and protests, of marches and blockades, they've got us nowhere.

I've been campaigning since I was nine years old and they fucked up the universities. For what?"

I thought about the sudden firestorm of media and the residual heat that still burned online and smouldered in the queue of interview requests. It seemed strange that saying none of this plastic fantastic wonderland we've wrapped over the world would be here if it wasn't for nature, could resonate like it had. It was such a basic truth. But sometimes songs surprise you too.

His taut face twitched like he'd made a decision. "I'd lain in bed all morning, skipped work and not even rung in sick because I couldn't face another day of beating my head against a colossal brick wall of apathy and Coalition corruption. Then the video of your speech popped up online. You reminded me we can tap into something bigger; people lived in awe of nature for thousands of years, all around the world. We can use that. It's why I quit the Foundation and came to find you."

So, if Michael was a psycho, he suffered the same delusions I did.

I laughed and told him if I had my way we'd all be shouting from the rooftops how outrageously amazing nature is. I didn't mean going 'wow' quietly in the safe dark of the cinema, with some documentary. And I didn't mean moaning about the bloody temper tantrum weather. I meant celebrating the glory of the sun and the beauty of the moon, the intricacy of fertility and the utility of death and decay. Nature rocks and our disrespect was backfiring badly.

We knew, then, we'd found what we wanted to do, both of us.

Reawaken awe.

I almost high-fived him, a new habit I'd caught from our roadies in the States. Clara had liked it but I suspected Michael would think it inane.

When he stood to go, I could see the poster for Earth Hour on the noticeboard behind him - a blue and green disc on a black background surrounded by the woeful headline 'Power-off for the planet'.

As someone who likes to play loud, I find electrical deprivation depressing. I left before it could bring me down.

I am to convince them I have been here some time and so I need to blunt my accent. When Pastor Brian's voice coach is not working with me, I watch British documentaries of strikes and protests, repeating the voice-overs to shape the vowels in my mouth. It is not so hard. The speed with which they speak is my main failing. I have to listen in double-time and rush my words to keep pace with them.

I have been here a little under a week now and have decided to maintain my journal as an act of faith; an account of my devotion that may prove a comfort to me in old age. Our work needs discretion and so I will keep no paper proof. Just these private notes online, locked secret by a password I will always remember.

I have a room here in a house across the way from the Chapel. They have only a small congregation. A dozen souls. Pastor Brian says the British folk have mostly lost the way of the Lord and those that have kept it commonly follow the Anglican or Catholic preachings. But our Church is here now and we are growing. In these times of sin they will find their way back to the Lord through us.

My room itself is fine; a narrow bed with an eiderdown instead of blankets and an old fashioned closet. There is a table beneath a small window with a view into a corner of the next roof, grey tiles under the grey sky and sometimes a pigeon, grey with purple, will land there while I am reading the Book.

We met at the cafe again the next morning. I'd offered to help Mum plant trees at Bramley Primary but when I rang to ask if I could meet a friend, instead, to plot the follow up to my speech, she banned me from joining her. I arrived before Michael and took the same table. The poster was still there, scolding me with woe. I swapped to where Michael had sat so I didn't have to look at it.

I started talking before he'd even got his coat off. I told him he'd been right about our eco-groupies - they were like 15 year old punks, all noise and no direction, firing angry rebellion - breaking windows because they didn't know any other type of power. I went through that stage too. Sam and I had a pop-punk two piece in the fourth form in which, largely, I swore and threw my mic stand off the stage. But I've learned there are ways of performing much better at drawing people in - most of us prefer fun and dancing to spit and flying equipment.

"So whatever we do," I said, "it has to be inspiring and it has to be fun. And no blowing anything up."

He was in an effervescent mood that morning and could barely get himself out of his coat or his tablet out of his bag for the fizz of his heated agreement. "But, you know, nature does do some good explosions," he said, when finally he was settled and we'd ordered. "Volcanoes and super novas are pretty up there in the awe ratings."

And there it was.

The hi-hat hit of inspiration, delivered by Michael like chocolate cake with sparklers.

"That's it," I said. "That's what I want us to do." I tried to get up to show him but my legs were tangled round the chair so it took me two goes. "This!" I pointed at the poster. The waitress came with our drinks but looked anxious I was leaving and I didn't want her vanishing with my tea so I sat down again quick, but to the side, so he could still see.

"Earth Hour. When they try and get everyone to turn their power off. We need to make it about wonder, not self-denial. Let's make it about seeing the stars. Pitch it like a huge global lightshow. Just think what it'd be like to stand in the middle of Briggate, or Times Square, and look up and see the constellations."

His smile started on the inside and brimmed out of his face like I'd lit him up.

"It could work..." he said, nodding.

He turned on his tablet and, before I'd even started on my tea, asked me if I knew how to use something called a Gant Chart and sighed when I looked blank.

Apparently a spreadsheet would have to do. He pushed the screen across the table to show me the template he'd created. There were dozens of rows of empty and colour coded columns in it, ready for us enter in the details as we fleshed out the plans. I pushed his tablet back over to him and said I'd never needed a spreadsheet to organise a party before.

"I have," he said and got me to tell him how I imagined it would be. His fingers flickered over the screen and occasionally he'd raise a sceptical eyebrow but mostly he just grunted in approval.

In the next two weeks we made my imagination and Michael's spreadsheet real.

We started with two phone calls - Michael rang the WWF guy and I rang Sinead. Michael had been on a climate protest in Bangladesh with the WWF guy so his call went better than mine. I pay Sinead a whack of my sales to make The Carnival Owls more famous which she does so successfully she thinks it gives her license to bully me. It took me twenty minutes of cajoling my way through her sarcasm about Bono and Geldolf and other old musos who wanted to save the world before she agreed to send a press release, and only then on condition I played.

Michael loved the idea and once I got over my niggle that playing put me too much at the centre of the night it triggered a whole bunch of new ideas - I am a performer after all.

From that first call, Michael kept WWF and the other campaign groups posted, seeking their trust we weren't taking over their show, just adding some rock and roll to their hair-shirt denial, though he didn't put it quite like that.

We turned the whole thing on its head. Instead of sitting at home in the dark on your own, feeling morbid about the world while you counted down the seconds till the power came back on, we asked people to organise Star Parties - to invite everyone in their street to turn the power off and go out stargazing.

Sinead did her duty with the media and unleashed the floodgates of interview requests. I quoted my Grammy speech endlessly and deflected dozens of reporters from accusing me of witchcraft. I tried telling the first few that witches had been old women with serious skills whose nearest patriarch resented their power. Sinead texted to say 'fucking stay on message'. She had a point.

I did a webcast and we put poster graphics on my HeadSpace page saying 'Don't spoil the party'. The downloads started and the 'shares' spread faster than last summer's fires had swept California, topping 12 million. People posted us selfies as they pasted the copies they'd printed in the lifts of tower blocks from San Fran to Shanghai.

We recut my Grammy speech onto NASA footage of nebulas and posted Star Parties into every event listing of every city we could manage and messaged my fans to do the same. The recyclable twins emailed to tell me they'd got Dusseldorf Council to not spoil the party - they were turning off office lights and street lights and asking all their ratepayers to do the same. It was genius. No one gets elected if they're seen to kill the fun.

I roped Stellar in and we pulled an all-nighter asking the mayors of the biggest cities to follow suit. Clara found us pale and giggly on the sofa at dawn with a promise from Paris.

Mum shooed me off helping to get her seed trays started, like I'd sworn I would, and Fate and Sam indulged me like they did when I took up the sax for a month after our South American tour. Sam even offered to guitar-tech for me but seeing as I had to go acoustic I turned him down.

Freed to be relentless, I posted Star Party promos to the HeadSpace walls of every muso I'd ever met and asked them to do the same. I did interviews about what I'd said in other interviews and in the gaps between I got Stellar to ask me questions and we filmed us on my phone and posted that instead. In the end even Leeds Council said yes.

We got City Square closed to cars and Northern Guitars built me a stage by the Black Prince's pedestal and as dark fell people started arriving. It was one of those spring nights where you can smell summer is coming - the afternoon's drizzle had faded with the last shoppers and the sky was mottled with clouds uplit from the city lights. At 10 seconds to 8.30pm Stellar started filming on my phone, feeding live to my HeadSpace page and I hopped on the mic and started the whole square of us counting down. At three I yelled 'Lights Out - Party!' in my best rock star style. Michael cut the juice to the stage and everybody yahooed and killed their torches and with a blink of surprise all the city lights around us, from the array of lit windows in the Queens Hotel, to the fairy lights round the dome of The Black Prince pub and the flouro tubes of the train station, went dark. Then everything went quiet too and we all looked up.

It turns out nature likes to party.

Between the charcoal smudges of the clouds, catching the hint of the distant moon, a million stars stretched away into an ancient forever. I like to think I heard a collective gasp but it might have been me. We'd persuaded an astronomer from the Uni to come down and she played Chinese-whisper stargazing, starting with Signus and Aries we could all see with our naked eyes, getting everyone who could hear her to tell the people behind them. The crowd I could make out nearest me was soon filled with pointing arms and bared throats, faces to the sky. Then she explained Leo for the people who had binoculars and all I could hear as I watched infinity sprawl behind the clouds were the murmured names of star systems, over and over again - a litany.

Michael tugged my sleeve and I groped for Elsie in the dark. Around me the shadow people we had all become were turned to each other, whispering, laughing, pointing. Away in the crowd a small child made the plaintive bleat I'd learned from Clara meant tears brewing. Michael nodded. It was time for a lullaby. I picked the first bars of *Twinkle Twinkle* from the strings into a sudden silence, then people laughed so I started again strumming the chords heftily and fast, as loud as I could play unplugged, throwing my late night whisky voice at the words and snagging everyone I could see into singing or shouting or chanting along with me. Across at the train station the lights came back on. It was over. We'd planned I'd say a few words on the mic but I know how to read a crowd and that night less was more. I shook my head at Michael and we packed away the gear.

Back at my flat, Leeds lit up again below us like a fallen Christmas tree, Michael scrolled through the world on his tablet. It was working. Not just here, where we'd been live in the midst of it, but the biggest Earth Hour ever, right across Europe. WWF had been sharing satellite shots of the fairy lights of the continent vanishing to black. They had a carbon counter running alongside it to show the number of hours by which we'd postponed a 3-degrees warmer world. I thought it missed the mood somewhat. HeadSpace was full of shared acoustic sets and celebration in the dark from towns and cities everywhere. I winced at the frantic posting in bright and power-hungry pixels then joined them. I plugged my practice amp in, turned the room lights off and got Michael to hold my phone and Stellar to shine my bike light on my face. I stood in front of the window with my Silver Sparkle Les Paul while he recorded.

"Did you see the endless sprawling glory of the stars, people, and thank the planet for such a fantastic view? How much splendour do you need?" I asked, then played an electro-punked up version of Twinkle Twinkle, snarling to the max. It didn't have a fraction of the potency of the version we'd all made, live in the dark of City Square, but it would have to do. I'd cherish the recording Stellar had captured in the darkness but pictures snag more shares.

We sent the video out into the world and as the night rolled on, the planet continued to do her bit, laying on a clear night down the East of the States and Canada. Not everywhere had wanted to party - among the squadrons of angry emails I'd seen ones from the Mayors of Knoxville and Charleston - but it seemed I'd reached enough fans in enough homes to make it work.

"Just think ..." Michael said, opening Stellar's beer and passing it to her.

"Dangerous behaviour, that thinking," Stellar chipped in, winking at me as she sucked on her bottle, glib and giddy from her first night out since the Grammys.

"No seriously," Michael leant forward in his chair, setting his bottle down. He rested his elbows on his knees and held his hands out as if he could catch us in them. "Just think what we did Ruby. We changed people's lives, for just a few seconds. Not to mention the mega-watts of power. Because of us, because of you, things changed."

I could sense what was coming, like birds are supposed to know about earthquakes before they arrive. Everything went slow, as if time signalled 'significant moment ahead'. I leaned back, my feet up, took a swig of my Hellfire and watched him. I'd set an old Joan Jett album of Mum's to play on the turntable. *Activity Grrrl* leached out of the speakers and set the hairs on the back of my neck on end, literally, one by one, like my hackles were rising.

"If you wanted to, you could change the world, Ruby. You've got the power and enough money to do something really big."

I laughed and said I thought we were into cutting power and took another, longer swig. Michael's face twisted like I'd hit him and Stellar suddenly got interested in her fingernails.

I got up from my chair and took my beer to the window, putting my hand against the cold glass. Sinead had managed as much of the angry mail and threatening posts as she could but had rung that afternoon to tell me, frankly, it had gone beyond cranky and into police-calling scary. Talk back radio had been mild by comparison. If you took the posts literally, I had been condemned to purgatory in the names of Allah and Yehovah and of Jesus Christ. I wasn't sure whether to be afraid or flattered I'd prompted calls for both a Fatwah and for excommunication. It wasn't the fictitious higher powers that bothered me but the anger and knowing the people who felt it were out there in churches and synagogues and mosques, maybe even here in Leeds.

It was frightening but it meant I knew Michael was right. We were onto something. For every angry Believer there were thousands of other people who'd rejected the same religions - or at least followed them kindly, with a pinch of salt. For every zealot there were many, many more of us who just wanted to live and let live. But we were silent. We had been too silent.

We'd respected different beliefs to the point where women worshipping everywhere were hidden under scarves and hats, whether they wanted to be or not. Even non-religious, white girls from Bradford were being heckled off the streets if they walked around by themselves after dark. I'd always felt they were connected, our loss of awe in the planet and its replacement with Big Religion. Our loss of wonder at women – how we swell and birth life into the world, again and again – and this faith in some chaste, male God.

Everywhere we relegate the awesome abundance of lust, fertility and birth to the bottom division. Sex is unclean, periods a curse and solo mums a burden or stoneable offenders, depending on where you happen to live.

I've never forgotten the fuss when I was 10, anticipating my first bra, and Janet Jackson's boob popped out at the Superbowl.

I don't think it's a coincidence that the harsher the heat waves and the fiercer the flooding and the more afraid we become, the more women are tied down.

Mum's always said, when people get scared, they cling to what they know. It seems, wherever you are in the world, there's always some old guy who'll preach fifties family values or fundamentalism. The corporates and the media love it. It lets them ignore the epic failure of the gleaming money-go-round way they run the world.

But it's not their world. She belongs to all of us and she's the only one we've got. No matter how many millionaires plot missions to Mars we're not leaving any time soon. If I could make a difference with a Star Party, one night of the year, maybe I shouldn't stop at that.

"I don't know," I said. "That was fun. We could make it even better, next year, with more build up. You could make a bigger spreadsheet!"

"Do you really think we can wait another year?" he asked.

Stellar fiddled with her phone then swore and scrambled out of the sofa, saving me from an answer. It was midnight and the babysitter would turn into a pumpkin any moment. I hugged her and Michael, dutifully, reluctantly got to his feet and left with her to flag down a taxi. I swapped Joan for Savages and opened another beer.

By morning my *Twinkle Twinkle* was scaling the free-download charts. I flicked through the stats narcissistically, still sleep-encrusted in a snowdrift of duvet, then rang Mum. She'd been itching to call but I'd scorched her so badly with my teenage tantrums at being woken she no longer risks it.

"You are ... fabulous," she said, when I'd finished the gloating you can only get away with to your mum. Her pause told me her approval was bigger than words and I basked in it like Furball in a patch of winter sun.

Then she asked me if I'd seen the news. Over 50 tornadoes had blown up overnight, raging from Missouri to Michigan - the most violent they'd ever seen, scattering cars like sugar and smashing buildings. Over 1,000 were already thought to have died as the twisters span trailer park residents from their beds into the wide, uncaring skies. I flicked my phone to CBS and watched the storms from the safety of my own duvet.

"I can't tell you how proud I am you're doing something, Ruby." I wasn't sure if it was the speakers in my phone making her voice wobbly. "It's getting worse so much faster than they said and it's always the poorest who cop it the most." The camera panned across huddles of families, clutching the remains of the little they'd ever had. A young black guy in a hoodie and basketball shorts approached one of the groups, carrying a small blonde girl in his arms. I couldn't tell if she was dead or just unconscious. I blanked the screen, cut the speakers and put the phone back to my ear. "You're a hero Ruby," she said, her voice still wobbly, and hung up.

I lay in bed and swore for a while till the need for tea got the better of me. I turned the TV on while the kettle boiled. The first three channels showed the tornadoes - the fourth, an infomercial for a plastic device called a Slap-Chop which you hit repeatedly to dice vegetables. I did think about hurling the screen through my window, wondering what size hole it would make in the glass and how far the pieces would travel when they hit the ground 60m down. There was way too much broken stuff in the tornado images so I threw all my cushions around the room and yelled 'fuck' a lot instead. Then I drank my tea and spent a long time in silence, looking at the bottom of my mug as if it held the answers. There is definitely a dark side to parental faith in our capabilities. When I ran out of excuses to myself I took three breaths to my toes and rang Michael.

"So, what's next?" I asked.

By the end of the following week I was funding the renovation of a three-storey red brick, gothic ramble, all high windows and scuffed parquet floors with pigeons nesting in the ceiling. Just ten minutes' walk - or three minutes' cycle - from my flat, it was crammed, ironically, into Church Row, the tiny lane behind St Peter's.

The first time we visited, Michael pried the hard-board away from the door frame to get us in. The paint had peeled from the walls, dragging chunks of plaster down with it. The hall smelt of forgotten hope and damp socks. He waved me ahead, to the room on the left. The door handle was crumbed in a thin grime. As we moved through the ground floor, the building complained to itself, like Grandad, when I wake him up and he's trying to establish where he is. Pale grey light seeped through the windows, muted by neglect.

"It's been condemned for ages, but your Council don't want to pay to demolish it."

"So who owns it?"

Michael shrugged. He thought maybe the Council, maybe the church at one time. Social Services had moved out in the 90s, followed by a string of bankrupt ventures in storage and finance and property.

"Well it's got lots of room," I said, floundering for something positive to say. I was still adjusting to the idea that there would be some kind of 'us', beyond Michael and me, tapping away in a café, and roping in Stellar while Clara napped.

"We'll only need a small team, half a dozen, to start with. But top people, the best we can find. People who can help us make this huge."

"Rent should be cheap enough," I said, peeling away a bedraggled flap of wallpaper, the plaster crumbling away behind it.

"We won't be able to rent. The place hasn't met any kind of standards for a very long time. That's the point. We'll squat."

"But I can afford to rent. And something a hell of a lot better than this." I'm all for retro but the place was decrepit and smelly, heavy with old graft, not bright with new beginnings.

"It's better we don't Ruby, that way we stay beneath the radar, as underground as possible."

I laughed. It felt like a long time since anything I did had been discreet, let alone underground.

"Not you," of course, he said, peering up the staircase, testing the first step as if trying to decide if he should risk the treads, "but the group. You're big enough to fly public, too popular to bring down. But the rest of us?" He shrugged, and abandoned the stairs. "Easy pickings."

I remembered the hate posts and didn't feel like laughing any more.

"We'd better get a builder in to check those stairs," he said.

I nodded and followed him back to the front door. April had started stroppy and the wind banged the ply board on the frame where he'd pulled it loose.

"We won't be doing anything illegal," I said as he held the board aside so I could step out.

"No," he said, fishing his hammer out of his bag, then looked at me, "we won't. But we can expect to be watched. It doesn't take much for the Coalition to start surveillance or the Fundies to get up a picket. We don't need to make life easy for them, do we? It's best if we keep the paper trail from you to us to a minimum. If we keep things strictly cash it leaves the lawyers guessing and makes it easier to skip out of the way if we need to. Just because its legal doesn't mean they won't try and stop us."

He turned and banged three nails in. I watched his back. The wind tugged at his shirt.

"You really are quite paranoid, aren't you?"

"Jail will do that to a boy," he said, turning and flashing a mask-smile at me. "We squat here and pay cash for anything we have to buy. We keep as much off the grid as we can." He reached into the bag again and handed me a phone.

"What do I need this for?" I called after him, following him down the steps and past the church. At my height I don't have to trot after people very often but he was pretty keen to get away.

"It's got some nice privacy wizardry built in," he said, as I caught up with him. "I'll get them for all the team and we'll do some things with the 'Net you don't need to know about. Don't pull that face. ISP jumping isn't illegal, yet, and it helps."

I caught his arm to stop him.

"I understand," I said. "I get why we have to do things this way. But if it's being done in my name, I do need to know." Michael squinted his eyes in the way I was starting to recognise as his calculating look, when he's weighing the odds and not loving the balance. "Promise me," I yanked his sleeve again and stared right into his calculation, as if I could sway the outcome if I looked hard enough.

"OK," he said. "We'll do ops stuff my way but I'll keep you posted. I promise."

"Good," I told him and patted the patch on his shirt-sleeve I'd been gripping and kissed his cheek, to show, wherever we'd just been, we were home again safely and then I took the dull little phone from him and slid it into my jeans next to my limited edition iTouch 8. The two together made my pocket bulge.

I left him at the Corn Exchange and went to Boar Lane and took out the grand maximum the cash machine would release to me in a day, and took it back to him.

I may have underestimated Pastor Brian. His shrugs and smiles are slow as a hot afternoon but his mind is like a frosty morning. He has set the first of my trials. To buy a tie at a store called Selfridges and pass as English. My accent must provoke no enquiry about my origins and I will wear a microphone so the Pastor can judge me.

When I was small, after my daddy had finished at the factory, we would watch the Simpsons and then, in the morning, we'd pretend he was Homer and I was Bart and say the gags to each other when he drove me to school. He used to say I was as good an impersonator as Jimmy Fallon, but still it will take me time to learn.

I go to the café on Charing Cross Road, not the Starbucks full of tourists, but Ronnies where the locals drink tea in big white mugs and order plates of fries, wide as fingers and damp with fat. There is a London sound to the voices, nasal and clipped like New Yorkers but slower, and with a falling 'oo' in place of a lifting 'oy'. As many again don't speak like that. The younger ones in hoodies, negroes and whites, talk and grip hands like they are in Detroit. There are harried men in thin suits gabbling rough, wide words into cell phones and a pair of girls in low cut tops and baseball caps the owner always has to tell to stub out their cigarettes. I asked him about them once, pretending I thought they were attractive to me. He winked and laughed and asked if I meant the Glaswegians. They talk so fast, mangling all the sounds, I thought they might have been from another country.

So my challenge is not just to make myself an English accent but to find one I can stick to and learn, all the way through.

They use it to judge each other. I've heard and watched them decide how they will be by listening to how someone sounds. I noticed it first sitting in the armchairs they provide in the banks. You can stay and listen for hours if you flick through their brochures from time to time. I've watched couples the same age as each other, wearing the same kind of clothes, approach the service desk and the same clerk react differently based just on how each pair sound.

Their accents signal where they're from, like ours, but carry with them extra messages coded from history. At home someone might think you're speedy if you're a New Yorker, slick if you're a West Coaster or slow but steady from the South. Here they'll sense what you do for a job, what your daddy did and how much money your family had a hundred years ago. Not just money, but status. England is full of people from Ivy League families who haven't been wealthy in generations but still get special treatment. Pastor Brian explained it as class. Not 'class' as in a polished high performer, but class as destiny.

I have to find a voice that will brand me in place and society and fit the story of the life I invent, where my American roots can seem buried beyond suspicion.

When the café emptied around me I dialled up the day's news shows on my laptop and played them again and again, mouthing the words silently to myself and hearing the accents in my head.

The news showed twisters but the whole wide state of Arkansas lies between them and my momma and I do not think the Lord will punish her sins that way. I rang on the way back to my room in any case. Her voice sounded anxious when she answered. I would have liked to hear her say a little more before I hung up.

We got in a builder, a mate of Stellar's. She sucked her teeth and scowled at Michael and fixed the stairs. On the first floor, we found the interior walls had all been knocked out. The space was high and wide and full of light, once we wiped the windows clean. The second stairs led to the attics, four small rooms, tucked under the eaves.

"It'll do," Michael nodded, coming down, his head bobbing as the plans fermented inside. "We'll put bunks in two attics for when people need to bed down and use the others for storage. "And this, Madame," he said, opening his arms to the wide space, in a rare moment of camp, "is Mission Control. Desks here, here, here. Sofas or bean bags or something by the south window. We can add meeting rooms over there, if we want."

"And a kitchen and a bathroom," I said, "in the back. We may as well do it properly."

He shrugged, as if eating and pooing were beneath decent activists.

It took Stellar's mate and her crew of men in muscle vests a week to make the changes and fix up the rotten plaster. Michael fussed about the mess they made. I paid them in cash, daily. Their last job was the front door. Michael had chosen the locks and told them how to mount them into a reinforced frame, clad in the old plywood. He made them build it at night, propping a temporary ply sheet in place of the original while they worked, to avoid suspicion. In the morning, nothing seemed changed, except, close up, the old board had a hinged flap cut in it. Beneath the flap, a keyhole gleamed. When I turned the key Michael had given me, the door opened inwards on silent hinges. Even I was impressed.

Michael was washing the windows properly - claiming he could no longer stand the smears and cobwebs but was afraid what would let us see out might also let the world see in. He didn't look like he'd slept.

I got him down from the stepladder, sent him home and rang Venus. She cleans my flat once a week and is tall enough to reach any spiders with the audacity to build a web while her back is turned. Height and reach seem fine attributes in a cleaner, besides, she makes me laugh and is part of a co-op, so no one gets ripped off.

I waved a broom about a bit while Venus and her helpers, Heather and Masumi, worked, but cleaning's not my strong point. At Mum's I always used to have problems getting the bath acceptably shiny when it was my turn. It always seemed like someone sprinkled pubes and belly button fluff behind me while I was wiping down the other end. There are times when you need experts.

It turned out Masumi was not only expert with the spray-and-wipe.

"They are only small poems," she told me, while she wiped the banisters and I swept the hall, "but sometimes, online, small is best, no?" She wasn't just a poet and master at online self-promotion but graffitied haiku in public toilets that caretakers found so touching they painted around them.

I told Michael I'd asked her to join when we met to collect the van from Sam. He gave me his silent scowl, his mouth pursed up just like Furball's bum hole, and busied himself adjusting the seat and the mirrors. He'd only agreed we could use the band's van if we dropped off the furniture after dark. She's an old ambulance we got painted with The Carnival Owls' logo when we started the band and she runs on biofuel made out of used hops from the brewery. We were half-way out to Meanwood before he could bring himself to speak.

"You said Operations was mine," he launched in, swerving to pass a timid Fiat. His voice was the petulant end of angry and instantly riled me.

"She's got skills we need," I told him, feigning boredom, watching out my side window.

"That, Ruby, is not the point. Recruitment is part of Operations!" He had to brake hard at the zebra crossing. I continued my careless stare. A small girl carried her Coke can to the bins in the park and dropped it in the recycling slot.

"In case you hadn't noticed, you are a star. A pretty big star. Hundreds of people are going to want to be involved. They will want a piece of the action, just to get a piece of you. We have to keep the team small. Just a handful of people we can trust. With your life. With all our lives. Don't laugh! I'm not joking."

I hadn't meant to laugh, but his melodrama on top of the petulance was just too much.

"We'll be taking on the big guns, Ruby. Right round the world protest groups have been infiltrated by mining company spies or secret police. That Kennedy guy was undercover for years, here and in Europe. There are arrests on false charges, intimidation or sometimes people just vanish. We have to be vigilant, Ruby. Your fame gives us some protection, but it doesn't make us immune. You can't just go round recruiting random strangers that take your fancy."

"I recruited you." I didn't look at him but I could feel him glaring at me while we waited at the traffic lights.

"I have the skills. And I know how to make this work," he snapped. "Your job is to bring the fame. We'll bring everything else."

"There isn't a 'we', though, yet. Is there?" I asked him, turning into his glare and smiling sweetly. "Except you, and me, and, of course, Masumi."

The lights changed and he pulled away.

"I need a small core team," he said. "Security, Tech, Publicity and Ops of course, that's me. We don't need fundraising because we've got you."

"So I'm a cash-cow PR stunt?" I'd grown too cross to keep the casual shrug in my voice. As I said it I knew he was right. I didn't have any activist credentials - I'd never been chained to anything or arrested. I hadn't signed petitions or waved placards or done anything other than make songs and moan, till the Grammys.

"Not just a stunt," he said. "PR dynamite. The trick is consistency. We need a team that plans everything and makes it happen and keeps you free to be, well, famous. Fronting it all."

"If I'm fronting it, I need a say. I want right of veto and input over key things...the team, and our approach. End of story." I looked away from him and glared through the windscreen.

He went quiet on me again while we turned into the industrial park and loaded up the desks and chairs and I handed over the roll of notes to the man in the corduroy suit. I thought the silence might mean he'd had enough. Perhaps he would walk away. I wondered, if he left, if I would keep it going on my own. As I slid the last chair into the van, Fate texted me again, wanting to rehearse. The building had taken up my whole week. I'd barely even played.

"Between five and seven," he began again, while he started the engine and backed us out of the loading bay. "That's the optimal group size for productivity, creativity and team bonds. Keeps the structure simple. We'll have a wider group of volunteers, of course, that we'll divvy up tasks to, but the big picture we'll keep to the five of us. No more than seven, even when we grow."

He nodded gently to himself, as if picturing the perfection of it. "I've already got someone in mind for security. I think you'll like her."

He glanced at me then and I thought I caught him smile. "She's as stroppy as you. Either that, or you'll kill each other," he shrugged, "but I wouldn't rate your chances. She's a black belt in something."

He knew someone already for the Tech stuff, too. It was only when he asked me about Masumi that I realised I'd won.

"I knew her work before I met her," I told him. "She's got this gift for social media, gets things shared because people fall in love with them and want to make them their own. And she can write. I think she'll be good."

"Fine," he said. "Publicity. When can she start?"

It seems the Lord sends the same grey rain to London as it sends to Louisiana - it falls on me here like it was falling at my daddy's grave the day I left. It's not really his grave. There isn't a body. But the cross with his name on it in the cemetery is as close as I'll ever get.

Today was the day the Pastor and I had set for my trial so I went out into the wet to practise one last time. I found a bar where it was warm and sat up on the high stool and tried out my new accent on the bar maid. It was quiet, in the afternoon, so as well as the words, I practised the ways I know to draw her focus to me. After a little while she came close and stood, polishing the glasses, leaning towards me while I talked. She was the kind of person weak souls confess to when they do not have God to hear their prayers for rescue or forgiveness.

When I got up to go she rested the tips of her fingers on my hand for just a moment. I knew she did not want me to leave. The ease of victory burned heavy in my gut, reminding me how badly I wanted the opposite once - a super-power to repel anyone from touching me.

I will now set down what I know of the task I have been given.

My Bishop, like me, once was fallen but now he is redeemed and become a man of grace and power, uplifted by the Lord. He leads our Church boldly, to be a beacon against doubt where others tremble. Our Church is beleaguered on many sides; the abortionists, the atheists and the faggots grow in voice and number. Together they think they can deny our Lord with equations and fossils, with wicked laws and promiscuity.

The heathens claim our world is changing, but deny the change as God's work. If God is sending flood and plague upon us it is our duty is to endure the purge and the righteous will be saved. Our Lord has many friends and though not all of them come to our Church, or attend our college, they pray for us and send patronage in other ways. I am here on a scholarship of sorts, at the behest of one of our patrons, and I shall do my duty like Daddy did his and make my Bishop proud.

In Selfridges, I chose a silk tie the colour of pondweed and while she rang up my purchase the assistant asked what part of Northampton I was from. I smiled and said we'd moved round the area when I'd been growing up. She chattered about her childhood in some place called Little Billing and smiled at me over the bag and the receipt as if she claimed me. I knew Pastor Brian would be smiling too. I am ready.

When I rang Momma she asked if it was me. It was so good to hear her say my name I almost spoke. I thought I could use my new accent and keep her talking but then I felt the heat and fury all over again and the words bunched up in my mouth and none of them got out.

Fate came to my flat that afternoon. I stood at the window and watched the rain paint the roads and rooftops silver while I listened to her berate me.

She can beat you with words like cudgels when she wants to. More than a week or so without drumming makes her bad tempered. I mean the real drumming, in front of an audience, where she'll transcend herself with a fury of hammering on the skins. It leaves her calm and smiling. Practising isn't the same. Especially not practice on her own because I'd cancelled and stalled as we got HQ ready for business.

I went to the fridge and got us both a Gold.

"It's only till we're up and running," I said, opening the bottles and handing one to her. "Just pretend it's a solo project I'm working on. I just need a couple of weeks."

She skulled from the bottle and looked sceptical.

"You're not writing, are you? That's why you don't want to rehearse."

"I am," I lied. "We'll practise soon, I promise. Just give me a break. We'll be better than ever, you'll see."

She pulled a face, doubt twisting her nose one way and pragmatism tugging her lips in the other.

"One more week," she said, in the end, like the gangster boss calling in his dues in one of the endless films she makes us watch on tour.

Some musicians collaborate online for years and never play together, but Fate and Sam and I had always forged songs in the fug of each other's sweat.

The day after we'd met at Sinead's party, I dragged Fate and our hangovers up to Leeds on the train and we locked ourselves in the practice rooms for a month, with Sam, playing music and thrashing the songs I'd been writing into some kind of shape. We lived on pizza and coffee and weed except for Sundays when I took them to Mum's and we stuffed ourselves on her home-grown vitamins. We ignored the news and ignored the crazy rain and played and played and played. I'd wake at 5am, buzzed on just a few hours' sleep with new songs fully-fledged in my head so we learnt to play those too.

It was 2013 and by the time we emerged, pale and blinking, like lost cave explorers, the city was baking in a stagnant July sweat, petrol had gone up even more and small crowds of angry men and women had appeared on street corners with banners declaring 'The end of everything'. We didn't care. The Carnival Owls had enough songs for a set and an encore. We were ready to rock.

I drive Fate to drink more vodka than she otherwise would, with my creative flightiness, but she trusted I wouldn't let her down when it counted. She even took my arm while we trotted down the stairs.

"Come up and meet the crew with me?" I asked her, when we reached Church Row. She glanced up at the pointy-arch windows, her own eyes set just as deep, then shook her head. She kissed my cheek, waved and headed off to catch her bus.

I watched her to the end of the street before I climbed the steps. It felt as if I was the one who was walking away.

I could hear them before I reached the stairs, a jumble of excited voices, punctured by bright laughter. As I climbed, their noise washed my worry away. This mattered. With Michael's help I felt I could actually grab a few of those unravelling threads and start pulling the other way. It might not change anything, let alone change enough - the road to hell was paved with good intentions way before they invented tarmac and we keep driving it - but I had to try. Once things were underway at HQ I could write and practise again. And maybe some of what I did, with Michael and Masumi and the others I was about to meet, might outlive *Peanut Heart*.

They were sprawled on the sofas by the far window. Michael spotted me as soon as I came up the stairwell. He rolled out of his seat and grabbed a beer from a box.

"No cold ones left, sorry," he said, handing it to me. "Come and meet the team."

Masumi waved to me, glowing, from her seat cross legged in an old wingback someone had covered in purple spotty fabric. I went over and hugged her, finding myself in the midst of Michael's introductions - Burt, who looked like he should play rugby but was apparently a magician with firewalls and mobile data, learning his trade with Barclays before they moved everything offshore to Jersey. Daisy, Security, despite her plaid frock and pigtails.

"Y'a'right, boss," she said in heavy Scouse and shook my hand like we'd made a deal for life. With me, we were five.

He asked me to sit and join them so I perched on the arm of Masumi's chair.

"Let's share some key points about the expertise we bring," he said, like introductory rounds were as normal as farting.

He went first with a hugely edited but impeccable list of credentials. I told them I brought fame, cash and ideas. Then I cheated and added my first real concert - Pink, Manchester Arena, 2006. I'd gone with Mum and spent the whole gig singing my head off, wanting to be on stage, and the months that followed learning the *I'm Not Dead* album lyrics and the guitar parts I could manage at twelve.

I glanced at Michael, who looked like he was getting a headache, but didn't interrupt when Burt copied me. His was Kings of Leon, which explained the beard, and Daisy's Atomic Kitten, of course, which she announced with loud parochial pride. Masumi's had been Little Dragon in 2017 which made her a late starter but one with excellent taste. I looked at Michael till he scowled then declared it was The Wiggles and wouldn't be budged. We all laughed and Michael passed more beer and the talk of change flowed among them like my muso mates' talk of effects pedals.

The next morning Michael had arranged all the desk chairs in a semi-circle facing a screen. A projector painted a glowing video of the planet from space, slowly turning.

When we had shuffled ourselves and our coffees into the seats he stood up in front of us.

"Once upon a time, 50 million years ago," he said, "the air got so laden with carbon dioxide it killed 99% of life on Earth. Only tiny bugs survived. It had taken 10,000 years for the gas to build to that level. Humans have achieved the same in just 200. If we're going to save the world, we're going to have to do it fast. Over to you."

The planet continued to spin and for a moment no one said anything.

Masumi spoke first, her voice clogged with courage.

"In China and India all the people have learned success means a big house full of fashionable things. Here, we still think the same, really, even though we call bankers wankers now."

She got a laugh and her voice opened up.

"All the other groups," she said, "they talk about energy and transport but none of them really talk about a more simple life."

"It's true," Burt cut in, "but a simple life doesn't keep millions of people in jobs, does it? We can't fight the economy." The discussion ranged around and around, to protests we could stage and ways we could help Plane Stupid and Greenpeace. But my thoughts had got snagged on those first two ideas, as if my new team were hiking on into the next field and I'd got stuck in the last stile. I thought maybe I needed more coffee. Or that I wasn't cut out for activism after all. Until I realised it was the same snagged sensation I get when a song is brewing.

The first few bars come like gifts from the universe, bleeding out of my fingers into the guitar strings like someone choreographed the notes for me. Sometimes the songs come when I'm shopping or eating out or at the movies without my guitar. I used to go mad trying to hold the notes in my head and my hands till I could play it out. It's like trying to juggle sand and puts me in a foul mood because I can't think about anything else or talk to anyone till I can get it out of me.

I had a lover, once, Bruno, a drummer from Mali. We were strangers riding the train from Liverpool to Leeds. He had the table seat opposite me and we'd fallen in lust by Manchester. We escaped the train and took a room at the Palace Hotel across the road for a few delicious hours before catching the 18.07 the rest of the way.

Bruno could compose his beats on any surface - the table in the train, a frying pan, my naked arse. He pitied my helplessness when a tune came and I didn't have strings so he bought me a 6-string purple ukulele I could tune like a guitar and take everywhere. I wrote what became *Peanut Heart* during a flight to Tokyo on that uke but Bruno was long gone by then.

The music might come clear as instinct, but writing lyrics means mining your soul. An oxymoron, Fate calls it. She's as taciturn as most drummers but packs a stunning vocab. An oxymoron, a conflict, a contradiction. The further you turn inwards to find the words, the more deeply you reach into the loneliness of your unspoken psyche, the further the words can spread when you bring them to the bright light of the world, ensnaring millions. It's an awkward, uncomfortable business, public therapy in flashlights from the rooftops, but hooked to the right beat at the right time, just sometimes a song will slip into the bloodstream of the people – broadcast, downloaded, strummed live and hummed in the street – a toe tapper, a chart topper, a hit.

Soul mining got Robbie rich in the Noughties and Taylor in the Tens and the start of this decade's becoming my turn. Wrapped in our crunching electro-rock, of course.

Except these days it's not songs that make the money. The Owls' first hit was *Scrappy Fight*, a million views in a week, 200,000 downloads and diddlysquat cash. What does sell for money are tickets and T-shirts and retro hard copies in custom cases that sit on shelves and look expensive. You tour your arse off and, when you become a trending name, your songs get bought for ads or movies and your band gets booked for private parties. Exclusive live shows, that's where the real cash is. I can broadcast live, worldwide, for free and everyone knows it, but there's only ever one real me, one live band you can touch and smell. Some people will pay more to hear The Carnival Owls play a private gig in a tiny room than we could make from selling out a stadium.

Anyway, Burt and Masumi had snared me the way inspiration does. That's why I felt left behind. And there it was, in all its simple glory. Our idea. If everyone else was trying to reign in the symptoms, maybe our job was to poke a stick at the cause? Who was better placed to challenge the fashion and passion for stuff, even recycled, fair-trade, organic stuff, than a rock star? I'd set trends before. The whole pantaloons thing was my fault, because I wore them in the *Killer Heels* video. And apparently Ruby has become a top 10 name for girls. If fame could do that, maybe it could do something useful. Maybe I could stop people shopping.

Michael had wheeled over a whiteboard and was writing up lists of climate change groups as people called them out. I took a diaphragm breath and got up. Michael felt me move and looked around, his face baring his uncertainty, so I smiled to reassure him. Smiling made me feel better so I did it some more. Then I took another real breath and told them what I wanted us to do. I phrased it like that too. If I was going to front this thing, I was going to lead it, not be just a dumb figure-head stuck on the prow. If I could be the face of the band and write the songs, I could do the same here.

So I told them I thought Burt and Masumi had set us on the right track. That given how fast we were running out of time we had to do something new and something big. If we, with my fame, couldn't challenge the crazy economy beast, with arteries of oil and shopping at its pumping heart, then who could?

Everyone looked scared. That pleased me. I'm a musician, I trigger emotion, it's what I do. I hadn't done fear before, but it wasn't that different from triggering joy or angst or melancholy - you just have to name the unspoken things. If the idea didn't scare us we wouldn't be able to spread it.

"We have to attack the heart of the beast," I said, "not just what fuels it. We have to get people to stop shop-ping."

Burt laughed. I liked that. We'd need a sense of humour. Then he stopped laughing. "You're serious, aren't you?"

I told them I was and then I asked them how we'd do it.

The Lord has been testing me. It has been two weeks since Pastor Brian put me on the train at Kings Cross, drawling away while we waited, blue and orange tatters of potato chip packets whisked around his feet by the wind. He had booked me a window seat, though not one with a table, and the train sucked me out of London and north, past long brown fields tinged green with growth and small drab towns. I kept my bag next to me but a woman with a hairy top lip got on at Peterborough with a ticket for that seat and I had to smile and move my pack to the luggage rack at the end of the carriage, out of my sight where anyone could steal it.

A strained, thin man in what they call a waistcoat pushed a trolley up the aisle selling coffee and tea and cookies and bananas but I didn't buy anything.

At Leeds the station was wide, white and cold, like being swallowed into a mausoleum. Outside, it was raining. I flagged a cab, or a taxi as I must call them here, for the address Pastor Brian had given me. The driver said 'oh great' in a sarcastic way when I told him where to take me for it turned out to be only three blocks away and I could have walked easy, even with my bag. I was ashamed of my weakness and my mistake and gave him more in a tip than the fare. He didn't smile but he did nod and pocket it.

The room is on the fourth floor of an apartment block large enough and humble enough, the concierge sufficiently weary, I can be anonymous. The building is old, red bricks stained by the city. It has been spruced up like an old man tucked into a dinner jacket for a high school reunion; nothing fits quite right or hides the elderly smell. The concierge, a woman about my momma's age, just takes the details for the credit card Pastor Brian gave me, hands me a key and waves me up the stairs. The card told her I am called Salvador for that is the name I must use.

A chipped door at the end of the landing opens into a room with a bricked up fireplace, a bed and a kitchenette, the tiny kind where everything's half sized. The one other door leads to a bathroom; no bath, just a shower, which suits me fine.

A window looks out onto the two lane snarl of cars going in or out of town. It doesn't open. Someone painted white gloss over the ropes that would let you slide the bottom section up. The room has a bed and a couch but no desk or table. I am typing this with my laptop balanced on my knees.

I have a cover story for how, as a rebel looking for a cause, I can afford my own place. An uncle, the unrelated friend-of-the-family kind, needs someone to look after the apartment while he works overseas.

Apparently this city is full of development companies with slippery names like Helium and Zeus, so they're an easy place to hide an imaginary uncle.

I've named mine Derek. He hopes I'll get a job in hospitality while I'm staying here. When I find Her, and am welcomed in, I will go to an interview every week, as if I were trying to please him.

'd planned to cycle up to Chapel Allerton before it got dark but the nights can still barge in and catch you unawares that late in April. At least the rain had finished falling and lay about on the streets, snaring the street lights in sprawling puddles I had to ride around. I chained my bike by Mum's front door and she came to greet me. She was wearing lippy, which she never wore at home unless we were celebrating. I could feel the excitement in her hug, the news bubbling to get out. She insisted I wait till we were at the kitchen table, a chardonnay poured for me to match the one she was half way through.

"I quit!" she said. Mum doesn't surprise me often - when there's just the two of you, you learn each other's warning signs pretty well.

"But you love your job."

"Loved," she said, pouring herself more wine to ensure her conviction was well enough oiled to run smoothly in the face of my scrutiny. Something had happened while I'd been looking away, my attention caught between the Group and my band. Mum has been the school gardens' coordinator since I was two and the council created the role, just one day a week. By the time I started school myself it had grown to full time. Whenever kids visited a school, for a match or competition, and Mum had been at work, they returned wanting beanstalks and black nero cabbages of their own. At the start I would hide when she came to Chapel A Primary. Already too tall, too pale and too ginger, I didn't need another stigma. But after a few weeks I learned the other kids thought Mum was cool - they clustered round her to see caterpillars or the first potatoes, to learn how to mulch lettuces and string up peas. I thought they got over-excited by things I'd known for ever but I didn't hide anymore.

She got up to stir the risotto while she told me, as if doing ordinary things would make the words more normal.

"It's been coming for a while," she said, "but I've been more persistent lately. It brought things to a head. In the end," she said, settling the lid on the pan and coming back to the table, "I had to promise to only plant where they said, or leave. So I left." She shrugged and tipped back on her chair, emptying her glass like she was the rock star. I wasn't sure if I was proud or worried so I poured us both more wine.

She told me how, when the PE teacher saw she had planted tomato canes behind the goal net, she was sure he would have a heart attack. The risotto burned. We didn't care - we were talking power and freedom, rulers and rebellion, Aung San Suu Kyi and Naomi Klein. By the second bottle, my pride and worry had become compatible.

Too pissed to ride, I stayed the night. I woke early, feeling I'd dreamed a song. The acoustic I keep at Mum's needed new strings so I slipped out, leaving a note by her microgreens.

Back at Clarence House, the power was out again so I got a killer workout climbing the stairs. There are definitely times when I think the 18th floor is a mistake, despite the sunsets. Panting as I walked to the end of the hall and into my flat, promising myself I'd do the stairs once a day to stay in shape till we played again, my phone rang. Sinead, with a booking for a private party for Shaun Ryder and a fee big enough my slice would fund the Group for a couple of months and leave something for me to slide into Mum's bank account. They wanted three live song debuts as a condition of the booking to which I offered a non-committal grunt and told her to book us. It was weeks away.

I drifted to the corner and picked up Elsie. Already a widower, Grandad had lost his mum to cancer about the same time my dad fucked off and our two gaps sucked us together. Grandad gave Elsie to me the day after I turned 9. I was grumpy with him because he'd told me he would try and drop in on my actual birthday and hadn't. The idea of a dozen squealing girls had probably defeated him. He did his best not to let me down, knowing how badly my dad had.

Anyway, the day after my birthday he took me for brunch at the Lakehouse and let me order chocolate cake. When we'd eaten he ordered me a juice, so we could tell Mum I'd had some vitamins, and excused himself.

An exit I'd assumed was a loo trip turned into something so miraculous I can replay it beat perfect. I saw it as soon as he came back into the café, wrapped in purple metallic paper, bulging with the excitement of a proper BIG present. He got me to shuffle my chair out from under the table so he could lie it on my lap and as I reached my arms round the parcel she spoke to me, chiming through the paper. I knew instantly. My own guitar.

'Oh Grandad!' I said, not daring to unwrap her in case I was wrong.

"Well go on then," he said, like he did when he was choked up but didn't want me to notice. "Open it!"

Then she was out of the paper and out of the long zipped case and in my hands, all the curves and strings and splendour of her. I knew just how to hold her, from all the videos, took a deep breath and strummed, one run with my thumb, right across the strings to make her sing.

"The E's a bit flat," he said. "I tuned it last night but it's shifted in the car. You'll learn soon enough. Yes, that's right, the top one, just turn the key a tad towards you, easy. Yes, now try again. Good! That's better."

"You'll teach me won't you?" I asked him, clutching her as if the wrong answer might magic her away.

"Well I'm rusty as hell, girl, but if you want I can try. Get you started at least."

I tested my fingers on the strings, imagining the calloused pads like Grandad's that would replace the thin line of pain.

"I do want," I said, giving him my serious look and making him smile.

Then I settled her on the seat next to me, with the same care Mum made me use when I had a hold of next door's baby. Then I stood up and hugged him, pressing my face into the gap between his ear and his leather jacket. "Thanks," I whispered, "Thanks a gazillion, Grandad."

Our lessons started the following Thursday when he collected me from school. He made a bunch of compilation CDs and played them to me on his old Discman, rigged with two sets of headphones so we could both listen - Dylan and Joplin and Lennon, all acoustic, all coaxing something extraordinary from their guitars

When I was 12, I went electric but I've still got Elsie. I like to write on her and when I'm in bed on my own I play her to myself before I fall asleep. I've never been much of a one for teddy bears but I'm pretty smitten with that guitar.

She was out of tune and a fine haze of dust had clouded her wood. I wiped her clean with my sleeve and tweaked her back into pitch and played *Wonderwall* to myself and wondered if I could find my way back to the smudge of new song I'd woken with. I thought back over the last few weeks, how strange it was to have Michael and now the Group tugging on my time and the splendour of the night we'd turned on the starlight.

A clutch of a lyric arrived - *the glare from a million rooms, burns the starlight from the sky, so we can dance and drink and sing, 'til morning.* My fingers started their quest for the right notes, a chorus trill of tenderness to tease before the crashing blame of a sequence of stomping verses. My phone cheeped again. I ignored it. 'Cheep cheep' it went till I swore and set Elsie on her stand and cleared the fluster of messages from Michael asking me PLEASE could I come in NOW so they could cement the ideas we'd floated into actions. When the writing is flowing, I can find a song at the bottom of every coffee cup or in the face of every stranger I glance at on the street. But I hadn't had that, not once, since the speech. Still, 'A million rooms' would have to wait. 'Yes', I told him. 'Yes, yes, yes'. I'd set this thing in motion. I had to see it through.

"It's all about endorphins," Michael was saying, brandishing a white board marker in one hand and a mug in the other, as I walked in. "People will only change if the alternative feels better." Burt, Masumi and Daisy all turned on their swively desk chairs to look at me. He had them clustered round the board and I slid into the empty seat, waiting pointedly for me, next to Daisy. I realised I was their figurehead not the naughty girl late to class so I threw a confidant wave and smile at them all and looked at Michael to model what I wanted them to do. The white board was covered in blue and green words, fragments of ideas, some circled in red. "And we've got to help them join the dots. When the Coalition is telling them shopping is the only thing that keeps the economy turning, and keeps anyone in a job, we've got to make them feel it for the lie it is."

"We could start with my network," I said, feeling I ought to contribute something besides lateness. "I could post an update to my speech, tell people what we're thinking, ask them for ideas?"

"We could ask what they are doing already, instead of buying things?" Masumi offered, the idea couched as a question. She was right. Even if it was small, more people made cards for friends or grew vegetables or kept a hen or knitted than they had when I was a kid. The magazines had labelled such errant behaviour 'Nana-chic' and pegged it next to 'Vintage', hoping that branding them fads would make them fade as fast. Neither had. And packed inside the practical budget-stretching was a complex and ancient bundle of human desire to create and to save. We could build on that, amplify it through the global sound system of the 'Net. It's one thing fame had taught me - we're each of us trapped in a little life with its own small hopes and pains and embarrassments, hoping no one else notices the weak or ugly parts. Unexpected things can happen when we find our little life suddenly connected to the 6.9 billion other little lives on Earth, all joined up by some sudden spark in common. Not that I had 6.9 billion HeadSpace mates, of course, but 480,000 would give us a decent start.

We agreed we'd kick off with a video asking what it would take to stop the viewer shopping. Was destruction of life on Earth and a return to swamps at the Poles motive enough? We would ask them to tell us about one time they *hadn't* bought something. And I would pledge to stop shopping myself.

"Even second hand?" I asked.

"I think swapping would be ok," Michael said.

The crew wheeled their chairs back to their desks and left me to gather my thoughts. I'd done my own video blogs for years, off the cuff into my phone. Having Masumi poke her camera at me shouldn't make a difference. Other than what I said had to change the world, of course. The nerves needled me into moving so I roamed over to the sofa. I lay along it, my head on one of the overstuffed arms so I could watch our newborn team beyond my feet, tapping away on their laptops, Michael fluffing about making everyone tea. Nothing I said into Masumi's mic would make a difference on its own. The bunch of us in our funny old building were just one little cog in the great big wheel of people working for change all around the world.

I realised I'd been holding my breath. Remembering to breathe helped me work out what to say. By the time Masumi came over, I was ready for anything.

The Whore is stupid.

She posted a vain video of herself playing a children's song and labelled the file 'View from my place after the Star Party'. There's only one tower that high in that part of the city. I just had to wait.

The first time I saw Her, leaving the apartment building, pushing a bicycle and flashing her legs like a stripper as She stepped astride it, I felt as a punch to my stomach. The sight stayed with me, burrowing, like the Devil had spawned a hellhound in me and it chewed my insides. Her skirts flapped, scarlet, as She rode away.

The next time I was ready. I had bought a used bike with racing handle bars from a trader at the back of the old markets. The handle bars were as low as the seat so I could ride tipped forward. I haven't ridden a bike since my daddy died and I stayed in bed so I lost my paper-round, but riding, like lots of much worse things, isn't something your body forgets.

At another stall, a woman with lipstick seeping into the creases around her mouth sold me a cap and hoodie.

When I rode behind Her, even when She looked back at me, She could not see my face or hair. I only needed to follow Her once.

Masumi posted my video and linked it to the new 'Stop Shopping' web pages she'd made. They, in turn, linked to hundreds of sites on making clothes and growing food and raising chickens, with space between for everyone to share their stories. Michael made her add sources on killing rabbits, filtering water with charcoal and lighting fires. "Just in case," he said, looking grim when I asked him.

Within minutes of the vid going up, the comments began to appear, flowing down the page in a crazy, crude, menagerie of imagination and sharing. It was heartbreakingly human and frighteningly fast.

We whooped, wide-eyed, as we watched the clicks ratchet up and read posts out to each other, liking and underscoring them with our own comments of encouragement. Until Michael shouted us to hush. He was standing, his phone to his ear, face pinched by the squeeze of bad news. I shared a clip on salvaging sequins to revive dull T-shirts on my own site, sent Sinead a quick update to help her keep any jealousy of Masumi in check and looked back up as Michael finished the call. Most of his face was back where it should be but the pinch still squeezed his eyes.

He came over, as if he wanted to only tell me, but we all looked up at him so he wound up telling everyone.

"I stuffed up," he said. "I forgot to tell WWF what we're doing. They're furious." Michael reckoned he'd overlooked them because we'd collaborated so closely over the Star Party. I said it was because he was over-worked.

"It's too much," I told him, "managing all the needy NGOs as well as organising everything. Let's just get someone in."

He argued for a while that we needed to keep the team tight but, snared in his own oversight, he gave in pretty fast. There was no point keeping the work close to our chests if we couldn't get everything done.

That night, I went to visit Grandad. The snow started as the dark drew in, as if the dusk shrugged itself into a white fur coat. It hushed my bike tyres on the road and feathered my eyelashes.

"It's snowing," I told him as I went into the room, hanging my jacket to drip on the back of the door and crossing to his armchair, kissing the dead leaf skin of his cheek before I hunkered down on his footstool, tucked in by his bony knees, rubbing the blood back into my fingers.

"Shall we play snowballs?" he asked me.

"Yes Grandad," I told him, "when I've warmed up a bit." And I asked him to tell me again his favourite snow story, the one he's told me so often I feel it in my mind more clearly than the ones I can actually remember.

It was 1995, the cold tail of January. I had just turned one and Grandad had been minding me for the day while Mum was up in Harrogate visiting a seed supplier. We had spent the afternoon finger painting, with me in the high-chair in front of the fire at his house, the skinny red terrace in Kirkstall.

"I got up to pull the curtains," he said, and I picture him, chiselled at 47 like he appears as he's lighting my cake in the photos from my first birthday, unfolding his skinny frame and pausing for a moment, his hand to the orange velour curtains, as he sees it. 'Ruby, it's snowing,' he had said and scooped me into his arms and into my coat and into the street where his neighbours on either side had stepped out too, to wonder at the fat, spinning flakes. They passed me between them, snug in my hood, twirling me and pointing up to the sky to show me where the magic came from.

"We had a few neighbours round after," he told me, back there in his mind with the teacakes held to the fire and the mugs of Horlicks spiked by a dash of the whisky he usually kept for late at night, "and the guitars came out and we waited for your Mum to call."

It was before she had a cell phone and in the end she'd borrowed one, trudging the line of snow-bound cars stuck in front of hers until she'd found someone with a phone and battery to spare.

And so it became my first snow and my first sleepover at Grandad's.

"Charlene from two doors up brought us a big dish of macaroni," he said, "and we left the curtains open so we could watch the snow. 40 centimetres in just three hours. Can you believe it?"

Of course I can. Most years since I left school we've had a snow that's stopped the traffic. He doesn't say it tonight but usually he'll tell me they called it the Night of the Big Snow for years. Back then it was a novelty. Now it's not even that unusual this late in the year.

The snow had fallen so thick and quick that night it sealed my Grandad's street of terrace houses and trapped dozens of cars in the roads at either end. When it stopped snowing they woke me up and we went out in it. Apparently, when Grandad set me down, I clapped my mittens and laughed. Norma and the other neighbours rescued strangers from their cars and gave them a warm sofa for the night. Grandad went in and out, carrying me in one arm, fetching blankets and coats, but he wasn't risking any strangers in the house with me.

"The whole city was drunk on Dunkirk spirit, that night," he said, like he always does. He wasn't born till after the war but his mum, Elsie, had volunteered, for an anti-aircraft unit that shot down Nazi planes so he sometimes talked like he'd lived through it himself.

I wanted to take him by the hand and lead him out of the numbing corridors into the bright reality of the snow. I was afraid he'd become confused and forget who I was and I'd lose him in the night. I squeezed his hand then hugged his bony shoulders and left before he could see my tears.

I slept sketchily and woke feeling as slushy as the city had become. Not even two coffees fixed me for the 'Stop Shopping' interviews Masumi had ready to go. NME were asking if I was crowd-sourcing lyrics for a concept album. Marie Claire's blogger wanted to know how much lipstick I'd stockpiled. The Telegraph was convinced some NGO was paying me. I almost told them WWF had me on their payroll, just to cause trouble - they still weren't talking to Michael because he'd forgotten to warn them. It's not like they're perfect. They might do good work with Coke and Avon but it still puts them in cahoots. I imagined Sinead yelling 'stay on message' and behaved myself.

As well as a stampede of email Q&As, I did six phone interviews in three hours. At the same time I posted a sparkly stream of HeadSpace status exclamations about them, to 'feed the flames', as Masumi said, like some samurai warrior poet. My fingertips were slick with keyboard and my shoulders ached.

"Enough" I said, pulling off my headset and standing up to stretch.

"We've got the Hackney Blogger booked for a live web chat in 20 minutes," Michael told me, hurrying over with his clipboard. I'd bought him a new, grunty tablet but it was still in its box. He liked to be able to scribble on his printouts and tick things off, he said. Pixel ticks just weren't as satisfying. And then he'd given me a little speech about the rare earth minerals mined for electronics and the perils of e-waste.

"You'll have to postpone him," I said. "I need a break."

I endured his lecture on respect for the media and agreed with everything he said and then I went home.

The Clarence House apartments each have a letterbox in the entrance hall by the lifts. Other than my Guitarist and Rolling Stone subscriptions, which Mum still gets posted to me, the old school way, mine mostly harbours junk mail but I check it anyway. Take-away menus are always handy. Beneath a sheet of ads for bad, cheap beer in cans was a postcard, golden with one of the Civic Hall owls, all Art Deco elegance against a moody sky. I flipped the card over.

'To the world's best singer and my golden Grammy girl. Here's to many more.'

Sam's methods of coercion are subtler than Fate's but generally more effective.

I took the card upstairs and propped the shining owl up against an empty mug on the coffee table, grabbed a notepad, found a pen down the back of the sofa and tried to write.

My words were all used up by interviews.

Failing to find any more flattened me into a sprawl on the couch. I lay there for a bit then prodded the remote to set the LEDs in my lounge to nightclub colours and sound-synch, turned up the amp and played Kimbra loud - she's remixed Chic with Woody Guthrie (it should never work but it does) - followed by Totems, the coolest DJ I heard in the States, luring the packed crowd at Create to dance their attitude away. They got me up and dancing round the furniture that afternoon but neither sent me inspiration so I rang Mum instead.

As soon as I talked to her I realised I'd been worried about Grandad all day. I don't expect him to get any better but I am afraid at how fast we're losing what we have left of him. Short of feeding him more blueberries and cryptic crosswords there wasn't anything we could do. Bouncing the worry between us just helped us both feel better.

She let me off more lightly for dropping cash into her account than she would have if I wasn't anxious and I distracted her with news of our Ryder gig. Mum had taken my money before - I paid off her house with some of what I made touring *The Black Prince Parade* - but she only accepted it on condition the house went in both our names. When I asked what she'd been up to, fishing less to discover if she was looking for work and more to check she was really alright, she fobbed me off with a dinner invite. I figured we could both use a hug.

"Stellar's booked me tomorrow but I'm all yours the day after," I told her and she told me she loved me back.

After more than a week of takeout food and waiting I have met the faggot.

Once She had led me to them I photographed them all, leaving or arriving at their shabby building. I wore a fluorescent worker's vest and weeded the old graves outside the church while I watched. Pastor Brian had arranged a special camera to be left for me in a locker in the station and I aimed its long lens carefully and when I had their pictures I sent them to him. The pictures gave him their names and their connections. The faggot called Michael has a friend at a charity in London with a taste for the sin of gambling that makes him weak. He told the Pastor where the faggot had failed and the type of work he would have for me.

Michael insisted we meet at a coffee shop to keep their location secret. I kept my smile inside. The coffee shop didn't serve filter so I had to order an espresso with a jug of hot water. He ordered something fancy and Italian that came in a cup the size of a doll's tea set. His suspicion engulfed him; the Lord showed it to me as if he was covered in spines, like a startled porcupine. I have always been good at soothing frightened animals. I once tamed a dog everyone thought had rabies with just a packet of Oreos and a bit of quiet sitting.

Underneath his spines he was soft. He has the sin of vanity, like most gay men, but without the looks to comfort him. Still, he hopes others will see beauty where he sees none. When he had lost himself for a moment, raving about oil and SUVs, I put on the same face I have seen others wear in the rapture. I shone all the idea of adoration across the table and the sugar basin at him, and when he had finished talking I touched his hand, like the bar maid in London had touched mine. 'You are awesome,' I told him, shaking my head softly, as if in wonderment. The Lord will forgive me for laying my hand on a sinner because I did it in His cause.

He said they had background checks to run. Pastor Brian had prepared the ground for those with the greatest care, so I knew I would not fail. Besides, I knew Michael wanted to see me again. I spent the rest of the day testing my mind against the city's street maps and bus timetables. I prayed for a swift deliverance and in his grace the Lord granted it. This morning, I got the call.

They have decorated their building with cast offs so it has a worn out look even before they have begun. The couch I was asked to sit on, when Michael gathered us around, has a blanket over it. When I stood to leave it moved so I could see the ragged patch in the upholstery underneath. Only when everyone else had been waiting, did She arrive. She was smaller than I expected.

With her looks and her clothes and her money and her fame She has a pull on everyone in the room, as if She is magnetic. Almost every time She speaks it is a blasphemy. And She speaks a lot. She flits her hands about as if She is undressing you and laughs, tossing her sinner's red hair and blinking her slutty olive eyes. She is Eve and She is Pandora and She is Salome. She is the temptation of chaos over order that has been man's undoing since Adam fell. It is my job to stop Her.

I rang Momma when I got back to my room. The first time since coming here. She sounded as if she may have a cold. I waited before hanging up but even though she said 'hello' twice more I couldn't be sure. Perhaps it was just early there. I will have to check the time zones before I call again.

Most of the media had already posted their interviews with me, kindling a spreading fire of interest, igniting more attention. The Guardian rang, wanting a face to face. I met their reporter at Calls Landing so we could sit outside and look at the river. We had to keep our coats on but at least it wasn't raining. They serve Kirkstall Pale but it was a bit early for beer to make a good impression, so I ordered a pot of tea.

"Let me check," he asked me. "Everyone's supposed to 'Stop Shopping', but buying coffee's ok?" I thought he had a cheek, seeings as I'd paid for his OJ too but told him, as a Yorkshire girl, tea was always ok, however you had to get it. That made him laugh and things improved a bit till he asked if I was an anarchist.

I told him I'd always voted.

"We want people to stop being consumers," I said, "not citizens."

He wrote that one down so I thought things were looking up again but then he asked if it wasn't just a stunt to sell my next album.

I explained about my Grammy and that our downloads were higher than ever but, as Sinead says, with the media, if you're explaining you're losing. I could have told him we didn't have a new album but if he wrote that down Fate would throw her drumsticks at me. She pretends she doesn't but she reads all the coverage The Owls get.

I fluffed and told him we hadn't even recorded the new album yet, which was true, but I could tell he thought he'd outed us in a grandiose promo ploy. Eventually the swan that hangs out on the river drifted by so I blathered about climate threats to wildlife before we stumbled to a close. You can't win them all, I guess.

It had started to drizzle and the clouds had come down to smooch the muddy water. I trudged back to the office and found them together on the sofas - Michael, Masumi, Daisy, Burt and a new boy, with collar length curls and Baileys skin and high-cut cheeks. He greeted me in a voice like comfort.

"Salvador," Michael said. "Outreach. He's going to take over our links to all the other groups." As I glanced from Salvador, in his dark curled prettiness and hipster jeans, back to Michael I saw how he watched Salvador - the efficiency behind his clipboard was chipped. His gaze leaked desire across the room, briefly, then it was gone. I wasn't sure Salvador would gaze on Michael in return - he didn't seem the type to be into clipboard and cardigans. He was giving me the kind of fevered puppy look I get from guys in the front row hoping for a backstage invitation, but I've never been one for crowding a mate's desire.

I reached to shake his hand, to welcome him in, and he held my gaze and traced his thumb across my knuckles so lightly I might have missed it. Neither of us smiled.

I took the empty bean bag and muttered a few words to thank him for joining us and affirmed that Michael was the boss. Salvador just needed to see the daring and glamour of him, behind his comfy clothes, so I asked Michael to tell us all about getting arrested. He blushed and I had to nudge him twice more but he was learning how stubborn I can be.

"Alright!" he said, brightening and tipping forward to rest his elbows on his knees, his clipboard forgotten. "It's the kind of stunt you can only pull off once, and you've got to have kept your nose clean or get your hands on a top class fake ID. Anyway, Davos Conference, 2011. I got a job as a cocktail waiter, serving gin slings to the global elite. Picture 80 odd top dogs from the world's biggest companies and 40 heads of state sucking up to them for jobs or investment. Only about six women – it's 90% rich white guys, right – and me in my white shirt and little black pinny sashaying among them with a silver tray and a sycophantic smile." I glanced at Salvador - tilted backwards in his armchair, cradling his beer against his hip, watching Michael. Good.

"Security is tighter than a Swiss watch but their protestors are precision engineered to match." I confess I did snigger at this, finding it hard to imagine activists more organised than Michael. He looked horrified so I waved him on and behaved. "This rather dishy sous chef served me up a hidden mic in a serviette and away I went, in among the thick of them, transmitting incriminating quotes with every glass. We had a signal booster hidden down a drain and a team in a van, a mile away, typing the audio feed straight into our blog. I was, I have to say, bloody brilliant."

He was into the flow now - the lure of an audience gets most of us if we can dodge our self-consciousness long enough, and his face was bright at the memory.

"You think those big corporates all work off strategic plans and rational forecasts but they're run by hairy mammals like the rest of us. It's all testosterone and deals. The politicians get their credit rating and their election donations just as long as they keep the cash tills pinging. Honestly, to hear them, you'd think the 08 Crash was a bad dream and climate change some bogey Del Toro dreamed up. The stuff I overheard! I was torn between wetting myself laughing and slitting my wrists with the corkscrew."

"So what happened?" Masumi asked, into his pause. I knew what came next. Michael had insisted he and I recount all misdeeds to each other so there could be no surprises, nothing they could use against one of us to ambush the other. We'd endured a long evening of confession at my flat, the lights dim to make it easier, fuelled only on coffee so we wouldn't exaggerate or forget. I'd told him about Dad leaving and the band, the experimentation with substances and bed mates, my broken grandad and my desperate mum. He told me he was a men-only guy, a failed maths student, a proven organiser and had only been arrested once, so far.

Michael shrugged, but his forehead creased above his eyes and he glanced away.

"I got caught ditching the mic. Three years in a Swiss jail, suspected terrorist reports all over the 'Net and a wrecked credit record. It wasn't easy but it was worth it." He was back with us now, sensing he could use this to motivate and bind us, mentally adding 'pep talk about sacrifice' to his checklist of achievements for the day. "We got some premier division quotes that the press actually ran. The Google servers in the Bahamas to dodge tax. That was us. And Pfizer telling Obama about the win-win of fertility drugs – good for profits and good for breeding tax payers."

"Three years?" asked Salvador in his steady, soothing voice. "Did they torture you?"

"Nothing military. Just the usual tied-up-in-a-holding-cell-needing-a-piss-for-five-hours kind. But, hey, Swiss prisons have great food. I've probably never eaten so well!"

Masumi used the change in mood to ask how my interview had gone and I told them the swan dropped by. She took the hint but bit back, reminding me how many I still had waiting and dropped an encore onto my 'to do' list - spamming my music biz mates.

She outlined what we would send and what I would say and I realised I could watch her talk and study Salvador at the same time, as he listened. There was a simple aesthetic pleasure in looking at his dark watchful eyes, the trace of his shaped stubble, the idle, ironic arc of his eyebrows. There was no doubt Michael had taste.

I spent the afternoon dredging through my contacts in studios and labels, venues and production companies. With the Star Party, we'd dressed it up as entertainment and I'd shared it like we shared our gigs, muso to muso. This time I rang, enthused, messaged and emailed everybody - managers, roadies, talent scouts and publicists, spreading the link to our 'Stop Shopping' video as if I was a desperate newbie with my first, home-made MP4 and no idea how to pitch it. Mostly they slicked a little politeness over their disinterest. Only the guy from Virgin radio laughed but he's always been a dick.

"Quick work," I said to Michael when he came over, nodding at Salvador.

"I told our WWF friend we'd recruit, to make sure I don't drop the ball again. He recommended Salvador. Flicked me his CV - Management at uni, grad trainee at BP but saw the light six months in and ditched it. He's been doing good stuff ever since. The references all stack up and Burt's given him the online once-over.

All clear. He's a lucky find." He glanced over to Salvador for a fraction longer than he needed to. "You were right, I needed help," he smiled, more surely than I'd seen for weeks.

If he was making Michael that happy, Salvador had already earned his keep.

In the depths of my HeadSpace contacts, I found a clutch of promoters I hadn't pestered yet and sent 'Stop Shopping' to them. Only two unfriended me. Finally, it was time for my date at the swings.

The sky was still snivelling so I almost stopped on the way to buy an umbrella, something large and luminous Clara would like, but I remembered I was stopping shopping so I just tugged my parka hood further over my face instead.

They had beaten me to Sovereign Park and before I could see them behind the trees I could hear Clara squealing 'higher' as Stellar pushed her. I took over pushing duties and Stellar produced a sneaky spliff which we stealth-smoked while Clara swung. It had been a big week – Clara had started poo-ing in the loo and written the first three letters of her name.

When our big, clever girl had enough swinging I got my hug, her grinning face, chilled from the wind of her ride, against mine. Then I had a swing to show her how high I could go. The afternoon was drying up as it dawdled to a close so the three of us piled on the round-about, Stellar and I trundling us around, idly while we lounged. My worry about Grandad and Mum's resignation leaked out of me to the accompaniment of its squeaking. Confessing my fears into Stellar's soothing calm restored me until I was able to invent a story for Clara about a fantastical merry-go-round, where the creatures were a unicorn, a gryphon, a dragon and even a phoenix that all came to life at full moon. She didn't know what a phoenix was so I told her it was a magical crispy chicken which made Stellar laugh till she cried, and that set me off, snorting with giggles, or maybe it was the weed.

The Group has set me to work. I am to collaborate with the quiet Asian girl on promoting their campaign. My job is to contact the other protest networks and brief them on our activities. I am to be charming and persuasive and to record their points of view. These are good uses of the talents the Lord has given me. I have been provided a desk, a phone and a laptop and am to note down who I speak to and what they say.

Michael keeps coming across to check on my progress. I smile and endure his attention and so far he has not touched me. He does not have the strength of the Lord in him and, as a weak man, I do not think he will reach out unless invited but none-the-less I pray I will not have to endure that again.

She comes every day.

Mostly the work is easy and I do what I have been told and watch, for now, but today was difficult. Sitting here, just thinking it over, I find I am holding on to Daddy's tags, running my thumb over the comfort of his name and whispering his Code: say your prayers, tell your truth and never hurt a woman. Today I dishonoured him.

Bishop Hamilton had warned me history is different for the Brits. They think they won World War Two, not us, and they think Iraq was a mistake. When everyone stopped for lunch *their talk turned to the Middle East and I had to nod and agree as they dissed what my daddy died for.*

    May God forgive me.

arrived the next morning newly energised, as if I'd mainlined toddler power. We shared and posted, emailed and phoned in double time, but the more I did, the more replies and comments there were to handle, like an ever-upward feedback loop. As the pale spring sun edged its way across our windows my energy leeched away. Michael had Salvador cornered behind his laptop, enmeshed in a spreadsheet of NGO contacts and whenever I looked at Masumi she thought of some muso connection I hadn't exploited. I chipped away, plugging our video, but when The Guardian article appeared online, a small and cynical column, I knew I'd had enough.

I didn't just need a break, I needed something real. I needed to play.

Before I left I texted Sam and Fate and asked if they could meet me at The Headrow.

As I walked back to the flat for Elsie and my bike, I tried to remember when I'd last busked. We'd done a spontaneous Owls gig in City Square the day we put *The Black Prince Parade* album online. The three of us had been so giddy we just needed to play. We got through three songs before the police turned up and then managed to vanish down into The Bank where we spent the rest of the afternoon getting arrogantly pissed.

If that was the last time, it would have been nearly four years ago. Too long. I was getting soft and disconnected, cushioned by money and glossy photos the mags touched up because they want the stars looking good, until they don't want you at all any more.

The clouds had got over their cold patch and hung fat with rain, slung low between the tower blocks with the weight of it. The wet broke through when I'd only cycled half-way up Park Row, plastering my hair to my head and making me fret Elsie's case, strapped across my back, would leak. The stands outside The Headrow Centre were bundled tight with bikes so I had to chain mine up across the road at the library. By the time I found Sam and Fate I was wet and cross. They scowled when I told them what I wanted to do.

"Fine," I told them, "pack up when we've finished playing if you want. Or don't play at all. I don't care. I need to do this."

We ripped *Scrappy Fight* and *Love Lupins* and *Tenderlust* apart. By the time we finished *Peanut Heart* we were grinning at each other like teenagers and the pavement was packed down the block. When the last applause kicked in a policeman, younger than I am, came up blushing and asked for my autograph. I scribbled something thick with kisses then flicked my eyebrows at Sam and Fate to give them fair warning. They exchanged a glance but didn't say anything. They didn't pack their gear up either.

As the cheers faded and the crowd shuffled, not sure if they should hope for an encore or resume their lunchtime shopping, I wished I'd brought a prop. Maybe a hat I could pass round distributing cards with the Groups's web address, something that would tell the story for me. But Michael was right, the power was in my telling. And so I began.

After I'd thanked them and introduced myself, which got a laugh and made a girl a few rows back wave her copy of that month's Rolling Stone, with my Grammy pics on page two, I started with a question.

"What are you shopping for?" I asked a woman at the front, blonde, about my age, wearing a grey coat that had seen a few winters.

"Eyeshadow," she said, laughing as she confessed her pleasure. They caught the game quickly, opening bags to remind themselves what they'd succumbed to as they bought their sandwiches; lipsticks, DVDs, magazines, scented candles. I kept it short, not sure how long I could hold them without songs and a microphone.

"Will it last?" I asked them. "Will it make you happy next month, or even next week? What did it cost you, really, added up alongside all the other lipsticks and magazines and irresistible pink stuff?" It didn't take long before one sincere young man told me we needed to shop - that it was the only thing that kept anyone in a job. But no one raised their hand when I asked them who made things for a living.

"I'm Alicia, and I work in a call centre," the blonde in the grey coat said. "People call us when their food mixer's broken. If it's under warranty, we take their details and ask them to send it in for repair, but I visited the warehouse once." She paused and looked at her boots. "We don't mend anything. It costs too much. It's cheaper to send everyone a new one, and of course they're delighted. But really," she said, looking back up to us all, "the waste is shocking. You should see them waiting for the dump, this great mountain of almost perfect mixers."

"But we need growth," the young man said. "The unemployment's killing us."

I agreed with him and asked what made them happy. Apart from the guy whose passion was his jet ski, everyone told me reading or gardening or playing with their kids or making love or hiking gave them their greatest fix. Simple things they didn't buy.

"So what stops you?"

"Hiking doesn't pay much." The crowd laughed again, riding the banter.

It turned out no one had enough time to do the things they loved. So we talked about the credit card chains we wore and the 40-hour treadmill that became 60-hours by the time you'd battled rush hour to drop and collect your kids and done extra hours because every boss was watching.

And they joined the dots, catching the thinking like an audience will catch a beat and add to it by tapping their feet or clapping.

"The profit and VAT from selling us foundation and painkillers, high heels and push-up bras is what keeps the world in drones and Kalashnikovs," I said and got meaty applause and a couple of whoops from the back row.

I left them wanting more, a Grandad trick, and said I'd see them online, told them to message me and tell me what they thought....

Fate and Sam had stayed. He gave me a hug but Fate just asked when she'd have something new to play. If I'd pushed *A million rooms* a tiny bit further forward I could have played it to her there and then - sent her off to work on the fat drum sounds to fill it out and Sam to weave in his narrative of notes and harmonies. But it wasn't ready. A song is a forlorn and half-baked thing until you've cooked it enough to share.

"Yeah, I've been getting loads of ideas," I lied, taking my time to zip Elsie away so she'd give up.

It was only when I crossed the road to retrieve my bike that I saw Salvador watching me.

"Masumi sent me to film," he said holding out his camera as if I expected evidence. I didn't need to ask how he'd found me. HeadSpace would have told them as soon as I hit the first chord.

He stood so close to me, the lunchtime crush sliding around us, I could see how long his eyelashes were.

If I leant forward, we would be touching. I shook the idea away like I'd shaken the worst of the rain from my hair, before we'd played.

Salvador had caught a taxi so I got to cycle back on my own, flying down the hill so fast it made me laugh and rekindled my adrenalin. By the time I was back at HQ I was as pumped as if we'd just played a stadium, not busked.

"We need stickers," I called topping the stairs "and posters. 'Stop Shopping's' gonna fly..."

"Stickers? How very 2010," Michael said. I stuck my tongue out at him and grabbed one of the office chairs, wheeling myself over the boards to Masumi and Burt, both tapping away.

"Let's go for a beer?" I asked them. Burt didn't even look up. He muttered something over his keyboard about the network. Masumi stopped and turned to look at me.

"You are very, very good, Ruby" she said, with a sincerity that made me squirm. "You want to see?" She turned her big screen towards me. "This someone uploaded already."

A low res phone video taken from close up in the crowd showed my face, filling the screen. She danced the playback along, letting flashes play for me. I got used to watching myself singing years ago, but talking, like this, to camera is different. Not talking in an interview about songs or writing or touring, or flirting with the audience at a gig, between songs, but talking to a crowd like this, trying to reach the heart of them and snag them into change. It was strange seeing me laughing and sincere, my accent broader than it sometimes sounds, making a kind of speech. I had to get Masumi to play it back properly, so I could try and judge it. It wasn't that good, really. But it wasn't bad either. And it was clocking up views faster than *Peanut Heart* had spread. The comments span away down the page, some angry, some afraid but many, many more saying 'yes, we need to stop'.

"It's working," I said, to help me make it real.

"It is," she said. "I've shared this one on our page and yours. I'll let it run for a while then I'll let this loose too." She toggled to the same scene but shot from further back to give a wider angle and show the crowd around us. Even from further away the sound was better. After a moment the image zoomed in to my face. "I'm cutting Salvador's footage in with other material," she said and touched the screen. It filled with a mosaic of gentle loveliness - kids playing in a rain shower like we used to get, before the angry downpours, and white foxes skipping across an excess of ice.

"You do know we're too late to save the summer sea ice?" Michael asked, coming over.

It was hard to remember what I was supposed to know. The changes were happening so fast and randomly since the Amazon and the tundra had betrayed us and both started chucking out CO_2. All 'the end is nigh' predictions of the last 20 years were hitting in a flurry, like rush hour buses. There were so many floods and heatwaves and unpredictable knock-on effects I couldn't keep up. The media would slay me in an interview.

"Is it … misleading?" I asked him. He shrugged. He said no one knew, not really. I think he was trying to make me feel better.

I had a better idea of what would settle the jangling post-adrenal mosh pit in my gut. A decent pint.

"Come on, pub time," I tried again.

"You go and when you are back I will have finished," Masumi said turning her screen away from me so its light flooded her face again. Burt had his headphones on and the slightly anxious look geeks get when they are battling a problem they are not entirely sure they can defeat. Given the heavy hits landing on the illicit network he'd woven to carry us into the world I thought I'd better leave him to it.

"We're celebrating?" Salvador asked, his dark head appearing at the top of the stairs. There was an elemental energy about him, as if the earth had sprung a leak and shards of magma flowed through its crust into his feet, leaving him shining and energised. He made me want to laugh. He made me want to dance. I knew why Michael wanted to fuck him.

I sprang up and grabbed Michael's arm.

"Get your coat," I said and watched him look to Salvador and back to me.

"No, you two go," he said. "You've done your bit for today, now it's my turn," and he stepped away as if surrendering. I tried twice more but there was no persuading him and I didn't want to make him seem weak by insisting. Maybe he was playing hard to get.

In The Palace we sat at the table by the window. Salvador told me how inspired he was by our work, touching my hand as he spoke. His skin was a pale glossy brown, like the gummed strip on the back of an official envelope, against my own, tracing-paper pale. The cigar smoke curl of his voice filled the soft, gritty place between comfort and danger. I moved my hand and drank my pint and locked my desire tight to my bones.

Eventually I leant across to him. "You're flirting at the wrong person," I said, carefully, into his ear. Then I downed my beer and left him in the pub, with half a pint to go.

I retrieved my bike from the hallway at HQ and rode a wide loop, south of the Aire, to pedal the lust away. After I dropped my bike home I walked fast back to Church Row so my heart kept racing and safely tired me.

"Next time, come," I told Michael when I got back. We let Masumi show us her final edit - the best slices of my speech, laid across Carnival Owls beats and strung between footage of us playing, me talking, images of nature's loveliness and faces from the crowd that morning. Mainly they were laughing but then, one woman, watching with tears poised in her eyes.

"And I ordered stickers," Masumi told me, flicking the last frame of the video from her screen to reveal the design - a line drawing of a handbag slashed out by a pink cross, its edges smudgy as if someone had drawn it in lipstick. Perfect.

Masumi hit 'upload' and I caught the bus to Mum's for tea.

She fed me pumpkin soup and let me fret about Grandad. She told me she loved 'Stop Shopping' and worried I wasn't getting enough sleep. Then she asked me if I'd go with her, to Garforth.

She'd been out planting, she said, every evening, along the verges, under the street lights, except the night it snowed. The slush had barely shifted and there she was, shrugging into her coat, tying the orange scarf I'd made her against the cold, her trug laden with margarine tubs of the seeds she saved each autumn, her trowel and a spare for me. I was warm and tired but of course I went.

We took the bus and planted lettuces and curly kale into the wet, shaved grass between the footpath and the kerb. The street lamps overhead turned us black and grey and orange. While we planted, she talked. She told me how sick she was of the rules that protected soccer pitches and kept food out of reach. Anything she had done in her job, she said, had been compromised. The Council didn't really want people growing food on a big scale because then they wouldn't buy so much. "If we were growing enough, the supermarkets would feel it,"

she said, "and Tesco and Sainsbury's all make big donations to politicians. She looked up from poking angry
divots in the turf with her trowel. "I had to get out, while
I'm still young enough to do the work properly."

Other people's mums in their fifties have affairs with
men my age or buy a used, red MX-5. Mine ditches her
job to grow more stuff. When we ran out of seeds,
I called us a taxi and dropped her home.

Back at my flat I sat in the glow from the city lights
scattered wide below me and played myself old
PJ Harvey vinyl. I worried about Mum driven to illicit
planting in the dark and Grandad slipping away from us.

To distract myself I went online and from the wide
and wondrous web I chose to read a post by a 10 year old
boy evacuated from Kiribati who was missing the dog
he'd had to leave behind. His island was underwater.
Clearly the dog had drowned. The boy thought it had
hopped on a floating log and would wash up on a beach
somewhere. He wanted everyone to share his message
so he and the dog could be reunited.

I turned the record over and couldn't imagine anyone
would ever stop shopping because I asked them to.

Until today, I have been compelled by obedience. Duty, my daddy would have called it. I had pledged to stop Her because Bishop Hamilton had asked it of me. But now I have witnessed the hot evil of her seduction first hand, felt its breath on me across the table in the bar, and my soul is fired by the need to douse her treachery against God. Only He commands the winds and rain. Only He sends life or death to fish and fowl and man. I will stop her blasphemy because my heart has witnessed the power of her corruption and today I saw the way.

It was easy.

Michael left his keys on his desk, a small set with a rubber rainbow fob. While he made me and Masumi coffee, I pocketed them. When I went to buy us sausage rolls from the Greggs store, I got the pale boy at Mister Minute to cut me a copy. I slipped the originals back on Michael's desk while he flicked through his phone for a number to give me. It was too easy. He never saw a thing.

I woke fretting about Mum and would have played the stress out but I'd left Elsie at HQ. I fingered my way through a couple of Gaga songs on my old Fender, still my second favourite stage guitar after the silver Les Paul, but it wasn't the same.

I left early instead and walked, through the concrete and glass wind tunnel Clarence Dock becomes when it blows from the east, dodged the cars on the Crown Point Bridge and up to the Calls. Everyone I passed was hunkered in their collars, head down, hunched in the chill and hungry for summer. When I turned into Church Row, Michael was coming out the door. He waited for me at the top of the steps, his face drawn tight.

"What is it?" I asked.

"You'd better see it for yourself," he told me and stepped aside to let me in.

All our chairs and tables were tipped and cockeyed, legs up amongst the debris of papers and cables. Some of the desks were broken-backed, as if the room had grown giant boots and stamped on them, crushing them to the floor. Anything that could be emptied out had been - shelves and drawers and the compost bin. I walked into the chaos, as if moving through it might help me understand. Masumi's large screen lay in shards like a smashed beetle. I stood her wheelie chair the right way up but it just made everything else look worse.

I hadn't been angry before, not like that. I'd had the big fear and frustration for a long time, overflowing at the Grammys. Michael's insistence we share survivalist tactics had placed a new foreboding in my gut, like the chill from drinking too much cold water on an empty stomach, that even the perky optimism of 'Stop Shopping' hadn't warmed. And last night, with Mum and her desperate planting, I'd got a new sense things were unravelling really fast and taking our sanity with them.

But the fractured desk and shattered windows, the broken screens and spoiled work ignited a new, bowel-deep anger. An anger at the waste and an anger at the invasion. How dare someone break into our space and trash it. I'd been robbed before. We once got all our band gear nicked out of the van and I was only 14 when I first got my pocket picked, but this was different. Pure destruction. Their message was spray painted across the wall in gory scarlet - 'Damned'. There was nothing artistic about that graffiti, just hatred in every stroke and drip.

Michael clattered up the stairs behind me and I realised I was hugging myself. I smeared the tears off my face and shook my arms out as I turned to him.

"Some Fundie sect?" I asked.

"I'd say so. Damnation is a pretty Christian concept."

"Christianity doesn't look very pretty today," I said and wondered if it'd make a lyric.

Michael flinched at my lame pun and told me he'd left Salvador downstairs.

"I've asked him to send the others home," he said, "while we work out what to do."

"Yes," I told him, "but just while we clean up the worst of the mess. I want the team back in, this afternoon. This is about them as much as us. They need a say in what happens next."

He muttered about it being my face on everything and him carrying the can but in the end he agreed.

Everyone met up in the afternoon, huddled in our jumpers on the sofas while a guy Venus had found replaced our windows. Most of the computer gear sat on the floor but we'd carted out the broken furniture and got two coats of paint on the tagging. Elsie had been safe where I'd left her, propped in her case in the cloakroom. I held her to comfort me.

Masumi had made a haiku about being damned by shopping and posted it on our site. She was similarly philosophical about the attack.

"If we move," she said, "they'll find us if they really want to. All our energy will go into watching our backs. Our work is too heavy for distraction. Besides, it will show them we are afraid." She spoke quietly, as if the ideas were written in calligraphy across her lap.

"Aren't you?" I asked, wondering if my anger was fear in disguise.

"I'm not afraid of anything," she said, looking right at me.

Daisy wanted to stay too, enhanced by security cameras and round the clock guards and explosives. I drew the line at explosives.

Burt was salvaging what he could from the gutted hardware. He sat cross legged on the floor, the mineral carcasses scattered around him.

"Computer stuff breaks," he said, when it was his turn to speak. "It's only gear. I fix it or we replace it. Michael and I had our laptops with us, so we've got those. I might get a couple of the others going again. All our content's in the Cloud. We can work anywhere." His focus was already back on the machine in his lap.

Michael thought a move would be distracting.

"Fine by me," Salvador said, shrugging the elegant angle of his shoulder. I noticed the line of shadow that traced his collar bone, leading from the V-neck of his sweater to beneath the wool.

"So we stay," I told them, standing up more to distract myself from him than for any dramatic emphasis. I put Elsie back in her case and zipped her safely in.

"Yesss!" Burt called, as if Leeds had just scored but he was watching at home with sleeping kids in the next room. "Here we are boys and girls," he said and turned the laptop on his knees to show us. Our 'Stop Shopping' pages sprawled down the screen. He'd saved one more at least.

I fished my phone from my top pocket and sat down again, thumbing my own social pages open. The HeadSpace stream showed splash after splash of support. It was Carnival Owls fans mainly - some asking if this was a new album, some declaring undying love, some telling me to stick to music. Jutting in between were comments damning us with the same fury as the rage written on our wall. We had enemies and we'd barely begun. I tried to follow the connection in my mind - why would hard core Christians attack us over shopping? I knew the churches all had gift shops but Jesus had picked a fight with the money-lenders.

"Is it because of my Grammy speech?" I asked Michael, showing him my screen.

I'd lashed out at the God-bothering but some believers are bigger greenies than me - even the Pope's gone all eco these days. 'Creation care' Mum says they call it, nurturing the fruits of their messiah. She's more patient with it than I am. We're not gifted rule of the planet by any super-powered deity. We're just part of it.

"It's their fear," he said, taking my phone from my hand, turning it off and passing it back. "The crazier the weather gets, the more afraid they get and the more they think God is punishing us. Denial is easier than confronting it all. And it's better for God and business. The big US-Fundy churches are all bankrolled by Chevron and ExxonMobil." He ran a hand through his hair and looked around the wreck of our office. "I wouldn't be surprised if BP had a hand in their growing over here."

I knew he was right, even if the connections didn't make much sense. It felt as if there were two very different logics at work in the world, gravity pulling in two directions. It had been a long day and, with a couple of thin nights' sleep behind me, I was as slow and ragged as when we'd toured too many towns.

"Bloody brilliant," Burt said, yanking me back to the room.

I wanted to go home and grab some sleep and start our revolution again tomorrow. Later I would realise how little I had understood about tiredness.

Burt had followed a HeadSpace link and found a video. I yawned and watched while he played it again, the sound turned up so we could all hear. The vid opened with two American high school girls, all Arizona tans and blonde tresses. One wore braces and was still beautiful.

"Hi," they said in unison, straight to camera.

"I'm Amy."

"And I'm Gemma."

"And we're both Rubies!"

I winced, still not used to what some fans call themselves. It was too sycophantic, too cultish. Just too damned weird.

"Cute," I said, "but I don't do cheerleaders."

"Shush," Burt said. "Just listen."

"We love you Ruby and what you stand for. We thank the planet every single day and do our best not to hurt her."

The two young women swapped, speaking in turn.

"Since your Grammy speech, we've got hundreds of girls biking to school every day, even though most of them can drive."

"There's so many girls biking heaps of the boys have started too, so they can try and score on the way," she giggled, blushing. I guessed one boy had succeeded.

"And we started recycling and composting."

"And got the cafeteria to stock loads more veggie food."

"But we wanted something to show what we stood for."

"Something amazing."

"Something unmistakable."

"Something that would make people notice what we said."

"But no lame T-shirts that have been done like a million times before."

"Something that would show how far away from nature we've got."

"Fuck, they're good!" I said, laughing, "The suspense is killing me!" I was awake again, wired from their energy.

"So first," they said, speaking together again, "we grew our pits!" They brandished photos of themselves into the camera lens. In the pictures they were beaming, arms akimbo above their heads, armpits lush with curly blonde hair. It was the most natural thing in the world but the surprise of it made me realise how rarely I saw it.

"Nice!" I said

"Wait," Burt said. "It gets better." The girls pulled the pictures away from the camera.

"And then we dyed them ruby!" The screen filled with swathes of teenage cleavage and four scarlet nests of armpit hair as the two of them lunged, laughing at the camera. The image cut for a second then returned to the two of them seated, side by side.

Amy, the one with braces who'd pulled a boy on her bike, spoke next.

"We did them in time for the first game of the season and worked our butts off to make sure we got picked for the front row." They really were cheerleaders! "Then we hijacked the choreography so we got to be in the middle. About half way through the first routine we all take off our hoodies and go straight into a star jump. So there we were flashing our hairy ruby pits at the whole home crowd!

"Coach was furious but there was nothing she could do. Afterwards we asked her to show us where in the rules it said we had to shave our pits. Of course it doesn't, though everybody does. So she had to let it go."

Gemma interrupted.

"But Ruby, the best part is, it's catching on. There's girls in every class growing their pit hair too and they're mostly the cool ones so it's becoming a trend. And we talk to them all to make sure they know what it means and send them to your website."

"So, we just wanted to let you know and say 'hi.'"

"And to tell you if you're out this way you HAVE to come and do a show."

"We love you Ruby!!" they both mugged at the camera and the image froze on them laughing and waving, their elbows high to show off their scarlet hair.

"Outstanding!" I said.

"I thought you'd like it," Burt said.

"I love it," I said, yawning. "I'm going home right now, to bed, to start growing my pits. I can revolt in my sleep. It's genius."

"You should send them a message," Michael told me.

"When did they post the video?"

"Last night, our time."

"They are seven hours behind us," Salvador said, his face closed, watching me. "If you reply now they will get it today."

161

"Alright, alright. But just text. I'm not doing video in this state."

"You are one vain woman," Salvador told me, spinning round in his chair, his voice deadpan.

I laughed, "Yeah right." I'm notorious for kicking around in my jeans and a green Aran jumper I knitted myself when I'm away from the cameras. It makes dressing up more fun when there's a reason.

I took the laptop from Burt and keyed in an effusive comment under the video post, telling Trudy and Gemma I'd started growing my pit hair the moment I saw their video. I shared the link to their vid on my Head-Space page. Then I carried Elsie home and slept till morning.

It was too easy and it wasn't enough.

I fear my Lord is punishing me for the sin of pride. I felt sure, as I walked away and heard the bang of the firecracker behind me, blowing the hole in the door to mask the silence of my earlier entry, that I had triumphed. But already they are rebuilding. The smell of the spray paint was worse here in my apartment, from the surgeon's gloves I wore, than it was in their office by the end of the day. I burned the gloves in the washbasin and left the bathroom door shut to suck the fumes away with the extractor fan.

Pastor Brian wanted a full report and the less he said to me the heavier my phone felt in my hand. I have let him down. He will report to Bishop Hamilton. Despite his disappointment, Pastor Brian is relieved I am not suspected. I think there is vanity in it for he prides himself on my disguise.

He says my collusion in their blasphemy must be my cross to bear each day. I told him how the sluts on the screen made me sick, flaunting the pubic hair from their armpits, the way whores pout and smack the lips on their faces to remind you of their cunts. I prayed for Gemma and Amy. They are so knowing, so young, as if they could not wait to leave their innocence behind. I fear for their salvation. Not only has the

Devil polluted their minds but he uses them as instruments of his decay. They are a wicked plague in their school and in their town and now throughout the world, infecting others without mercy or understanding.

I prayed for there is little else I could do - other than report as I have done, and place my confession here, before the eyes of God. After praying, I read Psalm 58:10 and it brought me some peace.

Hamilton will tell our Church in Arizona to bring the girls to God but I doubt those daughters of Eve will have the wisdom to hear his Word. Not while Ruby urges them on. She left us after She had posted her response to their video, but I stayed watching. Within no time the girls had replied, full of blasphemy. And as the Earth turned under Heaven and the sky went dark, fallen girls from across the planet left their own messages, promising to grow their vile hair and to dye it red.

As Saint Jerome wrote, though God can do all things He cannot raise up a virgin once she has fallen. I ask God for the strength to do my part in defeating this wickedness.

Tonight, when I phoned Momma, she did not answer. Perhaps she has taken up with men again like she did when Daddy died. She had no time for me then, either, and when I called out to her in my hour of need she did not hear. God give me strength.

I had the chorus and the video for *Scream for Justice* clear in my mind when I woke. I scribbled the lyric into my phone and padded through to the lounge, capturing the notes on Elsie before they faded in the sunlight. *Don't scream for me to get your kicks, Don't scream for me when the world's so broke, Don't scream for me - this fame's a joke, Scream out your lungs for Justice.* When I had it straight I played and sang it into my tablet and sent it to Sam and Fate to work with.

I often get a video concept at the same time as the song. I am YouTube generation, after all. The *Justice* video would start with tight-on face shots - girl fans all colours and sizes, singing into camera. Me, just intercut with them, doing the same. Then we'd pan out a bit so you could see we were in loads of different locations, all sorts of places to represent ubiquity. Then, for the last chorus every girl could punch the air, revealing a beautiful hairy scarlet pit. I'd debut my own new furry pets. Sadly that might be enough to give it news time cut through.

Michael had been bugging me to make an Owls song an anthem for the cause. This could be it. I set Elsie down and tucked my fingers in the warm cleft under my right arm and willed them to hurry up and grow. Then I went and showered.

There were two messages when I was dry and dressed.

Fate: Surprise! A protest song.

Sinead: Four days to Ryder party. Daytime wants you on. Call me.

Fate I ignored. Sinead told me *Daytime* didn't want me on to talk about the Grammy win like she'd hoped - they wanted to grill me about 'Stop Shopping'.

"You'd better know what you're doing, Ruby," she said before hanging up.

Do any of us, I wondered. I once saw the actor that plays Baldrick in *Blackadder*, narrating a documentary, saying there are three things societies have done, in the past, when their climate changed - sleepwalk to oblivion, innovate or rise up against the rulers. Oblivion seems likely but unappealing. There's shit loads of innovation but it's all too tiny because the corporations don't want it and the Coalition is useless. So, given Baldrick was always right, that leaves 'rising up'. But it's hard when you're rising to see what's above your head. So, no Sinead, I don't know what the fuck I'm doing but I have to do it anyway.

My phone chirped again.

Fate: I know you're ignoring me, bitch. Two more.

I put the phone under the fluffy grey cushion on the sofa where its chirps would stay trapped. I'd recruited

Fate between the vodka and the nitrous at a party Sinead had thrown, in London. Sam and I had been releasing some songs, on Trackcloud, recording as The Carnival Owls, but we were still finding our sound. Sinead had heard enough to be interested in representing us. The party invite was part of her pitch. Being Sinead, her parties had a practical purpose, beyond the hedonism. They were concocted not just to impress and close the deal with prospective bands, but to cook together different musical personalities and talents and see what might emerge. She is an addict for possibilities, be they sonic or romantic. Both make news.

Fate was in Sinead's kitchen, her back to me, and I heard her laugh first, a broad guffaw like something from a Shakespeare play. I'd pulled up a seat and become instantly smitten by her lips.

We'd matched each other shot for shot, others joining us in our rosy bubble at the pine slab of a table for a while before leaving us to the combative squabbling and flirting we'd begun even before we exchanged names. She won the argument - that bands with live drummers do better because humans evolved to feel the physicality of the beats in music. She said we quiver at the resonance of the soundwaves in a way you can't ever evoke through the compressed, processed beats of electronica.

I decided, around the third shot, that The Carnival Owls needed a drummer.

By the fifth, I knew the drummer had to be Fate.

I told her she was too soft and Southern for us - that I'd love her to prove her point by playing for The Owls but we were a Northern band. No Londoner would have the guts to shift to Leeds, or to hack our grit when they got there.

She told me she'd train up with me tomorrow and passed me a NOS from the box being handed round. I remember thinking, as the little patter of paw prints began inside my skull, that I didn't believe her and then my mind became a symphony of exploding galaxies, as my neurons fired in delight.

Giggling, later, we slid into bed and explored each other with the slippery erotica I think you can only get with another woman. The next afternoon, when she returned from her flat with her kit bag and a pair of practice drums, we promised each other - only music. But I do still like to make her laugh.

I hadn't made Fate, or Sam, so much as smile lately. I'd gone all activist on them, throwing my energy into making change not tunes.

Fate was right, of course. The Ryder gig was looming and two more new songs don't write and rehearse themselves. To top off *Justice* I needed to finish *A Million Rooms*, make one whole new song from scratch and get in at least two rehearsals. I swore, retrieved my phone and texted them both to meet at six for kebabs and a practice.

I chewed potential lyrics for *A Million Rooms* as I walked to Church Row, recording any snatches

I thought might stick on my phone, just in case. As I turned the last corner and the grungy brick of HQ came into view I had the genius idea there might be sound-grabs we could sample of the crowd and my vocals from the no-lights video Stellar had filmed. We could make *A Million Rooms* more a spoken word mash-up than the structured songs we usually release.

I stopped, where I was, in the street and rang Sam. He liked the idea, though, to be honest, I think he was more relieved I was thinking music than anything. Better still, he said he'd call Stellar to get the original footage and see what he could find. I didn't have to do it. It was what Michael called delegation.

I hesitated, a few steps from the top of the stairs, unsure if I could shoulder the weight of the Group's energy right then. It seemed to flow down the steps from the landing and smother me in responsibility. I could turn round now, go to Sam's and work on *A Million Rooms* with him, spend the whole afternoon lost in the buzz of creation. Maybe even record, if it came together. We could summon Fate, pack up the gear and go on the road, cocooned in the rhythm of travelling and playing away from news of reality.

The front door opened below me. Salvador came in, his dark curls in a flurry around his face.

"Ruby!" he said, when he looked up and saw me and in the moment of his surprise there was no artifice. His desire was plain. Even without Michael's prior claim, the last thing I needed was a fling with a collaborator. Once you start sleeping with someone there's only two things that happen - you keep doing it and lose yourself in lust or love, or you stop and at least one of you gets bitter and twisted. The times when you can pull off a return to platonic, like Fate and I had done, are rare as genius in my experience. One or three night-ers, on the road, where departure is explicit from the first raised eyebrow and no one expects to be friends, excepted of course.

I turned my back on him, with a courteous 'hey', and went up.

"Where've you been?" Michael asked, as soon as he saw me, jiggling his clipboard. Then he looked past me and blushed as Salvador appeared. "Oh," he said, and I could see the calculation run in his eyes, stacking up the two of us arriving together into a mountain of misunderstanding.

"Band stuff," I said and drew him away, to my desk by the window. "What's up?"

"'Stop Shopping's working," he said, "Daytime want you."

"I know, Sinead rang."

"Good," he said, "They called Masumi and we've booked you in, live-to-air from the studio."

"This week?" I asked him stupidly.

Masumi joined us, jittery with excitement, a grinning fidget of hands and feet. She was making me nervous. I asked her to make us coffee.

"I'm not ready," I told Michael, prodding into life the new laptop Burt had set up for me. "I need to do my homework, get a better grip on the facts. They'll rip me apart."

"So read up some more," he said, shrugging. "Start with Clive Hamilton, he's always good. And Monbiot. But it won't make any difference."

"I'm not thick!" I told him, thinking he meant I was too dull to learn. He explained, patiently, as you might to an amnesiac, that it wasn't my climate science the media wanted me for.

"It's just you, and your fame they want Ruby. You know everything you need to know. We've had enough of the problems. People need answers. 'Stop Shopping' is simple. It makes people listen. It helps them join the dots. That's the only story you need to tell."

"Thanks," I said, sarcastically and spun my chair away from him. I read the latest blogs from Monbiot, Hamilton, Stern and Hansen. Whenever I looked up, Salvador was smouldering at me from his desk on the far side of the room. I ignored him and read some more, typing a list for myself of some impactful facts I might remember.

By twelve I was tired of all the old men with their predictions of doom.

I flicked open my HeadSpace page and typed:

"Do they think we're going to dress up and go shopping while the world fries in our excess? Well they underestimate us, don't they?!"

I could tell Salvador was watching me again. Even rock stars aren't immune to flattery, in fact we're probably more susceptible to it - conditioned to seek approval. There was nothing subtle about his attention. I wasn't surprised it was making Michael jealous. If he was just a random, pretty guy admiring me in a pub on the road somewhere I'd walk over and kiss him, but any taste of Salvador would be poisoned with complication before we opened our mouths.

As if I summoned him with my mind, he got up. He kept his eyes on mine as he walked across the office, narrow hipped and contained, like Furball stalking, all his focus on his prey, before he got old and saggy of course.

"Can I buy you lunch?" he asked, leaning over my desk, his hands spread . The tendons ran up his arms, tightening the weave of muscles across his chest, plain through his thin sweater. He smelt of split sapling wood, sharp with potential. I wanted to touch his curls.

"I need you to go to London," I said, improvising. "Meet with Greenpeace and Plane Stupid and Climate Rush too, if you can find them. Take them through 'Stop Shopping' in person. We need them fully on board."

He looked wounded. Good. I was all for succumbing to lust but not right then. And not with one of the team.

"I've already got phone updates scheduled with them all," he said, moving away a few steps, watching me as he reassessed.

"It'll be better face to face," I told him, snatched up my bag and left.

One of the reasons I stayed up in Leeds, defying Sinead's advice again, is because not only can you get a decent pint, without the paparazzi sticking a lens up your skirt or people bugging you for a selfie, but we also still have proper music shops. Shops owned and run by guys who play and tune and mend instruments, not by chain store monsters. Two of the best are right here at this end of town.

Grandad always favoured Northern Guitars because he used to go drinking with Patrick, the owner. I've spent a bomb there over the years, but Patrick's never quite forgiven me for buying my first electric from Band Supplies. I take turns spending at both, which delights neither but keeps us all on speaking terms. The Owls aren't their only celebrity clients, there's the Kaiser Chiefs and The Music and Kalash and Hayley Gaftarnick. Even Andrew Eldritch still hangs out at Northern from time to time, fingering the merchandise. I am, however, their biggest famous customer right now, anyway, so it seems tactful to be even-handed.

It's also true that putting two of the city's icons in your band name makes everyone think they own a slice of you, regardless of whether they like your tunes. The Chapeltown Carnival had been shaking its stuff down the road from us every year since before Mum was born. Grandad used to take her when she was a kid and for years the three of us went. Mum reckons the first time they took me, when I was a baby, Dad came too, before he buggered off. As for the owls, well, just look up next time you're in Leeds and you'll see them peering down from rooves and doorways, plinths and podiums, all over the place. Mum and I used to make up stories about how they escaped the coat of arms and went on the rampage.

I needed strings and it was Northern's turn.

The only two things that have changed, from when Grandad first brought me in for strings for Elsie, are Patrick has gone grey and Flying Vs are back in style. The walls are still painted the same matt charcoal, adorned with guitars in candy colours, and the place still smells of warm electrics. Patrick was tuning a rather tasty Les Paul and nodded when he saw it was me. He knows I like to mooch and sometimes, if he leaves me to it, I'll succumb to a new guitar. I gathered up my Cobalt Slinkies and took them to the counter.

"Take your time," he called, testing his tune up with *Killer Heels* in my honour.

"Just these today," I said, leaning back against the counter to watch him play. He ran through the chorus once more then set the guitar aside and came over.

"Nice work with that Grammy, love," he told me, ringing up the sale to my account and shovelling the strings into a Northern Guitars carrier bag. I gave up asking him to put them in my own bag years ago - he wants the brand association more than he cares about my eco-conscience. "We could put the trophy on the shelf up there," he said, glancing above the racks of picks and other nickables he keeps on the wall behind the counter, "so people get to enjoy it, like."

I told him the engraved one hadn't even been delivered yet, but that I'd think about it. Band Supplies would offer me the same, next time I went in, and the thing would end up in the back of my wardrobe, because I wouldn't offend either of them. Unless Mum claimed it.

Only when I was back on the street, strings safely stashed in my shoulder bag so I didn't get busted as both a shopper and a plastic bag user, did I realise how grateful I was Patrick hadn't mentioned the campaigning. For a few moments I'd been just a muso again. I wanted to sustain the feeling, like setting a chord loose, on endless repeat, through a loop pedal at the end of the show because you don't want the gig to end. It was eleven. The Adelphi would be serving. So I did what I hadn't in months and took myself for a beer.

I scrounged a biro from the guy at the bar, settled into my favourite leather chair and scrawled lyrics all over paper napkins, spreading them across the dark varnish of the table top, between the damp patches from my pint of Pale. I didn't care where the words came from or where the words took me, just let them flow along to the fledgling melody for *A Million Rooms* I carried in my head. When I realised my glass was empty, I stood up, stretched, burped and looked down over what I'd written. I hugged my arms round my chest so I didn't make any hasty decisions. Then I squished four napkins to a ball and sorted the other dozen into a rough kind of order. I read them through once more, scribbled 'chorus' round a bunch of lines and swapped two napkins over. Then I photographed the lot and sent it to Fate and Sam, with the sound file I'd made the week before.

I slunk back into HQ like a truant. I needn't have worried about my absence. Michael was much more concerned I'd sent Salvador away without checking with him first.

"I had things I needed him to do, Ruby!"

"Like outreach? Well, he's reaching out," I said, but I caught Michael by the arm and dragged him with me into the kitchen where we could have a smidge of privacy. We really needed to get some meeting rooms partitioned off. I closed the door behind us and leant back on it, arms folded, so I both protected us from intrusion and guarded myself against Michael's frustration. Writing always leaves me tender, like a graze when the scab's come off, so I needed all the resilience I could feign. "I'm sorry," I said, right off the bat, so he'd know I wasn't picking a fight, "but I think we both need some space from him. I should have planned it and checked with you first. It just kind of happened in the moment."

"Space?" he asked, all innocent.

"Oh come on!" I said. "The man's a walking honey-trap. You've had the hots for him since day one and he's firing a guns-blazing hormone assault on me right now." Michael's face flinched from the jealousy punch despite himself. "Yes I know, it's not fun to hear.

I just don't think he's into you, or men, or can't admit it, or whatever. And I don't want him. Any triangle of lust, like this, is going to leave someone crying, let alone when we're working like we are. I might not be Agony Aunt at Marie Claire but I can spot this disaster coming a mile off."

"You do fancy him?" he asked, somewhere between sulk and salacious.

"I'm a sucker for shaggy hair and adulation," I said, shrugging. "So sue me. It doesn't mean I'm going to fuck him. This is working, Michael and it's too important for some pretty boy to derail us. You and I need each other."

"I know," he said, sighing. "You're right." He turned away from me, tapping his fingers on the benchtop as if typing himself a to-do list while he thought. I waited until he sighed a second time and was ready to face me again. "Salvador can do the stuff we need on his phone and his laptop while he's away. If he doesn't cool it when he's back, I'll talk to him, Ruby, get him to lay off."

"I think I might have given him the message," I said, laughing, and stepping over to fire up the kettle.

"If in doubt ..." Michael started, and then I chimed in, so we chorused together, "- tea!"

We laughed and hugged and when we left the kitchen with our mugs I thought we'd got through it ok.

"Try Harrogate," I said, to him, before we headed back to our desks. "Cute guys, and most of them gay from the luck I've had up there!"

I played with TV sound bites for the rest of day, my words as unsure and stumbling as they had been when I wrote my first lyrics in the 3rd year at high school. Then I paced around, testing them out, trying to remember them. Burt kept glaring at me until he retreated under his headphones.

He was doing the final testing on the Purse Pincher app he'd had an elven band of coders develop overnight, more or less. In the last few days, independent 'Stop Shopping' sites and HeadSpace pages, blogs and vlogs had popped up all over the web, here in the UK but also Europe, Asia, and the States. Swapping content feeds was easy – we were splashing their posts all over our site and they could take what they wanted from ours. Purse Pincher took the whole thing to the next level.

The app lets you set a goal for cutting your shopping and plug it into your own profile page. If you linked it to your bank account you got a running score with flashing flowers when you beat your spending-cut targets and bonus points for donations to charity. Masumi had designed the graphics with a saccharine-cute graffiti art feel – as if My Little Pony had run feral with a spray can. It was irresistible.

Burt's headphones must have been a signal. Michael and Masumi corralled me in the corner by the window to stop me pacing. They made me sit on the sofa, perching themselves, one either side.

"Practice time," Michael told me and started role-playing bad cop interviewer down to the steely stare and the flying spit. Masumi's supposed good cop was nearly as brutal. I was rubbish to start with. I mean, really lame. There was just so much I wanted to say and carving it into four second mouthfuls was impossible, despite all my sound bite scripting. I stormed off twice, stomping to the far side of the room, spattering swear words over everyone, but I knew they were right. If there is one thing you learn leading a band it's the power of practice. So I persisted. And the more I tried and the simpler I kept it, the easier it got.

"We're stuck on a treadmill," I said, "But it's not making us fit, it's killing us."

"We need to harden up and get serious about what matters. There's no excuse for not seeing how things join up."

"It's time to stop falling for the pathetic lies in the advertising – of course we don't need the latest tangerine cushions or a Kate Moss toothbrush or to upgrade the fridge for one with an icemaker. We don't need panty-liners when we're not bleeding. And we don't need 14 kinds of face cream. We're perfectly wonderful human beings without all those things."

I took a breath and started again.

"The ridiculous 'Must Have's are killing us. They make us work too hard, or feel too rubbish if we can't find work. It's hamstringing us with debt. And it's chewing up the planet to make all the crap that will end up in landfill six months later. We don't need fair trade, organic alternatives to everything. We just need to 'Stop Shopping'."

They were both nodding at me and I thought I was doing alright. Then Michael went for the kill and told me I was an eco-terrorist that wanted to destroy the British Economy. He spoke those last two words with capital letters, as if they named something sacrosanct.

I smiled. The most useful thing Sinead ever taught me was the power of the smile to disarm an interviewer or a hostile crowd.

"I don't do violence," I said, "but yes, we do want to take down an economy that's failing our people, not just here, but worldwide too." And then I smiled again.

Masumi laughed so hard I thought her head might come off and even Michael let a small grin leak into his face.

"Not bad," he said. "We've still got time. By then, you'll do."

I lolled back on the sofa and gave the purple cushion a happy hug. I think I managed a feeble 'yay', more in relief than jubilation. I was knackered. The happy hit lasted all of five seconds, till I turned my phone from 'silent' and saw the time. I scrapped the plan to call home for a guitar, swore and scrambled and was still 15 minutes late. I slunk into Halikarnas as if they wouldn't notice.

Fate and Sam had already ordered. As I asked for my own falafel and hummus roll I realised what hurt most was their nonchalance about it, as if, after just a few short weeks, they expected nothing better of me.

Their kebabs came first so we stayed out of synch.

"So what's the plan?" Fate asked, as she bit into hers.

"I think we should open with *Peanut Heart*," I said, "then *Fat Cat*, *Dead Heat* and *Combo*, back to back, like we did in Europe." I told them I thought we could drop in *A Million Rooms* then follow it with *Justice*, before wrapping up with a couple of our early singles.

"You reckon they'll think some of our old stuff's new?" Fate asked, as if she'd read my mind.

Most of those old musicians don't stay current with their listening. They get stuck in their own era and genre. They're too middle-aged and lazy to go to gigs, so they only pick up on new talent when it mainstreams. Then they send a PA online to buy the whole back-catalogue for them and load it to their phones. They might only get to know a couple of tracks, just enough to name drop in an interview.

I wouldn't say it was part of the plan, but it had certainly crossed my mind. I'd also built the set list on the tunes we knew best, either because we'd played them into our bones the previous few months or had been playing them for years. It meant we could use what little practice time we had for *A Million Rooms* and *Justice*. And the other one I hadn't written yet.

Finally my food arrived and I escaped into chewing.

"So," I asked them, after swallowing my first bite, "the whole 'Stop Shopping' thing. What do you reckon?" I watched their faces as I ate.

"It's your fame, Ruby," Sam said, licking chilli sauce from his wrist. "No one blames you for using it in a good cause."

Fate just snorted and talked about her solo project with a bunch of women drummers from Sheffield.

It's not that they weren't plugged into politics - we'd always played benefits and I'd written protest songs for us before - but our obsession was with the tunes, not change. Or at least theirs was. Now I wanted both.

We'd worked so damned hard to get our music known. Playing was all any of us wanted to do. Not that we'd had many other jobs to choose from. So we had played and played and played.

We played parties in houses and passed around Fate's old army hat. We played on buses and at train stations until they kicked us out. We were all 19 and we wanted to fill Leeds with our songs. We turned up at Radio Aire uninvited and played in the corridor outside the recording booth so snatches leaked in when the DJ popped out for a piss. When the guards came for us we sang and shouted the rhythm while they escorted us off the premises. Once we were arrested for disturbing the peace. We got featured on *Noise Control*, Yorkshire TV's reality hit, three times, an unbroken record both the Yorkshire Post and NME reported. When we weren't playing live we were online, feeding our HeadSpace pages. We pumped the video channels full of live footage we shot ourselves, always from just above ground level as we propped a phone up on my guitar case, and homemade videos for the songs. Those first videos were rough cut mash-ups of the city we filmed just walking around or in our favourite bars, or stills we grabbed from comic books and magazines and off TV. We tried to make the viewer feel what it was like to live in our heads, with the tunes we made, so they would never want to be without them either.

We played hard and it worked.

We made a living, we got signed, we got promoted. The gigs got bigger and better - there were roadies and lighting rigs. The merchandise sold and we started making more than we spent.

There are two kinds of performers. Those who play live to pleasure themselves, wanking their guitars in public, shoe gazing, and those of us who play for the hit of pleasuring an audience, striving for the psychic feedback loop between a crowd and a band that transports both.

There is nothing sweeter than feeding delicious noise to an audience. And I mean nothing - no drug or sex has matched the high of creating fat, tangy sounds that make a crowd dance. There's something sublime in the fusion of body, beat, tone and volume, flooding everyone with soundwaves. Making them move.

Nothing pleases me to my toes the way a crowd at a gig can. The right crowd of course, punters open to the spark I can sometimes ignite in them. Punters who'll sweat and bounce and punch the air for the sheer pleasure of it, swept up in the hectic moment we're making for them, up on stage with our drums and beats and strings.

I'm an addict to it.

But playing live's like any drug, you have to pace your consumption or it burns you up. The bigger you get, the more they want you and the more you want to please - the longer the tours, the bigger the parties, the more incessant the talk-talk radio. And the deeper the need to retreat, at the end.

Touring *The Black Prince Parade* right through '15 had taken us to breaking point. We learned from that. The last couple of years we've done three or four months max at a stretch, then, at the end, lounged in downtime to write, eat fruit and sleep before midnight. Besides, I might be old fashioned, but if I'm away for much longer I miss my mum. We learned to book every tour to the end before we start and to plan each year to ebb and flow.

But with the Group I was realising there is no 'end'. There is no ebb. Just flow, forwards, all the time, always on, always more to say, or do. Always more people to reach. At least most of it I could do online so I could still pop round to Mum's for a cuppa or Sunday lunch. But it was already squeezing my time and energy so hard there was only a dribble of juice left for The Owls.

For Michael, Daisy and Salvador, their lives were geared to making change. For Sam, Fate and Lucy, my psycho-synth-blues buddy, and Deano, who spins the sweetest ambient come down you ever heard, and all the rest of my muso mates, our lives are played to make music.

Or at least, mine used to be. Not even the fame had threatened that the way the Group did. There was always some place to escape, even when Rolling Stone stuck me on the cover. I hired a tiny cottage with walls half a metre thick, tucked in a cranny of Eskdale, and vanished for a week of writing and dominoes with the old farmers at the Startled Mare. Fred, who still ran sheep up the valley, kicked my arse every time. I beat most of the rest though, once or twice, and then I'd stomp back up the lane in the dark, between the narrow stone walls, with the owl calling, and back at the cottage I'd sip my Baileys and cradle Elsie in my arms and write till morning.

In music we made the ebb and flow, in and out of society work for us - weeks or months holed up writing and then locked in practice rooms 24x7 with Sam and Fate till we were beat perfect and tight as bees. It takes hours playing together to make the tunes a reflex, the hive-mind melded, so you can focus on giving the audience such a performance they'll be grinning to their toenails and raving about you for weeks.

When we were ready, we'd throw ourselves on the mercy of the world. Touring bares you daily, all day, to strangers, for months. It's your job to smile and sign T-shirts and do radio and play and play and play until you bleed, sucking up the massed adrenalin from the punters each night to fuel you through the after-party and the slow daylight stumble to the next town and the next gig.

And then there was the end again - resting, home, other friends, other music and writing.

But with the Group I couldn't see where it would end. How are you supposed to fuck off for a week to the Lake District when the world's at stake?

I'd only managed half my kebab but Fate and Sam were fidgeting. While we walked to the practice rooms I told them what I had planned for TV. They shrugged, accepted it. Sam made polite, supportive comments, but jangled his keys in his pocket while he walked, like he does when he's nervous.

I borrowed a guitar from Matt who runs the rooms and Sam booted up his laptop and played back to me what they'd developed around *A Million Rooms*. We began with that - layering Fate's beats and my guitars together with the loops Sam had made, all cool and crystalline for the verses then hot as lava for the chorus. When we had it coherent enough I plugged in a mic. My voice sounded like a duck. Fate cringed. I'd talked too much and not done any of the cosseting of my vocal chords

I normally do before we play. They waited while I boiled the kettle and inhaled some steam. It didn't make much difference but I blundered on then committed the same butchery to the gorgeous, potent thing *Justice* should have been.

"Oh yes, just two," Fate said, when I set the guitar aside. Sometimes she just has to state the obvious.

Sam looked up from zipping away his laptop, his eyes flaring with the fear we might erupt into a fight. His parents never separated but bicker like ferrets so he's sensitive to arguments. He needn't have worried. My energy was puddled in my flowery Docs, as if only their laces held me upright. I might manage a few desperate tears but any other retaliation was beyond me.

"Can you fit in another practice before?" he asked, filling the silence and slinging the bag over his shoulder.

"Yeah, course," I said, finding my phone and starting to slide through the patchwork of demands that filled my calendar, looking for a window where we could play.

"Just message us," Fate said, stuck her drumsticks in the deep pocket on the thigh of her trousers and left. Sam put the room hire on our band's plastic and rubbed the furrow between my shoulder blades while we waited for Matt to ring it through.

"It'll be ok," he said, but for once I didn't believe him.

I watched dull fields stream by, through the spattered glass of the window, and I prayed for forgiveness. I should not be returning to London while She becomes more powerful. I wanted my return to the capital to be a journey of glory for the Lord and it is not to be. The trial is hard to bear.

At Kings Cross I felt as if every stranger might stop and turn to mock me. I stood for a while, by the bank of payphones, all busy with the accents of Babel, and wished I could press my face into the vanilla smell of Momma's neck. I waited and waited, not caring what time it was in Shreveport and if I'd wake her, until I knew I would be late if I did not go right away. I saw then the Lord was chiding me for weakness and urging me to stay on the urgent path. May He give me strength.

My first appointment was just a few blocks away. The big protest groups run like businesses, all smart offices and tele-workers in cubby holes. I caught the elevator to the seventh floor and shook their hands and was shown into a boardroom with a projector and a screen. They looked concerned when I said I didn't need them but I know preacher style works best for me in telling stories.

When it was time I just stood before them and told them what the Group were working on. I could see they don't trust

189

Her from the way they held their arms folded across their well-cut jackets and kept their faces still. They suspect her fame and doubt her motives. All the same, they are entranced. They speak of her reach with envy. 'Stop Shopping' makes them afraid. It smells to them of chaos.

I saw three groups this morning and four in the afternoon and at lunchtime I visited Pastor Brian. We met in the back room of The Crown at Clerkenwell Green, all etched mirrors and polished wood. Our chairs had red velvet cushions tied to the seats. We each drank a small glass of beer and I told him She was gaining power. I told him my instructions are clear as scripture; She must be put off, however it is to be done. I have enacted what I can but it is not enough. As I spoke of Her I could feel my stomach tighten and churn, like a craving. She has bewitched me with her sinful ways. I breathed deeply and told Pastor Brian what I needed. There is no other choice. It is time for action.

He rang Bishop Hamilton to arrange the funding while I waited. As he spoke, droplets of sweat formed below his ears. As I saw the fear wet his skin, I felt my own anxiety settle and fade within me.

The wheels are in motion. The Lord's will be done. She will desist.

The next morning *Daytime* launched their promo for my appearance.

"It's not your best look," Masumi said as we watched it, all gathered beneath the big TV Burt had installed high on the wall between the windows. They had used an old photo, where I'm startled by the flash. The announcer sounded like they'd just climbed three flights, signalling flaky excitement. We left the TV on, the sound turned down and every time I glanced up the promo seemed to be airing. In its wake, the media clamour surged again, spilling from online onto radio. The next few days slid by in a spaghetti of social posts and interviews, strung long into the night as we sucked up every drizzle of interest we could. Every editor and blogger wanted their own soundbites, something exclusive to scoop more eyeballs their way.

Michael mustered a gaggle of comms volunteers to help Masumi and me. Daisy made us keep them downstairs. She installed a steel door on the first floor landing, so you had to punch a code into a keypad to get to the top floors, and security camera intercoms. It was supposed to keep them safe from our secrets as well as protect us.

As part of what Michael called the newbies' basic training Masumi had a huge map printed for their wall. She got them all to put a 'Stop Shopping' sticker everywhere they could find a group or event supporting us. It got them down and dirty with the coverage and they'd made the map a happy, global polka-dot by the time Michael summoned me down to meet them.

"We can't do this without you," I told them, wearing my best pep-talk smile and wondering how I was going to learn the names to match the dozen eager faces. I felt if I squeezed any new information in, all my hard-won climate facts would start to leak from my ears. "We need you to help us manage what's coming in and cycle it out faster too - every post we can comment on, or supporters' video we like, spreads the success."

Michael interrupted me to tape a checklist on the wall, next to the map and the whiteboard. "It's a cheat sheet," he said, "to help you sort the abuse from the gems. These ones you can answer," he pointed at the list. I tried to sit still on my swivel chair while Michael talked but his grip on the detail made me fidget. He held his clipboard but hardly glanced at it.

The new volunteers were sitting around an equally new swathe of desks and laptops. The hefty hole the ATM showed in my account when I got Michael the cash had made me laugh - so much for stopping shopping! The desks were all rescued from an insurance office, liquidated by flooding claims, but recycling was too risky with tech. Burt said even if he peeled apart every second-hand machine to check, he could never be sure they were clear of spyware fitted specially for us.

"The rest you flag for Masumi and Ruby to do," Michael looked to me and I nodded and smiled again, as if I was confident I'd be able to do my part.

Next he called out the names of all the journalists he wanted the newbies to follow. They had to share any posts each reporter or their paper made about 'Stop Shopping' and comment in support or correction, extending the reverb. Once every volunteer had a clutch of media to hound, it was question time and my turn again.

The first two were easy, and a giddy surge in my gut made me feel better than I had in days. Then an older woman with a bubble of brown curls round a kind face, who I think was called Claire, asked me what our new angle would be for *Daytime*. I started to answer then stopped and looked at Michael. He looked at Masumi whose lips were parted in a perfect O of surprise, like a manga hero under ninja attack. We didn't have any-thing new to say on *Daytime*. I watched the concern seep into Claire's kindness. It started in her eyes then leaked down to her lips. Soon it would be spoken into the group, loud as doubt.

"That's the next thing we need from you," I improvised, wheeling my chair forward so I couldn't see Michael. "'Stop Shopping' is catching on but you're right, we should freshen it up for Daytime. What do you think?"

They all talked at once, as if my question had squirted bubble bath into a hot tub and stirred up a foaming overflow of ideas. I let the soothing froth of it wash round me.

"One at a time," Michael said, getting to his feet and glaring at me before he turned to the whiteboard. Over the next half hour, under Michael's careful coaxing, they told us 'Stop Shopping' was too vague and floppy, too easy to start 'tomorrow'. They told us we had to make it more focussed. I got a visual then, of a magnifying glass channelling the sun's rays to one, bright point. They were right. We needed *Daytime* to be sharp enough to scorch through the indifference.

Masumi, our poet, gave us the answer, so of course it alliterates. On *Daytime*, we'd announce 'Stop Shopping Saturdays'.

Michael thanked everyone, then prodded me in the shoulder with his pen and I followed him back upstairs.

"Nice work," I told him as we passed his desk. He paused and I thought he was would tell me off for drawing the newbies into our planning but he simply nodded and went to his seat. His eyes were dark underneath, as if he'd slept in smeared mascara.

He confessed he wasn't sleeping, said his head was spinning from the cocktail of the campaign. I realised then we had just added one more spirit to the mix. When he'd been cross, downstairs, I'd assumed it was because my request for ideas had been the kind of surprise he liked the least, packed with potential disorder and risk. Really it was because Michael's brain was full too.

"No, no! The Saturdays thing is great," he told me. It looked as if only the taut pull between excitement and exhaustion held him upright in his seat.

"You're more knackered than me," I told him. "Go home."

"I can't, not yet. I've the volunteer plan for after Daytime to finish and Drew, the comms guy from Avaaz, is calling from the States."

"Please," I said. "You'll work on it better in the morning. I'll talk to the Avaaz guy myself or reschedule or something. It'll keep."

He paused, caught between the drive to do it himself and hearing the sense in what I said. I waited while he balanced it out until, finally, he stretched and smiled.

"All right," he said, "You win. But keep it short with Drew. I can call them tomorrow night. You've got enough going on."

"Only another gazillion replies," I said, checking my inbox. Masumi had already taken as much of the overflow as she could. "A quiet day. And at least they're more interesting than the emails I used to get, asking what I ate for breakfast." Neither of us quite laughed but it at least made him smile.

Michael switched his monitor off, waved and was gone.

I glanced at the time. It was only 50 minutes till Drew was due to call. Thirty-six replies left. If I dealt with them each in a minute I could be done before he rang. Speak to him for 10 and be home in time to talk to Radio 4. I like doing radio interviews curled up in bed.

I made a start, then found Masumi hovering at my shoulder.

"I'm the last," she said.

I told her to go - I had the codes and Daisy had two seasoned bouncers stationed outside. Masumi left and I turned up the speakers and blasted Pendulum while I typed.

I kept the replies zippy and upbeat, a few lines each, and I was doing really well until I got to 'Unhinged' from Illinois. How do you send a zippy one minute note to a 13 year old who has messaged you that her father rapes her every night?

You don't.

You spend the first 10 minutes re-reading the message. Not because you're a ghoul that wants to know how drunk he is and how much it hurts every time and that it hurts when she pees now too and she's afraid she'll get pregnant and that her mother will find out, but because you need to make the bytes of black and white on the screen into something real. You need to feel them.

You spend the next five minutes pacing the room, impotent with anger and cursing the stupid rules you made to keep these girls anonymous online and wishing the one school friend 'Unhinged' had told had helped her, so she wouldn't have messaged you.

And then you spend the next 15 minutes searching shelters in Illinois, trying to find one that isn't funded by evangelicals who will judge her, looking for the haven you can send her to where she'll be safe, and realising, as you do, that she might not read your reply for days and that 11pm here will be afternoon there and she's going to get raped all over again. No matter what you do.

Then you find Poppy, a grandma who runs a half-way house and counselling centre in Springfield. Her website is bright with photos of the flowers in her garden and doesn't mention the word God once, anywhere. The 'About' page says her daughter is a software geek who made enough on the NASDAC to fund the centre. So you smear the tears off your face. Poppy it is.

And when you've sent the reply to 'Unhinged', painting an escape route for her as gently as you can and breaking all your own rules by including your mobile number, you find it's three minutes till Drew is due to call and there is no way you can finish the other replies. So you make a cup of tea.

The kettle was just boiling when the entrance intercom buzzed. I pressed answer and Salvador's face filled the screen, pixelated in green and white in a way not even his looks could survive.

"I got back early," he said, his molten toffee voice set and fractured by the security system. "Is there anything I can do? Any admin I can help with or something?"

I thought about my replies and about Drew calling any moment. Salvador could talk to him. It would give me a little quiet time with my tea, to trundle through some more replies and re-find some calm after 'Unhinged', before I went home for the interview.

"Yes there is something you can do," I said. "I'll buzz you up."

I punched in the magic number and went to finish making my tea. When I turned round he was leaning in the kitchen doorway, smiling, like a break in the clouds and asking about my day. I made him the instant coffee he asked for and even mustered enough energy to tease him about his preference. Not shopping is one thing but if you're going to drink coffee it may as well be a decent espresso.

He was entirely proper when he took his mug, looking down to take the handle carefully. Watching the drink steam, he debriefed me on his meetings in London and what he'd seen travelling there and back. I followed as best I could while I sipped my too hot tea and worried some more about 'Unhinged.'

"The NGOs don't trust us, or you, yet Ruby. But their donations and their members are up since we started; Plane Stupid's supporters have doubled. So they are behind us, but wary."

There wasn't a crack in his decorum, apart from when he said my name, where I thought he enjoyed the feel of it in his mouth for a little too long. And then he told me that all along the journey, on toilet doors, on train tables, on red brick and corrugated iron he'd seen the words 'Stop Shopping', graffitied, the length of England.

It was working. Not just online, in the fleeting pixel world, but in hands and ink, on walls, for real.

Propane Nightmares finished playing and in the pause before the next track I heard the phone ring once, then stop.

"Fuck!" I shouted, Salvador stepping aside to let me barge past. The office phone blinked with a message. We'd missed Drew's call.

"Shit!" I swore again, dialling into the voicemail, scrabbling around the files in my mobile to find where I'd saved the password. The message was brief, tense. Drew didn't leave a number. I swore again and checked the address book on our network. His number wasn't there either. I thought about ringing Michael. He'd be more pissed off if I waited for morning. I could ring him now, get Drew's number if he had it. But Michael would insist on making the call himself. He'd huff politely, chastising me with silence and disappointment. I didn't need that right now. Drew would have to wait. He should have left a number. I'd tell Michael tomorrow.

Salvador was watching me, his head on one side.

"You had something for me to do?" he asked.

"Not anymore," I said and realised I didn't have any more replies left in me.

Outside, on the step, I stopped and breathed the night, as if the air could replace some of the strain I held in my chest. The two guards appeared at the sound of us and wished us good evening.

"It's late. I'll walk you home," Salvador said. It *was* late and I was tired. He'd behaved impeccably but just two days ago had been streaming lust like a bad porn star. Seeing my hesitation, the female guard said she would, if I preferred. It was ridiculous. If I was working with him I had to trust him.

"No," I said, "stay here. He's fine. He's one of us."

We walked in silence, Salvador an arm's length away from me on the pavement. At the bridge he paused. "Sometimes at night," he said, looking down the river, past the Armouries, "this city can be lovely."

"She's home," I said, stopping too, leaning over the painted parapet the way I have a hundred times. "I love the place, even when this river flooded and swallowed this end of town. I've never wanted to live anywhere else."

It was the end of our *Black Prince* touring year, the Xmas before I turned 22. The rain hadn't stopped all month. While we were all lolling among presents and pudding, it got impatient. A month's rain came in a day.

The river overflowed. By the 27th, Stellar and I had run out of weed and got bored so we ignored the warnings and trudged all the way into town, in our wellies. We got as far as Swinegate before the streets were cordoned off. I remember the red and white tape flapping in the wind and the water down Sovereign Street, all clogged with litter and choppy like Ullswater in the breeze. It was strange and terrible and everywhere down there stank for weeks. Leeds wasn't hit the worst. Carlisle and York both suffered more. Some places became islands, whole villages cut off.

I shivered and we pressed on.

"I'm fine from here," I told him, as we reached the Dock itself, half a dozen canal barges moored like memories of a happier Britain. I pointed to Clarence House, looming at the end of the Dock, past the boats at the end of the paving. "You can watch me go in." He fretted, briefly, but didn't try to follow me. "And thanks," I called out, over my shoulder.

I made it into bed in time for Radio 4. I left the lights off so the room filled with the glow of the city and I stroked my clit gently while I told all the listeners how their shopping was killing us. Afterwards I found I was too worried about 'Unhinged' to make myself come and lay staring in the dark, as if a vigil on the other side of the planet could help her make it through the night ok. Somehow worrying about one girl was easier than worrying about the thousands going thirsty or falling asleep with flood waters lapping at their doors or bush fires raging in the hills nearby.

I did my first radio of the morning from bed too, then picked out a silver Stella McCartney number to wear on stage and sang *A Million Rooms* to myself in the shower. I gargled warm honey instead of necking a tea and texted Sam to have him pick me up from HQ at two. I'd intended us to rehearse again right up until yesterday when suddenly there had been no more time. I knew the words, more or less, and we hadn't released either new track, so I could ad lib if I needed, but we wouldn't be good enough for me to look forward to playing.

I just had to get through today, put one foot and one chord in front of the other, and then, the day after to-morrow, we'd get 'Stop Shopping' on TV. I couldn't think beyond that. Everything else had to wait. Well more or less everything.

Walking in, I wore the best scarf I've ever knitted my-self, to keep my throat warm as if it was December. I slung my guitar case over the same shoulder as my holdall, to free up a hand, and rang Stellar, first.

"I can't talk," I told her. "I've got to sing." She told me Clara had entered a fire engine phase and please would I pxt her any I saw. I cheated and found a huge red one on Google Images and sent her that instead.

I rang Mum next. She was cagey and wanted off the phone before I did.

"What is it?" I insisted, stopping to push my attention on her, even when the lights blinked for me to cross. In the end she told me. She'd been arrested last night, out at Armley, planting 30 apple trees on the cricket pitch. "Mum!" I said, once I'd established she'd got out on a grand's bail and hadn't spent the night inside, not sure whether to laugh or cry. She told me she'd tried to phone but had just got voicemail. I would have been on the radio, preaching, and too puffed up in my own importance to notice I was missing her call. "I'll come over," I told her. She said not to. She had things to do and besides, I had a gig and a big day coming up. I let her talk me out of it.

The man blinked green a second time and I told her I loved her and started to move.

Masumi filmed me practising my soundbites and spliced them into a video we'd release after the show. I whispered my way through recording a mini podcast for a Strasbourg radio show. To rest my voice I did three interviews by email and wrote my lunch request down for Salvador when he did the sandwich run. All morning, my guitar case called to me from the far side of the room and my fingertips prickled to play.

I wolfed my blue cheese and cranberry on rye, made sure Masumi was done with me for the day and grabbed my gear to go.

"Don't come in tomorrow, Ruby," Michael said, eyeing the guitar case and holdall resentfully. "Take a rest day before Daytime. Daisy and Masumi will meet you at the station."

"You sure?" I asked, ignoring my Group phone's beep.

"Yep, and leave that here," he reached his hand to take it. "It's safer than taking it away with you."

"I'm only going to Manchester!" I laughed. He made it sound like I was abandoning them for enemy territory.

"I know, but you won't be focused. It's better to take a break while you do this gig. I'll bring it over tomorrow morning, if you want."

"Ok, just not too early," I joked and swung off down the stairs.

The Ryder bash was at Sound Control and the whole place stank of stale beer and nostalgia. When I was sure the guitar tech knew what he was doing I left him to it and went to find Fate and Sam. We plugged in his laptop in the dressing room and ran the two new songs through its tinny speakers half a dozen times. Fate finger-tapped her way through the drum parts on the corner of the table and I mouthed the lyrics.

"You didn't...?" Sam began to ask, hoping even then I'd have met the promise of a third song. He stopped when he saw my face.

I went for the pity ploy and told them Mum had been arrested. Fate called the police a range of inventive expletives. She's always been fond of my mum, chiefly because of her killer veggie chilli. I found I'd chewed my fingernails, black nail polish and all.

At seven, we did a sound check. By then the room was bedecked in orange and brown bunting, in honour of the seventies when Ryder had been born, just up the road. The MC strutted about like an anxious pheasant, as if no one who'd topped the charts had ever had a birthday before. He looked pale when we said we were going out for food and flapped a hand at the buffet, sealed under cling-film. Sam had heard of a new Mexican and we all had a yearning for a decently spiced margarita so we legged it before he locked us in the dressing room.

The margaritas were splendid and took the edge off my shame that we only had two new songs.

Peanut Heart worked, like I'd hoped it would, firing the crowd up in its familiarity, so they stopped pretending they were too cool to move. Fate and Sam played *A Million Rooms* and *Justice* like they'd toured them and I got through with my voice passably intact and only forgot the third verse in *A Million*. We'd hoped to head home as soon as we finished but the MC made us meet Shaun and mingle.

"We can't have you packing out just yet," he insisted. "It'll remind them they have beds to go to and that won't do at all."

Shaun was incoherent on coke and single malts. I realised I could only remember *Kinky Afro* but Sam saved the day with a decent ramble about how he'd been mesmerised by the cover and the sound of his dad's vinyl copy of Pills 'n Thrills when he'd been little. Fate looked bored. She is above feigned sycophancy even when she's being paid to drink whisky.

It was gone 4am by the time we were loaded and away. Sam drove, like he had when we started out. Fate, in the middle seat, watched the dark of the Pennines beyond the glare of the motorway like a sentinel, guarding him. I slumped in and out of sleep against the window. As we took the exit for Leeds, the first splashes of purple seeped into the sky. I closed my eyes again and made up the lyrics to *Velvet Dawn*, just a few hours too late.

They dropped me off. I scribbled down the new lines, showered and slept.

I received instructions yesterday on how to reach the men I need. Pastor Brian rang and told me the number to dial and the words to say.

I thought a lot about my daddy after I had gotten the message. It's 17 years now since he died. If it hadn't been for the eco-Nazis he might still have been assembling the gears on Hummers. Iraq made him a hero but it also made him dead.

Sitting on my bed, I held hard onto his dog tags while I prayed and thought about earning the right to wear them. And I thought about the CDs he'd left me, all lined up in their sharp plastic boxes on the shelf of my room at Momma's. I wondered if I'd ever listen to them again. I have each of the album names memorised by heart so I never download them by mistake. They're not something I want to stack up in my phone, like any old song. Other than his tags and his Code they're the only things of his I've got. The rest Momma cried over then put into plastic bags and sent to the church fair. I can still see her blue and silver nails flashing as she stuffed his jeans into the bags.

I thought about his Code too, of course, but couldn't manage that for long.

Today the Lord gave me the knowledge I have been praying for.

All morning I helped spread their lies; I telephoned all the organisations I had met in London to thank them for their time and shore up their support. I posted their photos of Her onto HeadSpace and I shared links from climate action groups in Peru and the Maldives, Perth and Moscow out into the Group's network. Releasing something on the Group pages is like unleashing a virus, you can watch the clicks as the infection grows, spreading their blasphemy, contaminating more and more unbelievers. Every message they send undermines the Lord and his will. Bishop Hamilton would quake and rail at me for assisting in their heathen quest. I can only trust that God in his vast wisdom sees I have had no choice if I am to fulfil my path.

While I worked I watched Michael in his weakness; pulled in too many directions, too easily swayed by my proximity. What with the new folk and the calls to make and her impending TV show it was easy to time my offer just right; to touch his hand in concern and radiate love for him from my eyes. Of course he said I could take her phone. Of course he told me the number of her apartment.

I went outside. I couldn't guess her password so I used my phone to make the call. Then I went to the canal and watched the brown surface of the water for a while and when I was tired of watching I dropped her phone right in.

I stayed holed-up in my flat all morning, crawling into my jeans and scoffing rice pudding cold, straight from the tin, my favourite comfort food. I stuck St Vincent on to play and skimmed through the print-out of my soundbites again for the next day. You can never rehearse too much. When I heard footsteps outside, I assumed it was Michael dropping off my phone. And then they kicked the door in.

There were two of them, across the room before I could get to my feet. They wore fatigues and stank of sweat and cigarettes, patches of munted faces in gaping balaclavas. They were sober fast and I had never been so afraid. The first one smacked the side of my head so hard it knocked me to the ground. It was only when the second grabbed my ankles that I realised why they had come. I pushed off the first, coming for my shoulders, and reached for anything I could use but all I did was pull a kitchen stool down on Elsie and then he had my arms and my jeans were off and the other one was beating his way into me while the one who held my arms grabbed my hair too to stop me swearing and biting and spitting at his face. They each took a turn, as if they had done the same a thousand times. When they were done, they stood either side of me with their big black boots and I was sure they would kick me to death. Then they were gone as fast as they had come.

St Vincent was still playing. It sounded like the rest of the world had stopped. At first there was just fear. I lay where they left me, drowned in it.

The music finished and the pain rushed in, like none I have ever known. I curled tight on my side, torn apart, and wanting to hide. I thought if I could just crawl to bed I could vanish under the covers. I tried to move but it made the pain worse. I waited. I tried again and got as far as the bedroom door before I started crying.

I cried and swore and waited some more, as if I was on pause. Then I reached the duvet and pulled it down from the bed to bury me. Every other instinct pushed me to a dead end. I wanted my mum but later, when I could tell her about it, not then, not yet. For what turned into a long time I just lay in my hurt and mess and gripped the duvet and cried.

I wanted to stay there but I was awash with their spunk. It kept oozing out of me, red with my blood, on my thighs and the carpet. Eventually, through it all, I remembered a little girl I'd asked to be brave. I thought about 'Unhinged' until I found a grain of courage. Then I crawled, dragging me and my duvet back to find where my phone had fallen in the tangle of my jeans. My hands trembled as if he still held and yanked my arms but I have Stellar on speed dial so I managed.

I didn't seem to be able to move again so I just stayed where I was and tried to breathe.

She called my name as she pushed open the broken door and paused, for just a beat, taking in the state of the room and the state of me.

"Jesus Christ!" she said, and was at my side, holding my head into her shoulder, warm and calm and steady which made me cry all over again. She guessed what had happened but I had to speak to tell her there were two.

"Someone sent them," I said and found I was sure of this.

It was a fact.

Something hard I could cling to.

They hadn't come by accident.

We stayed there, Stellar holding me and me holding the fact, hugging its heavy certainty into my body. As I held it tight, I became surer of its shape, defined against the pain.

They had come to make me weak.

The weight of knowing was too much. It would have crushed me, if not for Stellar's arms, keeping me safe despite its press.

They had come to stop me.

"We have to report them," I said, finding a thought behind the fact and laying it down like a stepping stone. I wondered if I could edge from where I lay and place a foot upon the stone, if Stellar held my hand. She watched me close while I sat up.

"You need a doctor," she said, "for a morning after pill and an HIV test."

She was right. I tried to imagine the next stone.

"You don't have to go to the police," she said. She was right again. With rock star money you can always make the world look the other way. I could get checked out at a private clinic, lie low till the bruises I could feel on my arms and face had faded. Money can always buy you privacy, if you're smart. But if I was going to move at all I had to follow the stepping stones. They were my only way forward.

"I want to," I said and found I was angry.

They had come to my home and forced their way in and there had been nothing I could do to stop them. I had been as helpless as 'Unhinged' before her father. I hadn't stopped them but I could report them. It was something.

I used the anger to make me stand up but the pain just about split me open and when Stellar scooped me off the floor again I had to lean on her.

I arrived at my building too early so I forced myself to walk to the river and back twice more to pace away the time. Everything around me seemed faint and distant as if I walked through a painting or a memory; nothing real apart from what was about to come. The thrill of being so close to victory made my skin crackle. I knew the Lord's will would soon be done. The Bishop would call my name in church and praise my deeds.

As I walked I found I had wound my daddy's dog tags tight around my fingers and they were paining me. I could hear him speaking his Code loud in my head. It made me afraid and I could not say to him why this thing must be done. If he was still alive, I could have explained to him why She must be stopped, the way the Bishop had made me see, so he might understand.

When it was almost time I came up to my room. I laid his dog tags out on the table and next to them I set the laptop to play the audio from the microphone I had given the shorter of the men. He didn't give me his name. Neither of them did. I did not want them. They are merely instruments as I am an instrument.

I listened to them climb the stairs, not speaking, just footfalls and the huff of their breath. The smash of the door made me jump. When She cried out I closed my eyes so I could picture Her. For a moment her whore ways triumphed; I saw myself there with Her, kissing Her then fucking Her and my hand was hot and helpless as I yanked myself, her crying out and my own gasps as one.

Afterwards I stilled the sound and knelt and prayed for forgiveness. I confess my sin of masturbation here to stem its worry in my mind. May the Lord's will be done.

"It is done," I messaged the Bishop. "She will not rally from this shame."

"My son you have walked in the company of evil and the Lord's mercy has delivered you. God bless you. When you are sure, return to my side," he sent me in reply.

I went down from my apartment and out into the street. Where before everything had seemed faint and distant now the world had been turned vivid, as if it was painted the colours of the fairground Daddy took me to before his last call of duty. Children ran down the sidewalk in technicolour raincoats and the sun burst through the cloud like the angel Jericho. I drew the air inside of me in gulps to my heart and praised the glory of the Lord. I wanted to walk, but not towards the city, out towards the hills and so I turned away from the river and strode a new path between lines of dark red houses until, on a corner by a grocery store, a woman, scarlet as an apple, took me by the hand and took me to her home.

She was named Joanna. In the sunlight of the afternoon she took my chastity but I knew it was meant and that I was blessed by the grace of the Lord in all I did that day. When I reached into my trouser pocket, for the notes to pay Joanna,

I found I had left Daddy's tags on the table at home and told myself it was just my hurry to leave the house and not that I had strayed from his Code that made me forget them. I resolved to leave right then so nothing became of them but Joanna promised more reward and so it was late by the time I returned. I walked back through the dark streets, tall with new wisdom. Within the week I will take my place at the Bishop's side, where I belong. My dedication is proven and new paths will open before me. The tags were where I had left them so I pushed them into my pocket, out of sight, before setting my trousers aside.

The room seems to pulse with God's energy and I am not sure how I will sleep tonight.

Stellar stayed with me through it all - through the cautious questions DI Lucy Braithwaite asked, as if any might explode the numb shell around me, and through the duty doctor's peering and swabbing and note taking.

By the time I limped out to the foyer Graham, my lawyer, was there, filling in forms, and Michael had arrived, pale and clench-faced. He told me he had cancelled *Daytime*.

"No," I said, suddenly desperate not to let them take that too. "This wasn't random. They want me to cancel."

They had come to make me weak, to make me dirty and afraid. They had come to silence me. I hadn't been able to stop them raping me. It was done. But I didn't want them to win. It wasn't fair.

The fear and anger surged again, metal in my mouth, and I reached out to Stellar so she could weave her fingers through mine and keep me from falling. I thought I might throw up.

It felt like I was looking at two of me - one trashed and terrified on the floor of my flat, the other here, shaking with anger. Neither was real.

They had taken what they wanted and I'd been helpless, but I didn't have to give them total victory. I didn't have to be ashamed. I gripped Stellar's hand. I wasn't alone anymore. I had to try to save what was left of me. If there was any way I could fight back, I had to try.

It was hard to think about leaving the brick vault of the police station. Going to London and doing TV was far too many stepping stones away. But I had to.

"I need to go on, if I have to crawl into the studio," the fear and anger said, through new tears.

Stellar said I was in shock. She was probably right. I didn't listen.

Michael looked even paler and went outside to make the calls.

Stellar had booked us a taxi to Mum's where our own doctor would meet us and I stood, waiting for it, propped against her like I have a million times when I've been too wasted to walk. When Michael came back to tell me we were on, again, I asked him for my Group phone.

"You've got it," he said, "Salvador took it over to you, this morning."

So then we knew and a whole new fear and hurt kicked in.

Doctor McKinnon was waiting with Mum. She'd tended Mum's childhood bugs before my own and I'd known her all my life. I'd never seen her cross before.

She took me upstairs and stitched my poor, savaged vag and doled out Tramadol. She told me I was brave for going to the police and terminally stupid for going to London, with the loving severity only the Scots can muster. She left and Stellar followed and then I was alone with Mum.

"I'm sorry," I said, like I'd broken something she loved.

She didn't say anything, just held me like she'd never let go.

Mum put me to bed and stayed while I fell asleep. When I woke in the dark, my heart racing and the smell of them all around me, she was still there. I watched her sleep, her face calm in the grey light as if nothing had happened. Awake, I knew I was right to try but overnight I had become sure I would fail. I would cower before the cameras and in my silence they would have taken all of me.

As daylight leaked into the room, I cast around for other answers. I should wait, take some time to heal, just delay the interview, like Sinead had asked when Michael rang her. Or I could get one of the Group to do it for me and before I could help myself I pictured Salvador. The thought of him made me cry out, waking Mum.

She fetched us both tea and watched me hold the mug with both hands and blow onto the surface, something familiar I could control.

"I want you to stay here today, Ruby," she told me, "but sometimes the wild decisions we make are the ones that keep us alive. The adrenalin saves us. If your instinct is to do the interview, I think you should."

I blew on my tea and watched her over the edge of my mug while the tears ran down my face.

"I'm so afraid," I whispered. "I'm so afraid if I don't go through with it I'll never do anything again." The broken 'me' on the floor of my flat felt huge and real.

"You would," she said. "You will. With enough rest and enough time you will mend. Not like before, but better than now."

I told her fronting up was what I did. It defined me. Performing wasn't a job I could change. I was suddenly sure, in the black and white of my shock, that if I pulled out of the interview I'd never perform again. They had come to silence me and if I let them have that too, I was lost.

I remembered 'Unhinged' again. Women and girls half my age survived this every day. They had come to silence me but they had also bound me tight to all those women all over the world.

Mostly we don't talk. Mostly we smother ourselves in the shame of it and hide our wounded selves until life becomes bearable again. I knew this and now I knew why.

A harsh, dark laugh broke out of me and banged around my old room, scaring me. Mum watched me like I might shatter.

"I need to do it," I said, "today. For me. This is the right time for 'Stop Shopping'. And Mum I'm going to ...I'm going to tell them what happened, too."

My anger howled.

Masumi and Daisy and two strapping Glaswegian's she'd hired as extra security picked me up in an armoured limousine.

I eyed it darkly from Mum's front step. It looked safe and brutal all at once.

"Yes it's a guzzler," Daisy said, mistaking my timidity for disapproval. "Would you sooner we went on the train?" That day the idea slugged ice in my gut so I kissed Mum and crept to the car, too sore to move despite the drugs, and got gratefully in. One guard, Sophie, drove, Daisy beside her. The other, Chloe, took the middle row. The back seat was big enough I managed to sleep past Leicester, till they broke in again in my dream.

I asked the make-up woman to leave my bruised cheek uncovered. Then Daisy, Sophie and Chloe half-carried me down a flouro lit corridor to the green room. Masumi was waiting there. I poured myself a shot of vodka, that the others declined, and downing that, over the Tramadol, numbed me enough to talk. To distract myself from what was coming I asked the guards about themselves. They were sisters. Not twins but dressed to match in black SAS surplus with tufty, gelled dark hair.

Sophie told me she kick-boxed, carried a knife and hadn't lost a client yet.

"Chloe's the sharp shooter," she said, laughing, but in a fond way that showed the admiration underneath. Chloe didn't smile, just flicked her eyebrows up and down once. She heard the presenter arrive before any of us and was on her feet before the woman made it into the room. I watched Chloe's hand pause over the gap in her jacket, near where her heart or a gun might be, until she was sure who had come.

"Ladies, I'm Lucille" the presenter breathed, unrufflable in her sheen of foundation and hairspray, thanking me before I'd done anything and air-kissing me. I pulled back, flinching to have a stranger suddenly so near, and covered it by helping myself to another drink.

Masumi had told her I'd cover 'Stop Shopping' first and then Lucille was to ask me a question about over-coming a challenge to make it on the show. That was my cue. I didn't rehearse it. I didn't want to talk its power out. Besides, I wasn't sure if I told a stranger once I'd ever be able to say it again. So we did it live on air.

I almost didn't.

The station had kept the crew small and Masumi stayed close by the camerawoman's shoulder so I could watch her if I needed to. I knew the 'Stop Shopping' phrases so well they became a small comfort as I spoke, each familiar as friendship. They tasted better than fear in my mouth. I saw the understanding spark in Lucille's eyes when I used my cliff analogy. When I talked about peer pressure and shoe-heel shapes she laughed, even though I didn't ham it up, like I usually did. I kept it simple, stuck to the script I knew as well by then as some of my hits. 'Stop Shopping Saturdays' had its own, new bundle of one-liners but they would have to wait. If the idea was good it would keep. I had something else new for *Daytime*.

When she asked me the opener we'd agreed, I realised how easy it would be to just tell her something trivial - that I'd overcome a flat tyre or being stuck in a lift. No one would know any different. Just my crew of course, but they would understand. I didn't think Michael believed I'd go through with it anyway. Sinead had rung us in the car, asking me again to wait until the shock was past, till I was sure. Lucille would be pissed off but would put it down to post traumatic stress or creative temperament. It would be easy.

And that, in the end, was why I did it. The time for easy was over. There wasn't any time left, to wait, to heal, to worry you never would. We each had to use everything, no matter the cost, before it was too late. I couldn't let them win.

So when Lucille asked me about the challenge I'd overcome to make it on air I told her.

"Well yes," I said "like thousands of people working for change around the world I've been... intimidated. They don't want us speaking out because the status quo suits them. So they try and stop us. With me, I got... I got raped but others get kidnapped or killed outright."

"So, you got raped to stop you coming on the show?"

It was harder to hear her say it than to say it myself but I breathed in and let the anger carry me.

"Yes and to stop me speaking out online. 'Stop Shopping' is having an effect and some powerful people, somewhere, don't like it."

"So do you know who...attacked you?"

"Two men, wearing balaclavas. But it was arranged somehow by a man who calls himself Salvador. He wanted to silence me. But I won't be silenced. We won't be silenced. This is bigger than me, bigger than any of us. We have to change and we have to do it now."

If I'd been making a speech, I could have left it there. There might even have been some applause. Instead, Lucille tilted her head and asked me how it happened. There's always a price. A talk show depends on salacious detail.

"He was bringing me something," I said, my palms hot and wet, seeing the door kicked-in again, "but they came instead."

My breath fluttered high in my throat, panicking to escape. The vodka threw me a safety-line. I kept talking.

"Before they left they wrote 'stop' across my wall in my favourite red lippy," I told her, and still I went on. "They must have totally trashed it. My lippy – and the wall!"

The safety-line broke. My tears started again and even Lucille stumbled.

Later, Masumi told me they had cut to a photo of Salvador, the one we'd taken for his security check.

She has broadcast her defilement. The Whore is more shameless than God ever let me imagine. I had to turn off the sound because I could not bear to hear but I watched Her, flaunt her despoiling on TV, as if She had won some pageant. The presenter fawned in sympathy and the papers and the blogs are also bleating in support. Can people not see the Devil thrives in Her? Do they not hear Her deny the Lord? What does it take to silence this blaspheming bitch?

Bishop Hamilton telephoned. He is displeased they have released my picture. He told me to travel here to Manchester where I am not known. A barber near the train station bleached my hair. I have thrown away my razor and bought a brown suit and three white shirts I can wear with a tie. The Bishop says I must do nothing more. We must not martyr Her. I am to hide and wait and he will send word.

I have not called Momma. I fear she will know it is me in the silence. If she has seen my picture she will have judged me before I could explain I do the Lord's work.

I hold Daddy's tags and I wait and I pray.

We were back in the car, limping out of London, through the traffic. I was curled sideways on the seat because I couldn't sit straight any longer, when Masumi got the call.

"It's Oprah's producer. They want us for next week's show."

"Holy fuck," I said. Outside the car, an old man in a turban sat at a bus stop, a huge Alsatian next to him, its head in the man's lap. The man stroked the dog gently across its forehead and looked into its eyes as if he were telling it his deepest secrets. Oprah was big. Bigger than ever on her own network. As big as you get, frankly. Asking Prime Time America to 'Stop Shopping' seemed audacious even to me. Even with so many jobless the other 75% kept the patriotic cash tills ringing loud as church bells. Going on *Oprah* would lay me bare before half the planet. I took another Tramadol and wrapped my arms around my head and wondered if we could ask our armpit cheerleaders to do the show instead.

"Ruby...?"

"Yes, yes sorry. Of course I'll do it."

It was too late for regret. I'd decided to use my attack against them and this was the reward. Going on *Oprah* would take this battered resistance and warp it to some kind of twisted glory. 'Eat that Salvador', I thought, as we inched forward. I wondered what the bastard's real name was and if he'd sold us out or planned to attack us all along but just the thought of him made my stomach clench and my face go hot and cold, blinking fear and nausea. I wound the window down to let in some exhaust fumes and swivelled round so I could see Masumi.

"There's a flight from Manchester every day," she said, fingers flickering across the screen of her phone. "We could catch..."

"No," I said, cutting her off. "Tell them it's a vid cast or nothing."

She looked at me, her eyes narrowed. We both knew it was a gamble. With Oprah, you showed. But I figured, just maybe, I was wounded enough and topical enough to pull it off. I didn't want to be a hypocrite, jetting in to tell millions of people to cut their impact on the planet. Even with added biofuel, flying's about the most eco-evil you can be. More importantly, the only place I wanted to be right then was Mum's. Perhaps Oprah would pity me.

I watched the curves of Masumi's cheek and jaw as she rang the producer back - the gentle line of her face, determined as marble against the charcoal leather of the car seat, as she spoke.

"They think you are too hurt to travel," she told me, when it was done. "I can book a high-res suite in Leeds. That is, if we're going home?"

"Yes, we're going home," I said and let the tears slide down my face while the car edged us forward and the first drops of rain slipped down inside the open window.

I slept again, most of the way up the M1. Between Nottingham and Sheffield I watched the cars and cat's eyes streaming past, as if tarmac and tyres were all that was left of the world.

When we got to Barnsley I decided I couldn't put it off any longer and rang Sam. He'd heard, of course. Mum had phoned Fate. In between swearing about the attackers he kept saying he was sorry and in the end I had to tell him to stop. It wasn't his fault any more than it was mine.

"But I will need some time," I said. "There's lots of media and stuff, you know ..."

He told me he knew. He said he understood. I had to bite my lips together to stop myself from saying he could never understand.

Masumi and Daisy dropped me at Mum's. It was only when we got there I discovered Sophie and Chloe were staying too.

They buttressed me up the path, one in front and one behind and didn't seem in the least surprised when another woman in Teflon and a puffer vest opened Mum's door. There was a fourth in the kitchen, draining the last of the teapot into a mug and wiping cake crumbs from a plate with her finger.

"She's upstairs, your Mam," Hu told me, after she'd introduced herself and Jasmine, who'd shown me in. The two of them were Mum's day shift, she said, in her kind, no-nonsense Geordie voice, and they were on duty now so Sophie and Chloe could rest.

The four super-sized women in their black-clad resilience filled the kitchen with confidence, bold and sure amid the clutter of seed catalogues and tea things. Their capability exhausted me, every move reminding me how weak and raped I was. Furball meandered around sniffing the toes of their boots, unperturbed. I scooped him up, over my shoulder, his warmth under my chin and in my ear like comfort.

I had to take the steps slowly, one at a time, and could only carry him part of the way. He swaggered up the rest of the stairs ahead of me.

Mum was making the bed in the spare room.

She didn't say anything, just came over and held me while I cried.

Afterwards, when I was too tired to cry anymore, she put me to bed again in my old room, with the trays of dahlia bulbs and seed potatoes, like I was something that could re-sprout after a nice, quiet rest in the dark.

We ate soup together, Mum cross legged at the end of my bed and Furball burrowed against my right hip, purring. She'd defrosted the last of my favourite pump-

kin and cumin from last Autumn. I sipped it, the mug
slightly too hot between my hands so it kept me from
thinking about anything else until one of our security
guards moved downstairs and reminded me I couldn't
pretend anything was normal.

Mum set her mug aside and stretched out her legs,
her bare toes flexing gently into Furball's well-padded
ribs to make him purr louder.

"You were so brave, darling," she said, eventually,
watching our cat. It was only then I realised how hard
she was working to keep her grief and anger bound
down.

"Not really," I said, remembering how close I'd come
to not saying anything. "It was just the only way I could
throw this back at them. Scale is the only thing that
matters, now. We need to make as much noise as we
can. All of us."

She nodded and held my feet through the duvet and
we both sat quietly together listening to Furball's purr
become snores.

The sound of Daisy and Mum arguing woke me. I lay
and looked at the ceiling for a while, as if that would
shut them up. Guilt I'd dragged this into Mum's house
got me moving and eventually I had dressed and shuffled down the stairs. There were two women I didn't
know in the kitchen with Daisy, as well as Jasmine and
Hu, Chloe and Sophie. Mum was wearing her dressing
gown - white and fluffy and fierce among the muscle-

tight heft of them all. When they saw me leaning against the door frame the guard women all stood up.

I thought I would just go back to bed.

Mum stopped glaring at Daisy and glared at me instead, then I saw her remember none of this was my fault and she sat, dropping the fight, into the nearest chair.

"She didn't know Jasmine and Hu are for her," Daisy said, realising she'd won.

The two new women had been the night-shift. They would stay with Mum from eight at night till eight in the morning, when Jasmine and Hu came on deck. Chloe and Sophie would go with me, wherever I went.

"I don't like it Ruby," Daisy said to me later, in the cab back to mine through the rain. "Those shites could find out where yer ma lives in a heartbeat. And the house is a right worry. Two at a time can barely cover it. We ought to move her. I'd be made up if we could get her into a flat like yours I can keep locked down."

"But it's her home," I said, "and without her job, well, the garden..." I pictured Mum trapped in a high-rise, battering the windows with her soil-engrained hands. "Do you think she'll be all right, if she stays?"

Daisy sighed.

"Oh probably, if she's not soft. Those girlies are good. If she lays low and lets them do their job...," she shrugged. "Besides, it's you they're after."

I'd told Daisy I needed clothes but really I needed to see it. I was expecting crime scene tape and planks nailed across but the door to my flat had been mended. I let Chloe and Sophie go in ahead and check, then asked them to wait in the corridor with Daisy while I went in. I left the door open behind me.

My heart thumped in my ears like the start of *Seven Nation Army*, daring me to flee. I clenched my fists and breathed, as if I was just facing stage fright. My eyes read the room while my brain tuned meaning from it. There was the kitchen bench and the stool I'd pulled over, the TV and my guitars. Slowly my body learned there weren't any thugs behind the sofa and my heart drum quietened.

"Fuck you," I said, out loud, to the space where they had been and punched the light on. Someone had painted over the lipstick on the wall.

Stepping into the room, I saw Elsie, tucked into the guitar stand behind my Fender and my Les Paul. Even though I couldn't see the damage I knew it was there, like a friend carrying her scar beneath her clothes. I heard Daisy slip in behind me.

"It's ok," I said, breathing again and going through to the bedroom. "I'm ok. I can do this." Daisy had followed me and stood in the doorway, arms folded, eyebrows cocked in scepticism. "Besides," I said, turning away from her scrutiny to pull a jumble of clothes from my drawer, "it'll help keep me focused, knowing the enemy was right here."

We'd already agreed I would stay, if I was up to it. Daisy reckoned she could secure this flat as well as anywhere and unless I went into hiding 'Salvador' and his thugs would find any new place again, soon enough.

"You're the boss," she said and left me to change. When I followed her back into the lounge and saw her ease in the room I guessed she'd been the one to come in and set things right. I was glad her strong hands had done that work, had set Elsie up on the stand and made things at least look safe.

"Will she mend?" she asked, following my eyes.

"Oh, I think so," I said, and crossed to my guitars.

Daisy watched me for a moment more, nodded, then went to join the others.

I picked Elsie up and settled us both on the sofa, laying her across my lap and stroking the dear blonde wood, savaged around the dark hole the stool had bitten when it fell. I laid my fingers on her frets and told her soon she would be mended and making music again.

I didn't tell her she would never be the same.

have still not heard from the Bishop so I am stuck here like Elijah in his cave, forsaken in a wilderness of my own making. Her influence grows every day. I spent the night in a room that stank of alcohol and vomit and the disinfectant that had failed to mask them.

I had nowhere else to go so I returned to the square I found myself in yesterday. 'Stop Shopping' stickers had appeared on every store window, like mushrooms pink with toxin. The shop-keepers have given up scraping them off. There is a small news stand by the bus shelter and I counted her face on six of the covers. My face itches where the beard is coming through.

Again, I have passed the day on this bench, my bag between my feet and the collar of my brown suit drawn up against the weather and I waited and I prayed, giving no heed to the wet. People came and went around me, carrying their umbrellas pointing forward to shield the worst of the wind and rain. My Bishop did not ring. I know he is displeased with me.

Only God knows how hard I tried. Words can never do justice to the truth in us that only He knows.

In my Bishop's eyes, I have let him down and failed in my task for the Lord.

Last night, when the waiting got too much and I could not call Bishop Hamilton because it was the wrong time, I rang Pastor Brian. He said I was a risk to the Church here. He told me not to call him again. He said I must do what Bishop Hamilton tells me. Bishop Hamilton tells me to wait.

This is my test. Yet the Lord calls to me to finish his work. I can not sit idly waiting to hear from Bishop Hamilton when my God is calling to me. His wisdom tells me the knowledge of how to stop Her is mine to find. Who else has worked alongside Her? Who else knows what makes Her smile and what makes Her cry? It is me and not the Bishop. I have waited and I have watched and I will not fail again in stopping Her. I pray to know what I must do.

When it began to grow dark and the first of the street lights came blinking on, the Lord sent me an old woman carrying the idea. She stumbled when she came out of the store called Boots and a younger woman, with the same look about her face, took her arm. The care that passed between them must be love. Women are weak so they feel it easily and show it off without regard. She is the same. She talked about her momma all the time. No mention of a daddy, though. Her momma must be another whore, breeding out of wedlock. I must not martyr Her but I must stop Her. I must target where She is weak.

I watched the old woman and her daughter until they were out of sight.

We caught a taxi to Church Row together, Daisy and Chloe and me. Sophie stayed to watch the flat, settled in a hazard-orange canvas chair outside my door. As we had left Clarence House I had opened my mouth to joke we all needed bikes then realised how sore I was. It would be weeks before I'd be going near a saddle and the anger made me sad and exhausted all over again. When we reached HQ, I let Daisy head up the stairs before me, 'just in case'.

Burt came over as soon as he saw me. The whites of his eyes were marbled with broken veins.

"What is it?" I asked, before he said anything.

"I have to go," he said, "get away from here, for a while at least."

"What happened?" I asked.

"You have to be joking?"

I hadn't understood I wasn't the only one trying to survive it, but of course, Burt was right. By raping me they'd attacked us all. I went to the window and looked out. I thought if the cab was still in the street I'd catch it to Mum's and go back to bed.

The taxi had gone.

It wouldn't be any easier another day. I asked Michael to bring all the men together first - he and Burt and the volunteers. I sat amid the eight of them, us all with our chairs wheeled to a huddle between the desks downstairs and all the screens turned off. I made myself hold Burt and Michael's hands. I'd only met the other six guys a handful of times and my body prickled with 'what-if' fear. I breathed and told myself knowing Salvador better hadn't saved me from him. Then I got started before I could change my mind.

"How does it feel?" I asked them, which pissed them off straight away. Even enlightened men hate the question, put to them upfront like that. "How does it make you feel that Salvador betrayed us and arranged two thugs to rape me?"

Burt got up so fast he knocked his chair over, which is hard to do with the wheelie ones - they tend to roll away. I flinched as if he'd tried to hit me, not just loosed my hand. His eyes flared wide, realising he'd frightened me.

"Steady," Michael said, letting go of my other hand and standing to right the chair. I could see him shaking as he set it down. Perhaps I was making things worse.

"You do ask some stupid questions, Ruby," Burt said, from across the room, his hands clutching the back of his head like I've seen him when a tech problem rears out of control, as if he's trying to hold his mind together.

"I know," I said, smiling a stage smile to make me look brave. "Blame the artist in me."

"For fucks sake! How can you sit there joking after what they did to you?"

"Would you sooner I just stayed home and cried?" I snapped.

"No, of course not, but.... well... are you actually ok?"

"No," I said. "It hurts like nothing else and I just about wet myself in fright when a phone rings or a car door slams. I expect to be celibate for a good long while and I'm sleeping with the light on. But I can't change any of that. All I can do is try to use it against them. And that is the only thing so far that makes me feel just a teeny bit better."

"I just can't believe they did that to you," said Tao, one of the new guys.

"Yeah, it's totally shit," I agreed. "But we all knew this wouldn't be easy. And surprise, surprise it isn't. Burt, tell me."

"We have footage," he said, still standing, primed on his toes like he was about to run from us. "Daisy had rigged the camera to show the door but the angle is wide enough." He was crying now, his red eyes leaking into his beard. "I watched it all, Ruby, and then I re-wound it and watched it again because I couldn't understand how that had happened just a dozen blocks away and we hadn't known it was going on. How is that possible?"

Masumi had already told me about the footage. She'd asked if they should give it to the police. I said yes. She'd also asked if I wanted to watch it. I said no. I had thought about it. I wondered if seeing it from a different perspective might help, somehow. But I didn't want to see myself trashed like that. I was afraid I'd look so helpless and defeated I would never be able to see myself as anything else again. It was already hard enough to see a way ahead.

"It's not only possible," I said, "but happening to women everywhere, every day." I was starting to shake and realised if I was going to finish what I started I had to have someone to hide behind. I thought about 'Unhinged' and how I'd been offline for days now and hoped Masumi would have noticed if she'd messaged me.

"Well it makes me *feel* fucking useless," Burt said, still standing but heavily now, full of sorrow, "that I was sitting on my arse, fiddling with our servers, while those total fucking bastards were doing that to you." Before, I would have gone over and put my arms around him while he cried.

"It's happening to some other woman right now," I said, instead, "and maybe she won't have friends and medical care. Perhaps she'll get an infection and die, or maybe she'll be thrown out of her house or set on fire in her kitchen. Being raped was by far the worst thing that has ever happened to me but, Burt, I will survive it. Somehow I'll get through it and so can we."

"It makes me want to go out and find them and smash their faces in," Michael said, "and I hate being full up with violence. Especially because I know it's how they want us to feel."

He was right of course. It's the added bonus of rape as a weapon. You scar the women, sow their bodies with your seed, if you can, and you drive the men to suicidal violence or despair.

We talked a bit more and Burt came and sat back down and took my hand again, gingerly, as if I might break. I squeezed his big fingers hard in mine.

"I need you to find a way through this. Each of you," I said, and I looked around them all and wondered if it was even fair to ask them to stay. "Do whatever you have to. Take up bare knuckle boxing, or see a counsellor or volunteer at rape crisis for a month, but get yourselves through this because, guys I need you. I need you more than ever. If you let this beat you, we've let them win."

With the women it was different. I needed to move by then so we walked, very slowly to my flat. I took Daisy and Chloe up in the lift to fetch the bag of clothes Stellar had brought back from the police and the zippo I kept for spliffs and a bottle of lighter fuel.

I led everyone to The Triangle, the little mown pocket at the back of the Armouries, and they stood in a tight circle around me while I sloshed lighter fuel over my torn jeans and the pretty bluebell bra and the purple Karen Walker hoody I'd been wearing and never wanted to wear again and set the flames to them all. The denim stank as it caught and Masumi held onto my arm and Sophie spat on the little fire so we all did the same, crying and laughing those short bitter laughs that are all you find left inside when the tears are done.

Back up in the flat, tear stained and smoky, I opened the vodka and everyone climbed on the sofa with me and we cried and held each other and Daisy told us she'd been finger-fucked once, when she was 12, by some guy who claimed to be an uncle. He'd followed her to the bathroom after her grandma's funeral. She'd been pliant with fear at the time but in the privacy of her silence afterwards she'd decided she'd liked it and felt bad because she knew it was wrong. Masumi said she'd come close once, at a party, after she'd had a quickie with a boyfriend on the coats in the spare room and another guy had barged in after he'd gone, while she was touching up her lippy, and tried to take her again. She'd only managed to push him off because he was drunk and fell over.

"I never told anyone" she said, "I didn't even find out his name. But I've often thought I should have. What if he tried it again and the next girl wasn't so lucky?"

"We do the best we can," I told her, and found her hand and kissed her knuckles and held her palm to my cheek. "How old were you?"

"16."

"Well there you go. A baby still."

"A lifetime ago."

I knew what she meant. She was still only 22, five years younger than me, but we'd both lived enough to learn you can tell your friends of unspeakable things and survive.

Sometimes it helps.

We regrouped at HQ the next morning. My body still hurt all over and that day my head was sore from the vodka too. I ordered us all a chocolate cake which doesn't cure hangovers but distracted me with comfort and sugar till the painkillers kicked in. I handed slices round the table and made Burt's slice extra big as a silent thanks for sticking with us. Michael stood up, his clipboard back in hand, to explain Tao was joining the planning team, to help him get the NGOs back on-side. Nobody said he was replacing Salva-fucker-dor but of course he was. I ate my cake and focussed on feeling some pleasure things were moving on. Actually things were charging.

"All our social stats are through the roof," Masumi told us, sliding her fingers across her tablet to push graphs lifted with sky-bound lines onto the screen, "and of course the media is now fully mainstream." She told us we'd made the number one spot on the six o'clock news both nights since the *Daytime* show and played us highlights of the footage. There was more about the mystery rapists than I'd have liked but enough on 'Stop Shopping' that it had sent our web visits soaring and left Burt scrambling to spread the server load.

It wasn't all good. The Fundamentalists were charging too, protesting at shopping malls with my picture on signs commanding 'Fear God' and posting hate messages to our pages as fast as Masumi and her team could moderate them away. "They are very international now," she said, claiming the spread as a measure of our success, "and very, very angry."

"The Christians really love their commerce and hate their women," I said.

"You think God and the Corporates collaborate?" Tao asked.

Michael shrugged. "It's anyone's guess who was paying Salvador. But Topshop isn't likely to send their staff out to protest us directly..." He jiggled his clipboard as if to shake himself back on track.

We agreed Masumi would step up the video-casts to three a day and pump the content full of as many success stories as we could find. We'd already linked to dozens of blogs by people who were buying less and feeling happier. The more stories we put out the more came in. Mostly comments and email but lots of video grabs from phones and laptops too, wonky head-and-shoulders testimonials, zero production quality but priceless.

A few came the old way, in the mail, cards or letters, mainly from the very old. Masumi had a pile on the table and slid them across to me. I opened the first I came to, a clotted cream card stitched with blue daisies and, tucked inside, a photo of a very elderly lady in a pink coat handing out 'Stop Shopping' stickers outside a Waitrose. I flipped the photo over. In careful pencil it read, 'Jenny Rose, Portsmouth, aged 92. Stop Shopping!' It took a lot less to melt tears from me that week.

"I'm going to find him, Ruby," Burt said, misunderstanding. "Him and his thugs. He's going to be sorry he ever hurt you."

I took one last glance at Jenny's picture and slid the card back into the pile.

"He's probably already sorry," I said. "It's making us – making this – bigger faster than we'd ever hoped. He failed. We're winning. Let's just focus on saving the planet. That'll do me for revenge. I just wish I wasn't still so bastard sore!" Michael winced and looked away. Gay men are, in my experience, by far the most squeamish about female biology. In different circumstances I might have lavished on some lurid details but that day we all needed kindness, me included. "Sorry. Black humour. It helps, you know?"

Michael fussed and apologised and we talked about what the police might find on Salvador's laptop and speculated wildly on what his background might have been. We asked ourselves yet again how he could have slithered through Michael's checks, and whether Burt should hack the DNA results from the police computers. Daisy looked like one of the storm clouds that brew above Ilkley when the weather's getting really bad. After a while I called a halt so Michael, Masumi and I could plan for *Oprah*, but really I just couldn't talk about it anymore.

I asked Masumi, as we moved to the sofas so I could sit more comfortably, if there'd been a message from 'Unhinged'. There hadn't. I guessed there might never be and gripped the idea of her tight between my thumb and index finger as if she was the plectrum of courage I'd use to play my way through the *Oprah* show and out the other side.

Before we were done, I could see Daisy was hovering. I told Michael the show was still a week away. We had 'Stop Shopping Saturdays' to launch and time to sort the details.

"It's yer ma," Daisy said, when I waved her over. I was out of the sofa, adrenalin surging, before she'd finished the word. "She's fine," she told me, holding my shoulders to settle my charge, "but Jasmine and Hu aren't pleased, mind. She's been dragging them half over town and there's no lying low going on."

I looked out of the window and wondered where she'd been planting.

"It's May," I said, noticing the rain had stopped. Blades of sunlight sliced through the grey sky, bleeding brightness over the wet bricks and pavement. It was beautiful. No wonder Mum wanted to plant. It suddenly felt more useful than cramming the world with more soundbites and pixels. "She needs to grow things."

"Well she'll be growing plenty with the fancy kit she's got herself now..." Daisy said.

I wished I could cycle but I made Daisy and Chloe come with me on the bus, instead of taking a taxi, so I could at least feel like a normal person and not some broken celebrity climate freak. The daylight was lingering a nudge later into the evening, dragging Chapeltown people out onto their front steps, hip-hop sounds and afro prints amped by some dry weather. Normally it made me smile but that day the whole thing seemed brittle, like even noticing might spoil it.

As we rounded the corner I saw the tractor and Hu outside Mum's house. The machine looked huge in the row of hatch backs and saloons along the street. It squatted yellow as a daffodil amongst them, a steely plough arched above its shoulders - a swagger of spades ready for work.

Hu must have called her because Mum came to the door while we were still looking at it. I reached out one hand, almost shoulder height, to touch the mud guard.

"You were right, darling," Mum said, coming up behind me. "We've all got to make the biggest difference we can." The mudguard was real. So were the enormous tyres and the glassy cab and the bared steel teeth of the plough. I took my hand away.

When we'd hugged and cried in the street for a bit we trooped into the house. The living room floor was spread with old Guardians, each open sheet carrying a cluster of seed trays. The sheets nearest the door were scattered with dahlia tubers, unearthed from storage in my room now the frosts were past. Mostly what Mum grew became food, but the dahlias were her winter duty and her summer delight. Each one would become an explosion of happiness, a party-popper flamboyance of a flower. The sight of her hope, laid out like that, was almost more than I could bear.

We ordered Indian, making Daisy, Chloe, Jasmine and Hu join us, and ate round the kitchen table, trying not to drizzle too much korma on the gardening books. Furball appeared, still staggery from sleep, and looped himself around my calves while I ate. As we mopped the last of the sauces from the plastic trays with our naan she told me about the tractor.

It seems you can't borrow much for agricultural equipment, at least not when you live in Chapel A, so she'd sold the Honda and borrowed the rest against the house, under the bank's out-of-work support scheme.

"They claim the loans are to help you find a job," she said, pushing back her chair and taking the empty trays to the sink, "but really it just traps people into more debt." None of the things I could think of to say seemed useful so when Furball jumped up I nuzzled him behind his ear instead and made him purr. "With your 'Stop Shopping'," she told me, "the whole finance world will soon come crashing down, so I don't imagine my loan will matter much."

She laughed and I realised she was proud. Proud of what I was doing. So proud it had prompted her to scale up her own rebellion, bail and income be damned. If buying a tractor seemed crazy, what did that say about how I was spending my days?

"I like the colour," I said, in the end. And that made her laugh again.

She reached for the kettle then chose a bottle of red from the rack instead.

"Fate rang," she said when her back was turned, changing the subject before I could say anything else. I watched Mum set out six glasses and Daisy wave aside wine for her and her team. She hovered for a moment then left Mum and me on our own. I pressed my face into the fur behind Furball's ears so I could fill my nose with his baked earth smell, and curled my legs up onto the seat beneath us. "She rang four times, Ruby."

Mum rummaged till she found the corkscrew and scraped the foil top to bare the cork. It might have been the way the very last of the sun fell in through the high sash window but I could see more pale grey strands amongst the strawberry than I'd noticed before. She's always been the blonde end of red - I get my pillar box locks from Dad, apparently.

"I can only guess how badly you're hurting, darling," she said, pouring the wine into the two glasses with studied care, "and you were swamped before this ... this thing, but just text her." She set the bottle down and rested both her hands on the bench so it might hold her up. "It's not fair, simply vanishing," she said looking at me and I was felled, yet again, by that false memory of Dad walking away, up the street - false because I was only eleven months old when he left. I have a particular tender spot, like the nucleus of a bruise, that he didn't stay for my first birthday. Even after all these years, Mum can't hide the hurt she holds. A tiny smear of earth had caught on her cheek, dark against the delicate lines on her skin.

They had met at the Warehouse, dancing to Nirvana. She'd just finished her first degree and he was already an arborist, following contracts round the country to see where he wanted to stay. If I ever imagine him, it's in the branches of a copper beech. I look up at him and he's laughing, hair rippling amid the crinkly leaves and I find I am holding a chainsaw. I'm never sure if the saw is to bring him back down to us or to carve him apart.

I'll never really know why he left. I guess the trees in Leeds turned out to not be good enough.

Furball purred, vibrating my ears and my thighs.

"I don't have anything to tell Fate," I said, rubbing Furball's chin till he spread his front paws and massaged my knees, snicking the denim of my skirt with his claws. "I'm supposed to be writing a new album but Mum, I've not been writing. Not even before this. Not properly. Not for months. I was meant to have three new songs for that Shaun Ryder gig and I only managed two ..."

I didn't tell her I wasn't sure I'd ever write again.

I didn't tell her I couldn't sleep at night and jumped a mile when anyone moved a chair or banged a drawer, in case it was them breaking in.

And I didn't tell her the idea of saying it all, once more, while Oprah nodded and smiled in profiteering empathy made me want to vanish under the duvet for ever.

"... and Mum, they broke Elsie," I said.

Mum didn't say anything. She handed me my wine, shovelled the seed catalogues and gardening books aside to unearth her laptop and in fifteen minutes she'd booked me four days in a cottage in the hills behind Coniston.

"No mobile signal and no wifi. Just take some other guitar and Daisy and write songs, Ruby."

She was right of course. Nothing heals me like hills and writing.

I telephoned the Bishop three times before he agreed to take my call. Between each attempt I read the cards in the payphone booth promising me sex. I prayed for the souls of the men and women for sale and breathed the cold wet tobacco smell, holding hard to my daddy's tags.

"I told you to wait," he barked at me, finally, more harsh than he has ever been to me before. I did not mind for I was so relieved to hear him and to share the burden of my knowledge from the Lord. I breathed hard and blinked away weak tears and asked God to help me for I had waited and could wait no more.

"I know what to do," I told the Bishop and explained how we would stop Her.

"I'm taking four days," I told Michael, "and I'm taking Daisy. I need a break."

He nodded and told me 'of course' but I could see the doubt I'd ever come back in his eyes and the drop of his shoulders. I ignored it like I ignored my own doubt.

"Masumi and I will do a dozen pre-records before I go. I've had an idea we can build them around. We'll film today and she can edit and drip feed them out. We'll leave this evening and I'll be back in time for *Oprah*."

"Where will you be?" he asked.

"Not far. Just away, so I can rest." Through the window I could see the yellow poppies in the church-yard shaking their heads in the wind. "I need to see if I can write," I said. I didn't tell him there wasn't any coverage.

I'd have liked to go to Eskdale again, to see if I could beat Fred at dominoes this time, but Mum hadn't wanted me anywhere I was known. I'd only been to Coniston when I was a kid and this house was eight miles from there. I'd only objected to taking Daisy once, then I'd seen the fear in Mum's eyes and backed straight down. If I was honest I felt it too.

Masumi loved my idea.

"It's not just saving money," she said, getting it right away, "'Stop Shopping' is also saving time."

She filmed me asking people how they spent the time they saved not shopping. We uploaded the video, and a graphic of a bright pink clock face exploding in flowers, asking the same question, then left them to rampage in the world while we headed to 'the mall'.

I was jumpy as a speed-freak, in the spacious glitz of the Trinity Arcade. Every mirror and plate glass pane flashed danger. Daisy and Chloe hovered close and Masumi gave me the mic, knowing she needed to keep me busy to keep me calm. She gave out stickers and we got people to tell us, to camera, what they were going to do on their lunchbreak instead of shop. Even people who hadn't heard of 'Stop Shopping' before were happy to pause a moment to talk to their local rock star. Most of them could come up with at least three things they'd sooner do than mooch around the shops.

We left them thinking maybe, tomorrow lunch time, they might do one of them instead. In just a few hours we had enough footage to last a fortnight, let alone four days. Hearing their stories and seeing their faces open up with possibility helped. My favourite was an old couple, in matching beige raincoats, who said they were going home to make love.

Daisy hired a dowdy Daihatsu with a full tank under a false name and drove right round the ring road twice before we headed north so she could make sure we weren't being followed.

At Skipton it began to rain, the fat wet kind we've learned to be wary of. It gathered force so by the time Daisy turned the car into the final lane, between narrowed walls, it felt like we were driving into a car wash. We sat at the gate to see if it would ease but in the end I climbed out to push the gate open, the cold splats falling so fast they streamed off my head. I was soaked by the time she was through, wheels spinning in the mud, and I had the gate closed behind her. That rain made me feel cleaner than any of the hours I'd spent under the scalding shower.

"This'll do you good," Daisy said, as I got back, dripping, into the car. She parked as close to the cottage door as she could.

When we'd got the bags and my borrowed acoustic inside, she went out into the wet again to move the car. "It's too close to the window. I want a clean sight," she told me. For a moment I thought she meant it was in the way of the scenery. I asked if it couldn't wait till the rain had stopped. "No," she said. "This is what I do. I won't tell you how to write and you don't tell me how to keep you safe while you do it. Deal?"

I nodded and found a towel to rub off my hair, then set to unpacking the groceries she'd had delivered. She must have talked to Mum. All my writing fuel was here -

Club biscuits, rice pudding, mandarin oranges and even a bottle of Baileys.

I poured us both a small glass and slunk into the chair by the fireplace. Daisy came back in, quietly, so's not to make me jump, towelled off her pigtails, and lit us a fire. Then she set up kitchen chairs at all the windows and ignored her drink. I sipped mine and watched the flames spread.

We spent the first night and day in silence. By morning, the rain had stopped and Daisy tried to find a station on the radio, scratching through the airwaves for tunes. I asked her to leave it dead. The static fell away and all we could hear again was the lonely wind and an anxious sheep. Sometimes a dog's bark would lift up the hill or a bird's cry would drift down from the moor but mainly we just sat on the hillside in the silence of the wind and sheep.

By the second day I wanted to drop notes into the quiet. I picked up the strange guitar and thought about my battered Elsie, then set it down, unplayed.

I ate the sandwich Daisy made then poured a large glass of Baileys and picked up the guitar again. That time I let my fingers lead.

By the fourth day I'd slept for 14 hours straight, climbed the hill behind the cottage, got soaked to my knickers, twice more, in the rain and written the outlines for nine new songs.

I wrote and I wrote and I wrote. I wrote lyrics so fast by hand I could hardly read them and found perfect moments of sound in every room, beyond every meal, in the bottom of every glass. I didn't want to be anywhere else or do anything else but to lay down all the words and all the sounds I was imagining.

All the writing made me yearn to sing. It's an old fashioned word, yearn, but it's the only one I know that captures the heart's hungering to open my voice and my soul, thumb in the harmony of the strings and raise up a room.

With the nine songs I'd made here, added to *A Million Rooms*, *Justice* and *Velvet Dawn*, we'd have enough for an album. And at least one chart topper - two if *Hard Hands* came out as good in the studio as it sounded in my head. We could lay down the tracks, release it quick and vanish on tour. I still believed it when I set the guitar down and told Daisy I was going to climb the hill once more, before we headed back.

It was late afternoon and the air was dry again though every footstep squelched in the bog of ancient peat and recent rain. At the top, a gash in the clouds showed the blue sky above and a sky lark spiralled up towards it, trailing notes like happiness.

I laughed out loud and turned to face the plummet and sweep of the valley below me, arms wide, face up into the wind, seeking any sunlight that might sneak through. It was easy to pretend this was all I needed.

Meanwhile, of course, beyond the haze of bluebells and the dry stone walls, reality was raging - an over-blown party, demanding and unstoppable. Michael and the Group were primed for *Oprah* and waiting. For me. I needed to do the interview tomorrow. And after that I had to follow through. Sure, I could drag Masumi out on the road with The Owls and we could post three 'Stop Shopping' vids a day and she could manage the media noise while I played, but I'd be forever split in two.

I just wasn't able to do justice to my band and 'Stop Shopping' at the same time. It was like trying to run two light bulbs in parallel, off the same battery, in science class - neither shines properly. Both flicker and dim. If I let my attention flicker from the Group other people might get hurt too. So far, it had just been me.

The skylark was still singing but there wasn't any sun for my face. Now I'd stopped climbing, the wind felt cold. I stuffed my hands in my Parka pockets and meandered a little way along the cracked limestone slabs, towards a hawthorn flourishing the first of its white. Past the rocks, a hare broke cover, flashed like whisky in firelight, and was gone.

"Fuck," I swore at the tree.

Then I took my hands out of my pockets and looked at the brave blossom amongst the crinkled branches in this harsh, vast place. I scanned the sky until I found the dot the skylark had become, its voice still spooling out its joy. Then I opened my mouth and I sang. I sang *Hard*

Hands all the way through, every verse and each chorus in between. I sang it like I was saying goodbye, and I was. I would gift my new songs to The Owls but they would have to take flight without me.

I took my Parka off, pulled my T-shirt over my head and unhooked my bra. I turned my phone on for the first time since I'd arrived and took a selfie, with my arms high above my head and the hawthorn behind me, showing off my curly new pits. I didn't smile for the camera. I looked into the lens of the world like I could change it.

After I'd dressed again, before I pocketed my phone, a single coverage bar appeared. I texted Mum an 'I ♥ U' then sent the photo to Masumi, like a promise.

It was time to work.

I am waiting for the Bishop to call, again.

This time it is different.

God has told me the Bishop knew I spoke His truth. The machinery is in motion to turn the Lord's will into action. Soon I will hear the time has come to play my part. While I wait, I pray. Sometimes I go to the cold stone vault of their cathedral, where enough people gather that I am hidden among the tourists, but its gilded fittings are too fancy for my taste so mostly I pray here, on the bench seat near the phone booth in case it rings or in case I change my mind and decide to call my momma.

At the Lawnswood roundabout I almost asked Daisy to take us straight to Mum's. I had a hug to deliver and I wanted to play *Bee Fury* for her. I'd summoned the notes one night, wrapped in Baileys and a blanket on the door step at the cottage, the stars smeared over the sky, and by morning I'd dreamed the words, waking groggy, needing a pen and a pee. Mum's kind about all my music, and she gets guitars and loud even though she doesn't crank out the Soundgarden quite so often anymore, but sometimes she'll really love a track we make. I thought *Bee Fury* would be one of those.

But then I also needed to start things up again on the right note with the Group. Mum knew I was a flaky muso on a mission. She'd wait.

I closed my eyes against the rain-splattered blur of the city while Daisy inched us through the dregs of the rush hour, replaying my rough-record of *Grike-tivist* through my ear buds again and wondering if I should tell Sam the idea I had for samples or just give him the lyrics and the guitar part and see what he came up with.

We weren't on Church Row when we stopped. Or anywhere near The Calls or the river. Daisy had driven us to a grey slab of a bunker, circled in a sweep of tarmac, marked into parking spaces and edged in three metre high concrete walls. I looked behind us to see electronic gates just closing while a steel rollover door cranked up ahead.

"Welcome to the new HQ," she said.

I was slow, still caught in chords and key changes. My surprise stumbled from a sudden shove of anger.

"What new HQ?" I spat, staying put in the car, as if moving would accept the change.

"You said 'no Group news', remember? I checked out a few places for Michael before we went and he messaged me to say they'd picked this one. We thought you'd like to see it."

"But why move?" I asked. She looked at me as if I'd become stupid then fixed her reaction just as fast. I know Daisy thinks I'm naïve but we can't go through life barricaded by hand grenades and braids. Even when we've been hurt.

"Church Row is just too vulnerable, Ruby. You know that." Then she told me they'd learned more while I'd been gone. "It's best Michael tells you," she said. "I'm just security. I listen, assess, respond. Michael and Burt, they did all the digging."

As she drove us inside the warehouse I saw Michael, sitting on a lone swivel chair by the far wall. His bike leaned against the grey wall next to him, a damp patch on the concrete beneath it and his hair still wet from the rain. He stood as we walked over, looking paler and younger than I remembered from the week before. I braced myself and made the hug I gave him decently grunty. He seemed to need it. While the three of us stood in the rude fluorescent light of the warehouse, Michael told us what he and Burt had discovered. His voice was damped by the suck of the concrete and Daisy listened hard even though she'd heard it all before. It felt like the floor of the world tipped and shifted beneath my feet.

When eventually I thought I'd got it, I swiped the chair and sat down.

"OK," I said, tilting back so I could look up at them, their skin fragile in the brutal light and my voice swallowed by the concrete walls and cavernous height. "I get it. It's not just fuckhead Salvador or whatever pretentious name he calls himself. He's got a whole nutty church of scary worshippers behind him. And now 'Stop Shopping' is working, we've got some serious corporate clout pissed off at us too. So you want to move?"

They nodded, shoulders relaxing in relief. It wouldn't last long. I understood why they wanted to hide and all the parts of me that screamed fear and anger, my whole body remembering the rape in the double paradiddle of my heart and the clench of every muscle, in the dry of my mouth and the sweat of my palms, all that instinctive, physical me, wanted to run and hide away too. But I knew it was wrong.

I would have ignored the knowledge if I could but I've learnt, in the last few years, to hear my intuition. In music, it's the only thing that counts. There aren't any rights and wrongs and some of the best sounds come when the rules are bent, if not robustly broken. Making music is to discover the beauty of anarchy, total freedom where anything goes and your tiny inner voice is the only guide you have to what is right. My inner voice is an annoying pixie tucked somewhere between my inner ear and my soul but she's a bossy bitch and I've learned I'm best to listen.

She was chucking a tantrum at the idea of hiding.

"I understand," I said. "I want to hide too. But this isn't about what we want. It's about what's going to work. We can't ask people to 'Stop Shopping' with us if we're hidden away in here. We can't shut ourselves off when we need to connect. Besides, the acoustics are horrible."

I was the only one that laughed.

They both talked at once and Michael stormed about.

After a while I upset them even more by suggesting they move out there and I stay at Church Row with anyone who wanted to. It was a dirty trick, flexing my fame and its hold on the Group, but I was more sure of my intuition pixie than I was of Daisy or Michael, right then. They were more afraid than me.

"Alright," I said. "We've got to stick together. But this place won't work for me. And there are risks in it, too."

Daisy stopped watching Michael and looked at me, alert as Mum's neighbour's Doberman at the smell of Furball.

I improvise better standing up so I pushed the chair away and told them my fame and our publicity was our strength. "We should use it more, not hide away. Out here they could vanish us altogether, fake what evidence they like and no one would know."

I watched Michael see, in the doubt on Daisy's face, he had lost.

"But we're all geared up to move," he said, holding his arms out as if his plans were a Lego model in his hands.

"We can move," I said, "wherever you like, but somewhere more public, somewhere safer – with light and windows and people. Not here."

"Oh, Ruby," he said, dropping his hands, his model in pieces.

Daisy took me to visit Mum and I delivered my hug. She was electrified from planting all day. I'd seen the mud on the tractor tyres outside. There was soil beneath Jasmine and Hu's finger nails, as well as her own. I didn't ask where they'd been. A tense top note to her energy fell away as I held her.

Mum loved *Bee Fury*, as I'd known she would. I'd expected it might make her cry, but I hadn't predicted the anger.

"You're all over the media, Ruby and *Oprah*'s only going to make it bigger. We failed your generation and now you're on the front line. It isn't fair." She slammed her mug down roughly so tea slopped across the open pages of the Veg Journal.

"Not all of you, Mum,"

The tears gone, her face crumpled round her frustration. Next door's Doberman barked and somewhere up the street a door slammed shut. It made me jump but I used my breathing so I didn't start to shake and I don't think she noticed.

"It pisses me off that we've left it so long," she said, pushing herself up from the table and going to stand by the sink, looking out to her garden. "We knew in the Nineties what we needed to do but we just slurped our lattes and waved the odd banner and moaned about it."

I wasn't going to get into the 'your generation' thing. I'd written *Blame*, about it. In the lyrics a Gen Xer, like Mum, accuses her Baby Boomer father of screwing the world and he rails at us Millennials, for our online addictions, as if we didn't have good reason to hide away in *Minecraft*. I wrote it at 16, in fury, during the week BP flooded the Gulf of Mexico with their greedy oil. I poured all my anger at our parents' and grandparents' climate failure into that song. Playing it drained the resentment from me. Blaming each other doesn't help. We need to stick together.

"I just don't know how much more I can take," she said, her voice calm again. "Sometimes I look at your Grandad and envy his oblivion."

"No you don't!" I was there in an instant, turning her to me, so I could tuck her head under my ear. She hugged me like she might never let go, then stepped back so she could see my face.

"I wish I could tell you to stop, to just stay here and be safe, my beautiful girl, making your amazing music, but I can't. We need you. We need what you can do."

"I know, Mum," I said, and she closed her eyes, as if that might keep the inevitable away.

"I love you so very much," she said, looking at me again, her hand on my cheek like I was saying good bye. "Promise me you'll be careful. You do know, if I could do this in your place, I'd do it in a heartbeat, don't you?"

"Of course I do," I said, and then she hugged me because I was the one in tears.

When we re-joined Michael we found the packing underway, the walls bare of posters and Burt entangled in bubble wrap. It seemed we were moving, after all.

"Masumi had the same idea," Michael said, picking his way between boxes and volunteers to join us at the top of the stairs. I looked round again but I couldn't see her spikey head. "She's gone to get the keys," he said.

My rejection of the warehouse meant Masumi had got her first choice - the old Cash Converters up on

Eastgate. It was a double-fronted store where we'd be on display like mannequins.

I wanted to help wrap things up and tuck them in boxes but Michael propelled me to the meeting table. It was strewn with magazines and he had stuck new charts to the whiteboard. I had a week to catch up on and my biggest ever interview to prep for.

When *Peanut Heart* made Number One I'd been on the covers of NME and Rolling Stone but, in the week since the *Daytime* interview, the women's magazines had draped me over a dozen covers. I slid them around on the table. Competing headlines shrieked: Eco Warrior Survives Rape Ordeal, Raped Rocker Tells All, Ruby Rape No Carnival. Sex, violence, rock and roll - my story had it all. Masumi had bought every mag and marked the sprinkle of 'Stop Shopping' references with post-it notes. There were five short paragraphs across 13 magazines.

A big fat fail.

I'd used everything, set light to my shame and my fear to spread the flames of attention, but the fire burned too fiercely. It roared on the sex and violence, the shock of rock star rape so loud, no one could hear what I was trying to say.

"It's not so bad," Michael said, sitting down, and glancing at the chair nearest me so I did the same. "You're topping all the search and trend ratings. Our online traffic's through the roof. That's where we can tell our story. All the articles mean is you've gone A-list. We can use that, Ruby."

And then he told me the story his new charts showed. We were making a change. It wasn't like the weeks before Christmas, when the news reports retail spending like football results, but the data he could access showed end of month sales were down for all the big European and American chains. Better still, the price of shares in retail stocks was falling.

"They've been slow," he said, "but the push back has started." He passed me a graph with an epic spike depicting media stories about 'buying green'. The chains' PR people had been spooling out stories to soothe their customers and keep them spending. It was bullshit of course. Buying eco-organic fair-trade stuff you don't need is still buying stuff you don't need. "This is 'Stop Shopping'," he said. "When they fight back you know it's started to work. We caught them by surprise, where it hurts, right in the numbers." He leant back in his chair and grinned, a genuine glee in his face for the first time in weeks. It wouldn't last - his anxiety would soon be back - but right then it beamed hope, like when the sun battles past storm clouds to shine just on you.

He talked for a little longer, helping me see the tee-tering we'd caused. I began to smell the potential of one more epic push, as if it was almost ready in the oven.

Back at my flat, in the entrance, three severe black and chrome mountain bikes were chained, next to mine, by the rack of metal letterboxes. Daisy wouldn't be let-ting me ride on my own again.

I'd asked Fate and Sam to meet me there. Daisy wasn't exactly pleased at guests – she'd banned takea-ways and mail order altogether – but marginally preferred The Owls coming round to us meeting over a pint. I had them bring pizza and I opened us all beers and we sprawled on the floor, round the boxes, as we ate with the new, rough-cut tracks I'd made sliding from the speakers all around us.

Together we picked apart the threads I'd woven, reshaping and colouring, making music and making each other laugh. Fate found the beats with her fingers on the table edge and I plugged my Fender into my practice amp and fixed up some of the chords. Sam captured the changes on his phone. When we got to *Hard Hands* they both looked anxious.

"You sure, girl?" Fate asked me, the crease deep between her brows as she listened for any doubt in my answer.

"Yeah, I'm sure," I told them. "Talking about it on TV was way harder than singing it." I couldn't help glance at where they'd written on the wall. "I think it might help, you know, to take it back from the media."

I'd recorded the track with a sparse scathing feel, drawing on the place beyond fear and anger where pity lurks, hoping it might take me further in that direction. They didn't want to change a thing and we agreed, just amplified acoustic. We'd layer in more drums as the verses got more explicit, to balance it out. Sam and Fate took more of a lead on the other songs, treating what I'd made for them the way Mum treats compost and seeds, the ingredients of a garden she maps to her will. They sketched out the album order and started on a set list, the new tunes making them itch to be on the road.

"Give us a week to learn them and flesh out our parts," Sam said, pulling his hoodie back on as he stood to go.

"I'll book us the studio, yeah?" Fate asked, "Tuesday week?" We've always worked fast.

"I can't," I said. The flurry of them moving, finding bags and jackets, stopped as suddenly as if I'd paused them.

"'Stop Shopping' is about to go really crazy. I'm doing Oprah tomorrow." I laughed, nervous, not about the interview but at what I was about to say. "It should send our track downloads soaring," I joked. They knew me well enough to sense I was stalling. So then I told them I had to commit. I couldn't stay in The Carnival Owls and be the poster girl for 'Stop Shopping'. There just wasn't enough of me to go round. Other people could probably do both, but for me it was too much. Something had to give.

"So finish the songs," I said, "I want you to. And tour. But you'll need another singer and guitarist. I'm sorry. I just can't."

"You quit?" Fate asked, the surprise naked in her face.

"I have to," I said, suddenly frightened I was running away after all, when I just wanted to free them to play.

"Thanks for the leaving present," Fate said, her voice reined in tight. She tucked her data-stick of the tunes in her flak jacket and stalked to the door like a wounded wildebeest too proud to show its hurt. I thought she might turn back but she just opened it and went out.

Sam gathered his keys and his wallet from the table, reluctant to leave.

"Maybe, Ruby, we could just hang out and jam, you know, till you've got some more time?"

I wanted to lie and tell him 'yes' but I didn't. He closed the door quietly behind him.

The Bishop rang and told me to meet him at an address near Heathrow. He had booked a flight for himself and the train for me. Before I left, I bought a new razor and shaved my face, for I am no longer forsaken, and put on the third white shirt I had not yet worn.

His plane was late so I found myself standing in a room high in a glass tower with a woman sitting across a wide table. She introduced herself as Ms Smith. I thought it rude she did not use her Christian name with me but I don't think she minds much about being polite to people. Ms Smith looked at her watch like she was angry with it for delaying Bishop Hamilton.

"We may as well begin," she said in a British accent from black and white movies. I wanted to ask her where she was from but she pointed at a chair and then touched her phone and made a projected image come into the air between us. There was a photo of me and lots of words written the wrong way round. She touched the screen again and the words came right.

"You can read?" she asked. I sat. The words were about me too; where I went to school, when my daddy was killed, where Momma lives now. There was a line under Momma's name and when I put my finger to it the projection brought up a photo of her I'd never seen.

She told me it was taken last week.

Seeing the photo of Momma like that, looking more grey and tired, made me sad and it was a while before I could read the rest of it. It was a surprise to see everything lain out like that and I had to ask the Lord to help me not to be afraid. It seemed they had written everything, even things I had not told the Bishop, like where I had lived in Leeds, and some things even I did not know, like the names of the men I hired for Her.

Ms Smith had got up while I read and stood close to the window. If you didn't know there was glass there, right to the floor, you'd think she was about to step off. Beyond the window the clouds were low and white, like you could touch them. I didn't know what to say when I'd finished reading so I didn't say anything at all. After a while she began to drum her fingers on the glass, like someone impatient will do on a table, as if she was in a hurry to be gone.

"What now?" I asked.

She told me it was down to Bishop Hamilton how he deployed his...people. She said it like that, with a pause before 'people', as if she couldn't decide what I was. I didn't know if she thought I was maybe a pig or a cow or some other of God's dumb creatures, or if she was thinking of a word for the kind of holy work I do and didn't know of one. I could have told her 'one of His faithful' would be a good way to say it, but I was afraid if she had meant pig or cow that she would laugh at me so I stayed silent. She talked again, anyway, saying it was unfortunate he was late and seemed for a while to be undecided. It made her fidget the way people do when they can't make up their mind and aren't used to such a thing. Maybe she prayed or maybe she didn't but she seemed to come to a decision.

"If Hamilton agrees, we'll renew the contract," she said. "The same terms as before but a lump sum in a bank account too, on completion."

I didn't know what terms she was talking about and thought the money must be for the church. I get cash for anything I need from the Bishop so I told her working for our Lord was reward enough and stood up tall from my chair while I said it so my daddy would have been proud.

She laughed then, a hard sound, like she thought I was being smart, and picked up her phone.

The image of my life disappeared.

As she passed me, on the way to the door, she handed me a card. It didn't have her name on it just a telephone number. "Please give this to Hamilton when he arrives," she said, "and tell him we carry on."

I asked her if that was all and she nodded and was gone.

When the Bishop came, all red and hot like he had run from the plane, I told him what she had said and he took me for a meal of steak and fries. I didn't talk about the money because I know such things embarrass him. The Lord provides. Maybe I meant to give him the card straight away and forgot or maybe I meant to keep it for a while.

When he went to the bathroom I took out the card and memorised the number. I gave it to him when he came back. He pushed it into his jacket pocket, out of sight, as if it were unclean, then handed me a new phone, the old kind, which just lets you ring numbers and type short messages.

After he had gone, I went to an internet cafe to write this and to search for the phone number online. It didn't come up so I changed the digits at the end for zeros, making it simpler. The Lord was with me and the search showed a website called the Global Economic Federation.

I found a page called Gallery and scrolled through the pages of photographs of men in suits standing in rows and smiling at the camera. There weren't many women so it made it easy to see Ms Smith, a few pages down. She was not named but the image was labelled Oil Sector Forum 2016.

I thought about dialling the number just to see what would happen. Perhaps Ms Smith would answer. Perhaps helicopters with military police would land in the street outside. Perhaps it would just ring and ring. I called Momma instead and when she answered I pictured her like she was in the photo before I hung up.

The start of the *Oprah* interview was pretty much a rerun of *Daytime*, with added whooping and clapping. She was all studied pro behind her teary cocoa eyes, even on the monitor screen.

When I couldn't handle her 'sharing my pain' any longer, I asked Oprah and everyone to help me beat my attackers by staying out of the shops that Saturday. I asked them to go to the park or watch a football game or bake a cake, instead. Naming the day felt solid, like a shield I could hold in front of me as we pushed forward. Oprah told me I was very brave and she'd ditch her visit to Bloomingdale's.

If I could stop time, I would choose that moment, when one of the richest women in the world said she'd stop shopping because I asked her to. I could hear the cash tills across America fall silent at her example, and the echo of their quiet follow her broadcasts round the world. It seemed as if, after everything that had happened, things would change, right then. The senseless shifting and wasting of stuff would slow, a new 'normal' would emerge and our suffocating climate would breathe and heal. That wasn't how the tune played out, no matter how hard I wish it had.

"So Ruby, before we close, can I ask, as a Brit yourself, how do you feel about the first sky-seed happening from British soil?"

"Sky-seed?" I thought maybe what she'd said had been chewed in the video feed.

"Yes, you know the Global Economic Federation has funded Cambridge University to launch 680 tonnes of sulphur dioxide into the stratosphere?" She glanced at her notes. "It's scheduled for June 1st, if the conditions are right."

I'd read about geo-engineering. Like most people, I'd thought shooting pollution into the sky to block out sunlight was just a sci-fi fantasy – boffins playing make-believe. It turned out they were playing 'Dare' instead. I must have missed it in the news, while I was away - there hadn't been time to read all my briefing notes. The only thing I remembered about sky-seeding was it would stop the sky being blue. The idea of no more blue sky, ever, was so simple and so terrible it had stuck with me, even when the rest of the science had blurred.

"Shit," I said. Oprah looked at me as if she expected something more.

"We don't need that shit," I ad libbed. "If we make enough cuts in using coal and oil right now we can make things ok again, more or less." My mind was flooded with vague sea level stats and I could feel myself floundering. I counted to three the way I do on stage if

I think I've forgotten the lyrics. It makes me remember to breathe and gets me back on track. The audience never notices. There's a power in silence. There's also a power in keeping it simple. I pictured Michael telling me people want basic sound bites they can understand, not techno babble. And then I pictured the sky in June from underneath Mum's sprawling plum tree and the sky at Christmas when the snow clouds have cleared. I would have counted to three again but Oprah was looking anxious so I just made do.

"We've all got to decide what's more important," I said, "driving the car to the shops or opening the curtains in the morning with some hope it might be a blue sky day." I could feel the hot beads of impending tears in the inner corners of my eyes and blinked twice so I didn't wipe them. "This sky-seeding, it turns the sky white, for always. Do we want that?"

Oprah opened her mouth to say something but fluttered her hand to her earpiece and said our time was up, instead. She cut to the break. The screen blinked as they cut the live broadcast, then Oprah appeared briefly, saying thank you and reaching one palm towards me, before the static wiped her out. A flurry of production assistants swept into my suite, one pouring me water, one calling a cab and one telling me Oprah was right, I was very brave.

I didn't feel brave.

I felt swamped and blindsided. Daisy joined us and I just held her hand, tight, until the cab turned up.

I wanted us to go back to my flat, to climb into bed with vodka and Elsie and cry and sleep till it all went away. Daisy just looked at me. I was the boss. It was my call where we went.

I am really trying not to be a person who runs away when it gets too much.

"Church Row," I told the driver. We would go back to HQ and Masumi would be replaying the interview and making notes. Everyone would have stopped packing up to dissect why I'd been so unprepared for the sky-seed question. I would walk in and tell them I was sorry. I would smile and endure their criticism because that was what they needed from me. Like it or not, I was their leader. I would not let them down because, even if I did, none of it would go away - no matter how much I cried or how much I drank or how much I slept.

As we climbed the stairs I heard their excited chatter above us fall away, leaving just the clomp of our boots on the steps. When we reached the room everyone was standing, solemn faced and silent, looking at me.

"I'm sorry," I said, straight up. Clearly I'd stuffed it up even worse than I'd feared. Then Michael started clapping, a slow, serious clap of respect and everyone joined in for a very long time until I did cry. Masumi was the first to reach me, hugging me and guiding me to a chair, pressing a tissue to my face.

"You were so good," she said. "So good it changes everything."

It was only later, when I'd grabbed a nap on the couch and eaten the vast bowl of mac cheese Tao ordered in for me, that I understood what she meant. Michael took me through it while I clutched a mug of tea.

"It's a step change," he said. "Getting Oprah to commit like that was magic. And then the blue skies thing. Genius. It tied it all together. The clip's gone global, TV and online." Michael was perched on the very edge of the sofa next to me, barely able to sit in his excitement. He began to show me the clip on some Hispanic network but I ignored the phone and he pushed it back into his pocket, without missing a beat. "Burt's had to pull in more techs just to manage the demand on the servers and we've the most interview requests, ever." I started to ask him when the next one was but he cut me off, telling me media could wait until tomorrow, to give me time to rest and for them to catch up.

"I've rested," I told him. "Now it's time to work."

I moved back to Leeds, to a guesthouse on the far side of town, on a street where the rumble of traffic from the York Road reaches all through the night. It does not matter. The Lord's spirit burns so bright in me I need only a few hours' sleep.

The days are long though the waiting has a different feel to it now. It is like the space at the top of a page of scripture, before the words begin. To pass the time and keep myself clean and dry I take the bus to the Trinity mall. I take a different number bus each day and sometimes ride the long way round the ring road. The mall is not as fine as the ones at home but sufficiently large I can use different seats in different parts so no one notices me. Its name comforts me with the three faces of the Lord and what sun there is gets focused by the wide glass roof. Spring is cowardly here. In Shreveport I would need only short sleeves by May.

I am careful, even though I look changed, because She is nearby. I move often and take care not to catch anyone's eye.

I think a lot. I think about Ms Smith and her Federation. I think about Bishop Hamilton and what she is paying him. None of it comes to me, like she expected; serving God is my recompense. The Bishop did not even grant me funds to rent a whole apartment of my own, like I had asked, just the room.

Perhaps he gives the money he saves to Pastor Brian. It must be a costly thing indeed to build a flock in a new country.

I watch the people and imagine, instead of the old stone of the Holy Trinity outside, a glowing church of our own, right inside the mall, where it is warm. Today, as I watched, I thought there were not so many people there.

Half of Fleet Street had wanted to see me, so Masumi had booked us a suite at The Queens Hotel and I'd entertained them in Art Deco style, one by one, while Daisy lurked in the bedroom with the door open. "If Oprah's stopping shopping, everyone can," I said, again and again.

Saturday itself we kept clear. I spent the day in the city centre, talking to anyone without a bag in their hands. One guy in an Ed Sheeran shirt asked me if I was 'soft', which I thought ironic, given his taste in music. A woman with cool purple hair told me shopping was the only thing that kept her sane and gave me two quid. Mostly people looked a bit embarrassed and said they thought they'd give it a go. A lovely lot of them wished me well and promised no end of suffering for the thugs when they were caught.

We ran it all as a livestream on Witter, filming till the shops had shut. Then we trooped up to the brick and leather first-floor snug of Smokestack. Masumi and I drank vodka martinis and bobbed around to the old-school soul while Daisy, Chloe and Sophie scowled.

Bazzer was behind the bar and put our drinks on the house so, technically, it wasn't shopping.

"The press has turned," Michael said, the next morning, pushing The Sunday Telegraph to me across his desk. In thumping letters the headline read 'Stop Shopping killing cities'. "The rest are the same. They reckon the retail spend yesterday was even less than in the '08 crash."

"So it's working?" I asked. "Shouldn't we celebrate?" I had a frivolous vision of us all taking off to the park for the day with Prosecco and pizza.

"It's working," he said, "but Ruby I don't know if it's a fight we can win."

"It's the magazines too," Masumi said, coming over. For the first time she looked unsure of herself, as if a misstep might send her sliding down a mountain. "One of the journalists you talked to on Friday just called." The woman had told Masumi to say she believed in 'Stop Shopping' and wanted to cover it but her editor wouldn't. "It's the advertising. She could lose her job. They will cover you, Ruby, but not the campaign."

The media need stars. We sell copies. But they need advertisers too. Ads for the big brands' sprays and lotions filled magazines every month, jostling to be nearest the front cover. The cash they brought paid the wages. But face cream and perfume were often the things people told us they had stopped buying. Just the day before, we had streamed a woman my age saying she had enough half-used tubs of facial goo to last the year. She'd ignore all the promises of improved formulas for endless youth and use up what she had. She wasn't the only one. My demographic bought a lot. Or they had.

Michael read from his checklist and I wasn't sure if it was because he was afraid to see my reaction or because he needed his notes.

"Claire's and Accessorize have warned staff to expect redundancies. Even The Observer's got a story on how the poorest are being hit." He brought it up online to show us the photo of Chinese factory workers getting laid off. He clicked again and the Mail on Sunday's home page filled the screen: 'Economy under attack'.

"Enough," I said, sitting down to think then, finding I was getting a hangover after all, dragging them with me to make tea. "We've got to keep pushing," I said, while we waited for the kettle to boil.

It was less than three weeks to the scheduled date for the sky-seed. They would only get away with it if no one was doing anything better for the climate.

I remembered Michael telling me, while we crafted the Star Parties, how the Paris Deal of '15 had been like starting to indicate, when the world had needed a hand brake turn. I poured boiling water into the mugs and poked my tea bag around to hurry it up.

"They've put their spin on 'Stop Shopping', that's all," I said, as Michael passed me the milk. I knew I was over-simplifying. The evil empires of the world were built to prop each other up and would lock together tight to survive our rattling. "We have to spin harder, that's all. They might keep us out of the media but they can't stop us online."

They seemed to believe me. "Just go for the biggest mainstream reach we can get with our time," I told them, "even if they'll only cover me. It will all drive our web traffic." Michael started to summon all the comms volunteers he could reach, to help Masumi. I texted Sinead to send us anybody useful.

Michael arranged them to meet us up at the new offices in the morning. I wanted to stay and help with the last packing and loading. They'd hired a beast of a truck that could have swallowed the band van we'd started the Group with. Instead I got sent home with Daisy and the links that would tell me all about Professor Rees and his Cambridge sky-seed project.

When the afternoon was almost done, and the sun made a late appearance, flooding my flat like a special guest on stage for the encore, Masumi rang. Oprah's PA had messaged to say they had invited Walmart and Macy's into the studio for a right of reply. So much for support, girlfriend.

The next morning was the kind that makes even Leeds pretty - May in full swagger, a lusty promise of summer. It was a day to ride.

I was flanked on either side by Chloe and Sophie. Daisy rode tucked in behind or suddenly ahead. If Sophie had put as much effort into peddling as she did bitching about having to ride, she'd have left us all for dead. It's a combination that always makes me happy - a pack of women swooping through the city, though that morning I longed to be away, freewheeling on my own. I chaffed to be off like I did at the end of a too-long tour with The Owls when everything any of us said grated on the other two. Thinking about my band made me miss them so, subdued, I stayed dutifully in place. I did my best to ignore my sore and sorry crotch and gently curs-ed Masumi for finding us a new location uphill all the way from my flat after I'd been off the road.

There were 20 people waiting for us, ranging from a silver haired gent that ran an ad agency to a pair of pri-mary kids that made YouTube documentaries. Michael introduced me and they were all mine.

One thing I've learned from the thousands of hours on stage is how to change a set when you sense you're going out of synch with the room - when to kick the playlist off the monitor and play the gig by ear. Some of our best-ever shows were the ones where we leapt be-tween songs on instinct, like boulder hopping along a beach, and slung in a cover we'd only ever jammed before or a new song that wasn't really ready, just be-cause it felt right. As front woman it's my job to lead it, to take the band into the surprise of the unknown, and keep them tight and happy while we do it.

I'd realised in the night, sleepless after a siren had woken me, thinking over what Michael had said that, despite the impact, 'Stop Shopping' was stuttering. It felt like a new song that thrills your heart when you re-hearse it but dies quickly in the bright lights of a stage. As they read the onslaught of headlines every day, people who had stopped shopping would start to become afraid of their power. Their friends who lost jobs in shops would accuse them. Spending would creep back up, egged on by guilt. Our Saturday focus would only drag out the decay.

I had let the dark night thoughts circle like vultures until they landed on the carcass of my greatest fear. The sky-seed. Taking the blue sky away to patch up the mess we should be fixing was just one step too far. It was for me, at least. If enough other people felt the same, we should target that.

I brought Masumi's clippings onto the big screen for our new volunteers, sliding each away in turn to reveal another critique beneath.

"We can't sustain this much longer," I said, "So it's time to change tack." I stood, as if by moving, I could take everyone with me.

I told them we needed something that built on 'Stop Shopping' but was potent enough to derail the sky-seed - something active people could do, wherever they were, rather than the passive abstinence of not buying more. And then we set them loose.

They laughed and argued, broke into small groups and reformed as a whole, covering the whiteboard and dozens of flip chart sheets. I never knew whose idea it was. The room had become a chemical magic box, a chrysalis, and 'Car Dump' emerged from the cauldron of discussion.

It was one of a cluster we short listed, but unparalleled - a compelling butterfly, simple and lovely enough to make us all afraid.

"It is perfect," said Masumi, nodding. "And it ties in exactly, see?" She replayed the *Oprah* clip of me again, asking the viewers to choose between 'driving to the shops, or opening the curtains with some hope'.

"How long till we start?" I asked her.

"Two weeks, if we crank it," she said. The idea needed logistics and pretty pics before it was ready to roll. I felt like I did when The Owls had finished recording and all we had were the rough tracks and the producer kidnapped them for the mixing and the mastering so they were fit for consumption.

"What if we made it one?" I asked. She looked to Michael, eyebrows raised like calligraphy question marks. He scrubbed his fingers through his hair and nodded.

Meanwhile, we had to switch tack, ease off 'Stop Shopping' and really get the Sky-Seed story out there...when it was running hot, we'd be ready.

"Just tell me what to say," I told them and went to sprawl in a bean bag with the two million messages that needed clearing.

When the day was nearly over, Michael and Masumi took me through the plan. 'Stop Shopping' saved people money but 'Car Dump' would cost them. We had to get it right.

"Will it work?" I asked them. Michael nodded, opened his hands to the future and smiled.

"It'll be the biggest flash mob the world has ever seen," he told me, amped on his own hyperbole. "People will get sucked in on the spur of the moment, even if they don't plan to." Outside, Eastgate was gripped by rush hour, cars chugging helplessly on the spot, while just outside our window the pavement flowed with people.

I left Masumi shuffling her flamingo flock of Post-it notes across the wall and Michael snaring fresh pages into his clipboard and escaped to Stellar's for the soothing, ordinary mayhem of tea time and bath time and *The Wild Things* before *Eastenders*. When it finished I asked if she'd do it.

"Of course, silly," she said, but she wouldn't meet my eye. Chloe and Sophie had waited outside. I could have sworn Stellar's old Fiesta glared at me when we left.

I thought about the messages that would be mustering in my inbox and how we should ride back to the office so I could answer some more. We cycled to Mum's for Horlicks instead. She told me 'Car Dump' was genius before shipping me home to sleep.

There has been a flurry of meetings in the back rooms of dark bars, half-introductions to men who are only trusted with the shard of information needed to take us to the next meeting, with another man. I should be tired but the Lord has breathed sweet air beneath my wings and I am carried by His grace.

Finally we have a house and we have a team and soon it will be done.

A series of bright blue cartoons of sky-seeding, complete with a grimacing sulphur dioxide cannon, had appeared along the bottom of our windows overnight. Michael was already hunkered over his desk, phone to his ear. After just a day he was oblivious to the passers-by and their curious stares. Half a dozen of the volunteers from yesterday were working away on laptops or scoping concepts in felt tips. Not only were we open to the street but in here we'd become open to each other, too. Our original group, minus Salva-fucker-dor, of course, piled in with everyone else, together. Daisy had a permanent frown but it made me feel we could do anything. I made tea and posted a cascade of perky comments before I went over to Michael. I could hear the indignation from the other end of the line and Michael's calm sympathy burst in frustration when he hung up.

"You'd think we'd *asked* for a frigging saboteur," he swore at his laptop as he keyed in notes from the call.

The protest groups and NGOs had been furious when they learned the person we'd given them to deal with was the infiltrator who'd betrayed us. Michael had managed the most difficult liaison, spending hours listening to stressed directors splutter about security and confidentiality, soothing them as best he could. The friend from WWF hadn't returned any calls.

I didn't blame the other groups. It wasn't like we had any track record. Some of them had been working on this shit for fifty years and we turn up and grab a load of limelight. They'd all done well out of us - we don't take donations and refer anyone who wants to give to them. But we'd still turned up late, made a lot of noise and set them up with Salva-fucker. They had a right to be pissed off.

"I thought I'd give them a head's up on 'Car Dump'," he told me "but they're still pretty freaked. He nodded at the phone. "That guy was panicked 'Stop Shopping's about to crash Wall Street and we don't have a plan for afterwards."

"He's right," I said, "We don't have a plan for what comes next. We just need to make sure there *is* a next."

"Vacuums are dangerous," he said, tipping back in his chair to look up at me. I wasn't sure if he was testing my nerve or testing his own. I decided it didn't matter much.

"Humans have brains and the Internet and at least a half-arsed democracy in most places," I said. "If the fantasy they call the economy falls apart, we'll figure something out between us. The most important thing, right now, is to show the goal posts have moved, for ever. It's not ok to shaft the planet anymore."

He surprised me with his laugh and I saw the tension slip from his neck and shoulders like snow slumping off a tree.

"You're irresistible," he said and smiled, basking for a moment at what he and Masumi had created in me. He stood, suggesting we get everyone together to look at the first 'Car Dump' ideas, but as he was about to flip off his laptop, he stopped.

"Just a moment," he said. I fetched my phone from my desk and when I returned he was back in his seat, flicking his way through the Government website. I poked him in the side and whined. I wanted to see the new concepts. "You and Masumi do it," he said, shrugging me off. "I need to deal with this."

There is, of course, always something to deal with in this game. The album of activism is never mastered, never complete, so you always have to be the one to walk away each day or after years, when you just can't do it anymore. Plenty of people never do, they just live their whole lives trying to make things better and die trying. I didn't know if that was me, but for Michael it seemed likely.

"What is it?" I asked him, pulling up a chair and sitting astride it the wrong way to show I wasn't settling in for more computer work.

"Well, we've had the Minister for the Arts, and the Minister for Climate interfering, but this is different." He brought up the email that had interrupted him - three crisp lines requesting his presence in London for a meeting with the Minister of the Interior. "It's like Homeland Security in the States," he said, "but more secret. I doubt this is to politely reassure us Britain can balance emissions and the economy or to offer you an Order of the Garter."

"I'm getting an Order of the Garter?" I pictured myself at Buck Palace in a drop dead Westwood frock and my Docs, shaking hands with King Will.

"Of course not. Royalist bollocks."

He hadn't even looked up from the laptop. I swallowed my disappointment like a last swig of tea that's gone cold in the cup. I'm a rock star. I like a bit of pomp and grandeur and the Royals were the least of our problems, as far as I could see. Of course, with the economy wobbly, I was fast becoming more public enemy than potential Honours recipient.

"Do you need to go?" I asked, remembering what he'd told us about Switzerland. If it could happen there it could happen here too. It would be easy to ignore the Coalition - having created so much of the mayhem they sit on their hands and let the chaos run, especially here in the North. But they have the power to make people disappear. There are still teenagers locked up after the 2011 riots for nicking a pair of jeans, except they're not teenagers anymore.

"I have a feeling they'll come and get me if I don't," he said. "It's on Friday. I'll just go there and back in the day." I said I'd go instead but he looked horrified. "I need you out here and free to talk," he said. "Just in case." But he did agree to get Daisy to send someone good with him.

"My pick is Treasury know 'Stop Shopping' is hurting," he said, pressing 'send' on his reply. "So they've briefed the heavies to reign us in."

"Or maybe they're pissed at us targeting the Sky-Seed. Perhaps there's export potential?" He laughed at my joke, a light snort of incredulity, but his eyes crinkled at the corners like they do when he's thinking.

"Maybe," he said, and sighed.

We pulled our chairs into a circle and spread all the ideas on the floor. When we had picked the ones we liked best, Masumi commandeered me for Sky-Seed interviews.

We did them all from Leeds, exhausting our phones and our fingers and earning the lifelong adoration of the video conference suite. They ran all day and half the night as we chased peak viewing hours around the globe. In between, I slept - ragged snatches harried by dream interviews in which I repeated myself or started to sing.

Sinead kept leaving me messages but I ignored her. I didn't want to talk about the band. In those three days I was a relentless one hit, blue sky wonder, a single-minded soundbite slave.

On the Friday, we hauled ourselves into the unreasonable heat of the afternoon, dodging the sodden downpour that whispered flood, to the Belgrave for a debrief. We sat amongst the bright beach huts on the roof garden amid the bunting and puddles, gambling with sunburn. A pint of Withens Pale on top of the tiredness made me giggle. Masumi opened her laptop, loading a wash of charts onto the screen but then she looked at me, changed her mind and closed it down.

"It's worked," she said, simple as one of her haiku. "Not since Prince died has one story trended so strong, so fast, worldwide." I swallowed the impulse to sing *Purple Rain* and made myself picture what that kind of coverage really meant. It wasn't just us of course, the whole save-the-planet brigade had come out behind us, decrying the Sky-Seed, but it was the red headed rock star the media wanted most.

Fame, like rain, is relative. Since *Oprah* I'd been drowning in it. The negative headlines after 'Saturday' had only increased the deluge - the media loves conflict. There was so much attention it flooded into me, filling me up and leaving me clinging to the little rocky island left inside myself. But the world bores fast. In another week, me and the blue skies would be supplanted by Russel Brand's latest spiritual proclamation or Kelly Osbourne's alien baby.

The world hadn't bargained on 'Car Dump'.

We were ready to go.

Michael messaged Masumi to say he was back in Leeds so we sank the rest of our pints and limped back to HQ. Masumi and I slung our arms round each other's shoulders like we hobbled, wounded but victorious, from a battlefield. Daisy stalked behind us.

I could hear the chatter from inside through our windows - a dozen or more people talking and the strange echo of my own voice, the playback from an interview, on the sound system.

I'd never got nerves too bad when we started The Owls - I'd always been just so damned hungry to be on stage. But there had been one time, at the O2, where I'd grown up watching amazing bands, our first headlining gig in a proper three tier theatre. Just as I was about to step out of the dark someone announced our names over the PA. Generally they just cut the background tunes and the house lights dropped and out we came, but this time some cheesy announcer gave us a big build up, calling us on, and calling out my name like I'd just won *The Price is Right*. I had frozen, the reality of what I was about to do crystallised by my name in my ears. Listening to my voice playing now felt the same, as if some weird sound-ray immobilised me in the street.

At the O2, Fate had poked me with her sticks till I moved and as soon as I grabbed my guitar from the stand I was fine and loving it. That afternoon, standing in our doorway, all I could do was listen. The odd soundbite bumped through the glass intact, making me wonder where I'd found the words, like waking to find lyrics I'd written drunk the night before.

I turned my back on our windows and leant back against the glass, closing my eyes in the delicious, betraying sunshine. Masumi had gone in ahead but Daisy waited, watching me.

When I stepped inside it would become my job to lead the Group onto a new stage. I knew exactly what we had to do but I had no idea where it would take us. None of us did.

Daisy coughed. I looked at her as if she might have plaited courage into her pigtails for me.

Behind her, a skinny Grime kid passed Snoring Ned, the homeless guy in our new neighbourhood. When the boy was almost beyond the old man he stopped, slid his hand deep in his jeans and pulled out a few coins, returning to drop them into Ned's cap. Ned startled and woke. He raised a salute to the boy, tipping fingers to his eyebrow. The teenager shrugged and loped away.

I dug my fingertips into the headache mustering at the bridge of my nose then tried to smear it away across my face.

If faking courage was the best I could do, at least I would have tried.

"Let's get on with it," I said, as if Daisy was the one lagging back.

Buried in the tortuous bureaucratic language the Ministry had subjected Michael to was the lie they would review the Sky-Seed and the promise that, if we didn't officially cancel 'Stop Shopping', they would press economic terror charges against me.

A t the guesthouse they call me Daniel. They boil eggs for me at breakfast time and in the evenings serve scoops of meals from large oven dishes. Last night we had shepherd's pie. When I went to bed the memories came and no matter how hard I tried, everything I had swallowed down instead of telling Momma, because she was with Mr Miller, leaked out, like it does, with his damp hands trembling inside my shirt and his chewing gum breath on my stomach and his hairy pink legs sticking out of his black robe and all the rest I can not type. I had to get up and dress myself again to stop the shaking and let myself out of the narrow little house to find some clear air in the yard.

I gripped my arms through my sweater and held my face up to the thin rain that was coming from the glowing clouds. They sat low over the yard wall so I thought maybe it wasn't raining at all but just the cloud making me wet. I didn't know if they glowed from the city lights or the holy spirit. I thought maybe the cloud might lift me up and carry me to God so I prayed. When I opened my eyes again I was still in the yard and the knees of my trousers were wet from kneeling.

I don't know what Momma would have said if I had told her. She had known him all her life. He is in the photo she showed me of her first communion, smiling behind a row of girls in white dresses. Momma is the one with the longest white socks. I do know that first night, trying to sleep, the memories spewing back out of me, took away any courage I had to tell her. I was young then and had not learned how some men in some churches are consumed by the Devil so I blamed God and I blamed my momma. I strayed from the Lord's path until the Bishop found me.

I went back into the guesthouse and took off my trousers and laid them over the chair so they might dry by morning. Then I found my sweater was wet too so I hung that over the heater. The bed covers were heavy and warm but when I closed my eyes all that came afterwards arrived; the disrespecting Momma and finding I could take the rum from the back corner of the local store without being seen and, if I drank enough, it let me sleep without remembering.

I got out of bed again and knelt and prayed for strength then drifted in glowing clouds until morning came through the window.

It was just a plain, grey house, set by itself on a back lane, away from the main highway. A row of bushes with pink flowers ran along the path to the door and the grass had been cut. I knocked two-four-two like they had told me. My phone buzzed and I keyed in the code we had agreed. After another minute the door swung in. A big man in a grey suit stood behind it so he could not be seen from the street. He handed me a neoprene balaclava the same as the one he wore. Like his, mine fitted tight over my head and stopped halfway down my face, with holes for my eyes, leaving my nostrils and mouth uncovered. He nodded once then tipped his head to show me I should walk down the passage. The doors on either side were closed and the grey carpet ran ahead, straight up the stairs. On the first floor, at the back of the house, I could hear two men laughing. I pushed the door open and went in. They had her on a steel legged chair, set between the two wall lamps that would once have bracketed the bed. She faced the wall, her knees touching the pearly pink paper, wrists bound with tape behind the chair back. It didn't matter that she faced that way; the windows were boarded over and she wore the same head cover we did but on the wrong way round so her red hair stuck out the eyeholes in random tufts.

The men sat in a pair of easy chairs, the high backed leather kind, cans of Coke open on a low table between them. They were dressed the same as the man who had let me in but seemed even bigger.

"Come to check on the merchandise?" the far one asked, pushing himself out of the chair and crossing to a refrigerator. It was plugged into one of the chimney alcoves, where you'd usually put a set of drawers. He got out two Cokes and held them out to us. The man who had let me in took them both and passed one to me. Its cold metal helped clear my mind. I pulled the ring, releasing the hiss and drank three long swigs.

"Is she eating?" I asked.

The third man told me she was, when she could stop talking long enough. Apparently whenever the gag was off, she told them about all the jobs she was missing in the garden and *fretted about watering the plants. "As if that's what should be worrying her," he said. "Still, at least she's not a screamer."*

I kept looking at her hands, clasped together with silver tape where Momma wore her silver bracelets. Her hands were ugly. Even from where I stood and drank my Coke I could see the skin was dry and worn and her nails were chopped right away. Momma always had fine hands, with nails like fluttering birds. Once she got tiny jewels put on them, like diamonds from a wedding ring, one on each nail, and they sparkled in the light.

I didn't want to look at her anymore so I went back downstairs with the first man and watched soccer on TV. I thought I should read some scripture so when the advertising came on I got out my Book but I opened it at the fifth commandment which startled me and then I couldn't get the image of Momma's hands out of my mind, fluttering behind the neck of Mr Miller. He was supposed to be helping us with a loan, after Daddy died, but came round to the house far too much and was there, pressing her against the kitchen bench, when I got back needing to talk that day. I was so angry I could not speak. I could not tell her how hurt I was that she had forgotten Daddy and I could not tell her what I needed to. I put my Book away and when I finished my Coke I screwed the can up tight and threw it against the wall. The man in the grey suit laughed.

When the time came, I let him make the call. I watched them from one of the high back chairs; the first man, smooth voiced, so I believed he had done the same before, like he said, and the others, one by the door, one with the pistol tight by her ear. He clipped her with it when she shouted but the sound leapt into the phone line and was gone.

"A pity," the first man said and took me down to the kitchen.

"What now?" I asked. He had made coffee and I held the cup firm to still my hands. It was no different from when there was a ransom, he said; we waited.

There's an old book from the Nineties called *The Tipping Point*. Mum had a copy. It was a book she held dear, alongside *The Bean Trees* and *A Practical Guide to Companion Planting*. She said it gave her hope that little things could make big ripples. Its optimistic patter reassured her, I guess, while the weather got wilder and she raised her daughter and got her gardens growing.

I hadn't thought about that book for years but in those bewildering days I remembered it. It wasn't just us, of course that were tipping things, there were thousands of other groups all around the world, a great web of pressure and effort and hope that had been growing for decades, all pushing, in the same direction. Sooner or later something had to give. We just applied a bit of celebrity heat in the right place at the right time.

Maybe Mum remembered that book too, when she gave me her terse, four letter message.

She'd chosen it carefully from among all the words she could have gasped at me in that heartbeat before they yanked the phone away. She might have hidden her Masters in Plant Biology and her fluency in Hindi

315

behind old plaid shirts and gardening gloves, but she always had an abundance of brainpower.

She knew she'd made it easy for them, slipping away from her protection. She knew I'd ditch it all in a moment to save her, that they'd got to me the best way they could. And she knew she was the only one who could stop me. Maybe. If she told me not 'love!' or 'help!' but 'DON'T!'

It stunned me, the same urgent bark she'd used when I was little and poked a knife at a plug socket. The same word and tone as when I'd tried to catch a sparrow in the net she'd given me for catching cabbage whites to release at the park. Not that the sparrow would have hurt me, but she knew how broken I would be if I trapped and injured it. 'Don't' she'd said then, firm as thunder, to save me from myself.

A man's voice followed hers on the phone, blurred with fury, then the insolence of the dial tone in my ear.

I looked at the phone, silenced. I don't remember dropping it. I just found myself on my knees, face wet with tears. Then Masumi rushing over, pulling me up, saying things I couldn't make out, my mind not letting anything in over the memory of my mum's voice, as if the sound of it in my mind could hold back the tide of the world, stop time, save her, even though she'd told me not to.

There was a lot she'd disapproved of - my coke years and my celebrity shags and even my moving out, finally, to the Dock - not because I was leaving home, but because Clarence House didn't have a garden. She might have disapproved but she'd never tried to forbid me. The only times she'd ever told me 'Don't' had been to protect me.

"Ruby," Michael said when finally I could stutter my way through what I'd heard, "we'll get her out."

I was on my knees again, my body remembering her holding me, my memory replaying her voice on the phone. 'Don't!' she had commanded me. And when I had got back from Coniston, she'd told me she'd 'take my place in a heartbeat'. The two played over and over, remixed in my head, till I was bent to the ground, hands on my ears crying 'no' to rewind it all.

We had to get her out. Stopping 'Car Dump' to save her would break her heart and shatter the hope she'd kept through everything.

"Can you call the Police?" I said, fighting the panic with every fluttering breath, "and that guy you met at the Ministry. And see who Daisy knows. We have to find her." I got to my feet, willing my legs to work.

"We'll cancel," Michael said, "work out some other way."

'Car Dump' had taken a week to get ready and we only had a week left till they shot their sulphur load. The noise about the Sky-Seed wouldn't stop it alone. If we didn't start 'Car Dump', they would fire their cannons and a line would be crossed. They would subdue the sky and, having once bent it to their will, they would do it again. All the urgency to change our ways would be lost. We would keep burning the oil. Clara would grow up thinking the sky was meant to be white.

We would live out our lives under the dismal clouds they made.

When I was little, on the last day of the first proper holiday we had away together, at Ravenscar, Mum had a sore throat. She took me to the lighthouse anyway because, she said, you never know when you will get another chance. We climbed the spiral stairs round and round and emerged into a magical prism of light, the sun bright through the glass and reflecting in the mirrors. It was high above the sea and we could see for ever. I blinked and laughed in the wonder of it all and watched the gulls wheel below us and above us and span around and around and around with them.

When we went back to Ravenscar, the following year, the lighthouse had been ruled unsafe and closed. We prowled around the base together and had to console ourselves with hot chocolate. Mum had been right. Timing is everything.

We couldn't cancel. But we could delay.

We had picked Saturday because we thought people would find it easier to leave their cars if they didn't have to get to work or school. It was a risk because a weekday rush hour would create a faster gridlock, but making it easy mattered more. If Saturday would work, then so could Sunday. We could delay a day.

Michael was already on the phone and Daisy was barking sharp Scouse through hers at somebody. I couldn't wait for someone else to do it. I had to find her.

"We go tomorrow, instead," I told Masumi, grabbed Daisy by the sleeve and flagged a cab in the street. I rang Mum. It went straight to voicemail. The sound of her was comfort and calamity.

The police were at Mum's before us, unravelling crime scene tape. I pushed past them and ran through the house myself. I found her keys but I couldn't find Mum and I couldn't find Furball. By then I was starting to shake. Another policeman came and made us go outside. She wasn't in the garden. Daisy made more calls, summoning her people to scour the city. One of the policemen brought me the blanket that lived on the back of her couch and put it around my shoulders. It smelt of my cat. I called his name but he didn't come. Neither did my mum.

"We'll go house to house," I told Daisy. The policeman told me they were doing that already. I had to leave it to them. They had the training to find her. Someone might have seen something. They were doing everything they could. It was best if I went home to wait. They would send someone with me. There might be a ransom call.

I didn't want to go home. I wanted to ride the streets calling her name until she heard me and struggled to a window where I would see her. I thought if I started right then, took her old bike and rode in fast, wide loops, for long enough, I would find her.

"We don't even know if you're mam's still in Leeds," Daisy said, wide-eyed at the idea of me rushing off.

Daisy and the policeman who'd brought me the blanket took me home. Two more officers, with a laptop and headphones, were waiting for us. The laptop gave me a new idea. We'd post online that Mum was missing - share her photo everywhere and ask for help. Someone somewhere would know something. As we rode up in the lift, I flicked through my phone to find the clearest picture I had of Mum, then I rang Masumi. When he heard what I was saying, the kind policeman put his hand over mine.

"You can't," he said. "It might panic them."

And so we waited.

When it became afternoon I asked Daisy to go and look for her. She glared, carefully at the three police-men, their laptop wired to my phone, then nodded, and left.

There wasn't another call.

When it got dark, I went down in the lift with one of the police. He watched quietly while I stood by the canal, head back to the sky and called 'where are you?' An up-lit haze of clouds slid across the dark. There was no answering cry. He took me back upstairs.

As I watched daylight leach across the city below me, Daisy came back. At some point in the night the policemen had changed.

We left the new shift to their listening and we drove, in the car Daisy had brought, back to new HQ at the Shop. All the way up through town I kept expecting to see someone who looked like Mum, that would turn out to be a stranger. I didn't see anyone like her at all.

"We'll call it off," Michael said.

It was the only way to be sure. To save her. The only person who'd blame me, for ever, would be Mum.

I thought about the steel of the knife and the lure of the dark slots in the plastic of the socket.

I thought about the tempting flutter of the sparrow around my net.

I thought about her bees.

They led me beyond the front of the stage into the dark unknown.

"Don't!" I said and with her one, short word, I fell.

Everything I had known dropped away, like I would tumble in darkness for ever. My heart screamed. Somehow I was still breathing and still standing. I focussed on that while the dark-bright dapple close to fainting cleared.

"We can't," I said, eventually finding words to place into my terrified breath. "Not if we have to stop this." I waved my arm as if it could encompass all we needed to do. Maybe it was hopeless, fighting something as determined as gravity, but Mum didn't think so. She would never forgive me.

"So...what?" Michael said and he looked afraid. "What the fuck do we do?"

"Unleash chaos," I said.

I posted the Incite at 10.45, 26 hours later than we'd planned. We kept it simple. Tao had organised translations into Spanish and Mandarin, Hindi, Arabic and French.

In English it read:

1 Write 'ENOUGH!' on a piece of paper.

2 Take a car, put the note in the windscreen and drive to a busy road with slow traffic. Blow your horn three times and stop the car in the middle of the street. Take the key, lock the car and walk away.

3 Keep the key safe until you hear the Sky-Seed is stopped. Or mail the keys to your president, prime minister or king.

We listed the postal addresses of every leader we had been able to find. My phone started jumping with messages. It had begun.

"I haven't got a car," I said. There had been a shocking pink Porsche at Brooklands I had meant to buy the day before. I had thought it would look good clogging the ring road on TV. Instead, I had got that call.

We caught a taxi back to Mum's.

All the way the driver swore in Russian at the cars abandoned down Chapeltown Road.

We went to her ridiculous yellow tractor, still parked outside her house. While Daisy spoke to the four policemen waiting there and consoled Jasmine and Hu, distraught with their failure, I took the can of black paint we'd brought. Grim with action, I sprayed 'I Love U Mum' over the back window and the bonnet.

Masumi posted pictures of me with the tractor on HeadSpace and told the world Mum had been taken. I didn't care what the police said. There might still be time to save her.

A woman Mum's age in a leather jacket and the young guy with the Doberman came out of their houses. I put my note in the windscreen and climbed into the tractor cockpit, Daisy and Masumi wedged either side of the seat because I insisted on driving, even though I could barely see for tears. The woman and the Doberman guy got into their own cars and followed us in convoy. I blared the horn and theirs blared back and by then we were on Chapeltown Road and there were dozens of cars with their horns sounding and people stopping and getting out. Eight young women, all long brown limbs, spilled out of a red estate car, yelling my name.

I climbed out of the cab on to the bonnet and sang out 'Mum!' joining my voice to all the horns and all the shouting so she would hear us and be saved.

Nothing happened.

Even though there were curtains we had to keep the lights off when it got dark. I did not mean to sleep but I was woken on the sofa in the lounge, by two of the men arguing.

"Not until we're sure," I told them and lay back down as if I was going to sleep some more but I prayed instead.

Once it was daylight, we put the TV on. The first man had the remote and ranged through the channels like a coyote along a fence, looking for a way forward. Nothing had happened.

As the morning ticked away it became harder to hold my mind back from rushing to triumph. I had done my part and now must pray for patience while the Lord did his work.

I heard one of the men in the kitchen and then he brought us a hot dog each wrapped in a thin, white slice of bread. Oil soaked through the bread and burned my fingers. I looked down to see where I could put the sausage I did not want and when I looked back up it had started.

The news showed a helicopter above the streets of Leeds, choked with abandoned cars. Pictures from cell phones in London and Delhi and LA followed, filled with the same. There were police cars caught in it and some cars trapped with drivers still in them, shouting. Policemen walked among the empty vehicles and wrote license plate numbers into notebooks.

I found I had knelt on the carpet so the first man had to step round me when he left the room. I followed him back up to the bedroom and he nodded once at the man with the gun who pulled her hood off then shot up underneath her chin. The blood and mess arced high across the pearly paper.

It was a much brighter red than in the movies and thick with her flesh. I thought she would fall but the ropes still held her up in the chair. You could walk in the room and think she was unhurt except she wasn't. We had killed her. Everything in the room seemed still except my body which pounded like I was running and pricked like I would faint.

The first man took my elbow, turning me to the stairs. He said the other men would clean up. Outside, among the roses, I realised it could not have happened. She was supposed to choose her momma. Instead she had led thousands into devilry. I turned back to him, my mouth full of foolish questions; perhaps we had called the wrong number? Perhaps she was still alive despite the blood?

He pushed past me before I could speak.

"Vanish, now," he said, his face fierce. I followed but by the time I reached the gate he was gone. By then I knew I had failed.

We left the tractor in the middle of Harehills crossroads and walked fast, Daisy and Masumi and me, past the marooned cars and the disbelieving drivers stuck between them. We cut west, over Scott Hall Road and through the cricket club. Daisy pulled a brown striped beanie from a pocket and made me pull it over my hair. Masumi's thumbs flickered as she walked, posting the video of me ditching the tractor.

It was all about the numbers. We needed a lot of cars, fast, more than they could tow away, more than there would be trucks to take them or places to store them. We needed enough to close the roads.

When we got to Buslingthorpe Lane, where the stone walls leap the Meanwood Beck, I stopped, the breath staccato in my chest, fear, adrenalin and disbelief drugging my veins. I held the tractor keys very tight in my hand over the low stone wall and I watched the slide and tumble of the beck below, swollen from the repeated bashings of sudden rain. The keys twisted as they fell, her acorn fob turning and tumbling. As they splashed into the slipstream of the current, I knew she had gone too.

Daisy grabbed me around the shoulders as I cried out and between them they half carried me to The Primrose. She sat me at a table with a pint, Masumi holding my hand, while she rang Michael. I could hear his voice, thin and fractured through the phone speakers, telling us to stay away. There were military police surrounding the Shop. Burt had been tracking the radios so they'd got everyone out, just in time.

"They know it was us," Masumi shrugged, her voice rough with pride.

I was shaking and the sight of the beer had made me feel sick so we walked the three miles to Grandad's. I wished I'd brought my bike. I could have cycled ahead of the fear and grief in gulps of speedy air - fled into snatches of normality before it all caught up with me again.

Daisy and Masumi waited outside, standing anxiously next to the bench by the flower bed as if the aged were waiting to grab me. A blackbird was singing in the holly tree. The receptionist knew me but barely glanced from her television. The screen was full of cars. Grandad was up, in the chair in his room, the blanket I'd knitted him over his knees. He opened his eyes when I went in and took the headphones from his ears.

"Pink Floyd," he said, fumbling for the pause.

I asked him which album and we talked about Syd for a while and then I told him they'd taken Mum and I'd called their bluff. It turned out he was having an away day, after all. He patted my hand and said 'That's nice, dear'. Then he put the headphones back on and pressed play.

"You tell him, boss?" Daisy asked, at my shoulder the moment I stepped outside. I nodded. I'd told him. And to be honest, right then, there was comfort he hadn't understood. Even Grandad's love for me might have limits. If it did, I didn't want to find them. His confusion cosseted him and protected me. It's only now, writing this, that I wonder if he'd hidden in his dementia to protect me. He asks for her sometimes, but then he still asks for his mum too and he hasn't seen her in nearly thirty years.

Michael had messaged Masumi directions to an abandoned gym in the top of the Core Centre so we trekked through Burley, keeping to the back streets, then cut amongst the hospital buildings. The roads were almost empty by then, like a scene from *The Walking Dead* where a city is scattered with abandoned cars but all the people are gone. Somewhere a siren blared and a police motorbike came towards us, riding the far pavement. We ducked into an alley and hid in the smell of pee till it had gone.

We ran behind the library then across into St Anne's Street, like Michael had told us. There were police checks at the doors to The Light so we hurried past, risked Albion and the Headrow, running full tilt by the time we reached King Charles and the fire-escape doors. Burt had rigged them with a videocam and lock release.

We were too out of breath to talk as we climbed the five echoing concrete flights.

The gym weights and machines had all gone, but you could still see the indents in the carpet. There wasn't any furniture. The dozen volunteers who had stayed with us sat or sprawled on the floor, as far as they could get from the windows. Burt was cross legged behind a laptop and Chloe lay on her stomach watching down into Albion Street through the glass with a pair of binoculars.

"We left cameras up at the Shop," Michael said, waving us to stay close to the innermost wall. "They haven't found them yet." Burt rolled to his feet and came over.

"Have you got a laptop for me?" I asked.

We hacked our demand for the Sky-Seed to be scrapped into every news site in the UK and onto every MPs' HeadSpace page. We emailed it to every journalist and every politician and every civil servant.

Masumi had printed thousands of posters and, during the week, we'd sent them to as many volunteers as we could find addresses for and to every flyposting company The Carnival Owls had ever used, here and overseas. 'Now!' we told them. 'Get them out now!'

After the first few hours the police had the city properly locked down, so we stayed.

We had injected thousands with potent hope but the adrenalin high of protest fades fast. People tire. They

330

weary of taking a stand. Daily life is tough enough. The grind of trying to carry on, in cities seized by cars, would wear everybody out.

Touring taught me stamina. When I have to I can run and run. We needed my staying power to keep everyone on their feet.

We posted more video, shot tight, so no one could identify the room and I called all the journalists we'd spoken to from a phone Burt had rigged so it couldn't be traced. I explained our Incite again and again and we replied to the landslide of comments and questions and every half hour, throughout that long, long day, I called Mum's phone.

Every time I let it ring till it went to the message and I could hear her voice.

I followed him to the gate and looked back at the house but there was nothing there for me to do. Instead, I walked.

I would go eight blocks then find a busy street and a cab to take me away. I was still walking and had lost count of the blocks when my phone rang. As I got it out of my pocket, drops of water pooled on the screen. It was raining. My hands were shaking and even when I saw it was the Bishop's number calling I could not still them enough to answer it. I pushed the phone back in my pocket. It buzzed with a message and still I kept on walking, glad it was raining because if anyone had come by it would have masked my tears.

Eventually I stopped, in a bus shelter. I sat on the narrow seat at the back and dialled the number for the message. I remembered pushing open the heavy oak of Bishop Hamilton's door and kneeling on the rug before him and promising I would not fail. The message said 'Don't come back'.

I took the SIM card out and crushed the plastic case of my phone beneath my heel until it shattered. My fingertips scraped on the sidewalk as I gathered every broken piece and then I pushed them below the fish and chip wrappers in the trash can fixed to the bus stop sign. A few yards down the street I slipped the SIM into my jeans pocket and felt the dog tags.

I gripped them while I walked back to the trash can and pushed them in too. The tiny SIM card I carried, sharp edged between my grazed finger tips, for another two blocks until I saw a drain grate and dropped it down.

When I reached the little row of stores, I could see a small crowd had gathered outside one. There were a dozen or so cars abandoned in the street and the traffic from both directions was trying to share one lane to get past. As I approached the gathered people I thought maybe there was a preacher but they were watching the bank of TV screens in the store window. I couldn't hear the sound but pictures of Her were intercut with the talking head of the newsreader and then they moved to a journalist interviewing the Prime Minister.

A man in a beige padded coat watching next to me spoke, shaking his head.

"You've got to admire the lass," he said, "now anything could happen."

I went down the alley behind the shop, past the dumpsters, and was sick. The alley led to a scrap of park with ragged trees, a rusted roundabout and a bench with most of the slats missing. I didn't need to be comfortable so I sat down there while the people walked their dogs and the day got dark around me. I thought about Ms Smith in the tower and remembered the number she had given me but there weren't any words to say if I dialled it. I wanted to pray but when I closed my eyes all I could see was the blood and I was too ashamed.

When it was truly dark I went back to the TV shop. Most of the screens had photos or footage of Ruby. I looked at them and felt she was a stranger. It didn't seem to matter. The phone box on the corner was bright, its light still working.

She answered on the third ring.

"Momma," I said, "it's me."

It took all week. People died because ambulances couldn't get to them. Houses burned. A few young men looted. But mostly people went to work and took their kids to school. They walked and cycled. They did their laundry and bought what they needed from the emptying shelves and they listened to the news. They heard the Coalition railing and the police helpless.

On the second day, the Coalition declared a state of emergency and sent the army into the towns. They towed cars onto verges and cars into parks but behind the openings they created were just more cars. In some places, streets were cleared but people dumped fresh cars in them overnight. Everywhere sold out of bikes. The squaddies leant against lampposts or sat on kerbs, smoking. They knew they were outnumbered. We hid away, stayed high, flitting from apartment to empty office, under hoodies and sunglasses, and always posting.

I kept calling Mum and whenever I slept I jolted awake, to try again.

On the third day they issued the warrant for my arrest, under 9/11 laws, and the news sites crashed with comments. Plenty raged against me, against us and the 'Car Dump', but more, a lot more, called for the Coalition to go.

The six o'clock news showed Beijing and Washington, Mumbai and Sydney still locked with cars. The tanks couldn't get through. Helicopters circled overhead. In Bristol, two looters were shot.

The Coalition stopped giving interviews.

Then, in a brief, binary flicker of black and white, a three line release on the newswires announced the Sky-Seed was cancelled, for 'technical reasons'.

We had won.

The UN called a Special Assembly to shape a moratorium on sky-seeding, like the Convention on chemical weapons. The Internet boiled with demands for fresh democracy. Scalded Governments everywhere scrambled to promise an oil-free future, fast - our Coalition included.

We asked people to go back to their cars.

Some never did. Perhaps they decided they didn't need a car any more. Or perhaps they were amongst the people who died that week, their bodies carried on doors to the crematorium by the neighbours who found them.

I didn't have a body to bury.

I waited till the streets were nearly clear before I went back to the tractor. I carried armfuls of poppies and foxgloves I had cut from her garden. I laid them across the bonnet and the roof, lit a taper to the petrol tank and sat on the verge, watching while it burned.

They never found her. The police tried but eventually it was one of Daisy's team, a bouncer turned PI, who worked out where she'd been held. Laurence held my hand, lost in his huge paw, and told me they'd pieced together the route they'd taken from CCTV footage. They tried every house in the street. At one place there was no answer so they broke in. It looked as if whoever held her had left in a hurry.

"There were takeaway boxes and stuff," he said, "Typical hostage set up, but Ruby...I'm sorry. There was blood too, like you get from a gunshot."

"It might not have been her," I said but I knew it was. The police would test the blood and then there would be proof but I had known she was gone as I dropped her keys. Maybe they'd dumped her in the Aire. She wouldn't have minded. She'd have laughed and pronounced herself fish food. Mum always had an easy view of mortality. She saw people as perennials - sooner or later they die. Perhaps it's a gardener thing. I haven't inherited it.

If she had to be gone, I would have preferred to tuck her in the earth, but I couldn't. So later, after the insanity of the first day of the UN Assembly, in a stifling room because I insisted, zealous with grief, that we would NOT talk until the air conditioning was off, after

I left the NGOs to make sure the delegates met their promises, I came back to Leeds. I collected Elsie from Patrick's tender repairs and spent the day in Mum's garden. I planted delphinium and lupin seeds and I planted peas and beans and I buried her copy of *The Tipping Point* among the first of the dahlias and I sang to her all the songs from my childhood - *The Bear Went Over the Mountain* and *Lady Marmalade, The Lion Sleeps* and *You are My Sunshine, Paper Planes* and *If I Let You Go* and eventually, through my singing and my crying and my laughing as I remembered her, I felt a hard, furry head butt the back of my leg. I scooped him up and cried in his fur and sang till I got cold.

Then I came in. I had a long bath and I wrapped myself in her robe and I sat down here, in her reading chair, with my legs curled up, like she used to sit, and I began to write it down so her part in this, lifting a little girl up to see in a nest and everything since, is known.

THE ENCORE

I t's scorching beyond the shade. Mediterranean hot. Too hot for Leeds, even in August. My skin is turning pink at just the idea of stepping into the sunshine and lights baking the stage. For now I can watch, from the sticky shadows, through the chink I've found in the backdrop curtains. Temple Newsham smells of suntan lotion and beer, or rather the crowd does. My city is out to celebrate and my band is topping the bill. The people are banked right up across the park, swathes of waving arms and floppy hats stretching past the row of azure flags that rim the sloping lawns. Behind the flags are the trees and above the deep green oaks and horse chestnuts is the brilliant, baking sky itself - intense as hope.

Savages are nearing the end of their set but there's time before The Owls need to muster. I track down Daisy and Michael at the backstage bar. They're both flirting with Jamie xx who's up next and should be getting his shit together. I shoo him off and drag them to my chink. They peer through and I picture again the vivid sprawl of summer they can see.

Michael tells me it will keep getting hotter. But – and this is hard to believe – this past year we managed to not layer any more tog ratings into our climate duvet. It will get hotter, but, if we can keep up the good work, the heating will slow, then settle. It's not a done deal - Australia's emissions went up, even with Perth empty, and the fracking companies are suing everyone. There's still the last 200 years' of smoke-stack damage to sweat out, before the gauges stop rising. It won't be easy and it might take us till we're old, but most governments, convict colonies excepted, are now acting like it's urgent. They proved more scared of their people, and the power we can wield when we shut our wallets and ditch our cars, than of the corporations - or their evangelical stooges.

So we're here to celebrate, with a solar-powered show.

I leave Daisy and Michael watching the crowd and go to work on my breathing. At the bar, I find myself a director's chair with a good view of the backstage mingling, stick my Docs up on a handy hay bale and summon a beer from a cute, star-struck waiter. Yes, I am looking again, but not touching. Not yet. I've got knitting to keep my hands busy. It might be hot today but winter is coming, with promises of brutal snow, so I'm making Michael a beanie to match his favourite, tasteless cardigan. I knit and do my breathing exercises and at the end of every row I take a swig of beer.

It has been a whole year.

I still haven't packed up her house. Instead I crammed my old room full of her books and clothes and the ornaments I never liked - the curly-iron candle holder and the fake-African figurine. I took down her bedroom curtains and put away her blankets too. Behind the door. Claiming the space. Moving in.

I redecorated, shifting the colours from her summer yellows to grey, shot through with the hot, dark purple of a summer storm. It gives me calm to write.

It's been the same in the garden. She always said you were meant to live a year in a new home so you could learn the surprises of the seasons before making any change. This home isn't new. I know what grows. I've kept the plum tree but mostly I've planted dramatic shapes that stay green through winter. The dahlias I'll unearth before the frost and pack away, then plant out for her again, each year.

Sometimes, when I'm working in the garden, the hurt of losing her will get too much. I'll set aside my trowel or secateurs and lay my body on the ground, so I can't fall. Then I'll take the memory of her I've found, behind the bean stalk or underneath the flower pot, and I'll tune it into the seed of a song. I can't bring her back and

I can't rewrite the day I let her die but I can make, in her honour, the best damned album I have ever made.

I keep the Group part time now, so there's space for The Owls. When the charges against me were down-graded to disturbing the peace, the Coalition desperate not to martyr me, we moved back into the Shop. I was still bloody-minded with grief and commissioned a doz-en guys with pneumatic drills to destroy the carpark at the back. We've made it a veggie garden, with hens and Mum's hives, abuzz with new bees. I'm bad at leaving Furball on his own so I take him along with me, in a special basket on the front of my bike, so he can see where he's going. He presides over the digging or sprawls in the shopfront window, to supervise the street.

We use the Shop for afterschool classes on climate care and wind turbines and growing food. It will take a while for curriculums to catch up, so we fill the gap for now. We teach peaceful protest too, just in case. I leave that to Michael. I teach guitar. (That's a secret. I'm not supposed to teach anything at all until my probation's over. I can't help it if the kids grab ukes whenever I play and copy what I do.)

Masumi streams the legit classes live, as they unfold. Then she edits the best segments into nuggets for us, and the other centres like us, here and overseas, to show. Parents, who come to drop off their kids, often stay. Four of them teach now, too. Most people know some-thing useful.

The pre-schooler sessions we keep upbeat - muddy forays into nature, mostly. Stellar's brought Clara since we began. She starts 'big school' next month. Even though she'll be one of the youngest, she is more than ready - when she's not bragging I'm her aunty, she's scaring the littlest ones with her dark tales of the last polar bear.

Luckily kids handle the grim stuff better than grown-ups. If we weren't so good at avoidance we wouldn't have got in this mess.

I reach the end of the row of what can, most kindly, be called mustard and change yarn. I'm adding a gold band eight rows up. In my eyes, Michael is a rock star and deserves a little bling.

The lurex is the same soft gold as the envelope the card from my supposed dad came in. The stranger's writing was as anonymous as any other Masumi might have plucked from that day's sack of fan mail and hate mail, the week we moved back into the Shop. He had sketched, in black ink, a hawthorn tree on a limestone crag. I've seen worse drawing.

Inside he had written 'I am sorry it took me so long. If it's not too late, I would like to buy my daughter a beer' and a mobile number.

I closed the card and put it back in the envelope. That night, I slid it under my pillow where it will stay until I know if I will call.

I begin the new row, counting the stitches as I draw the air – one, two, three – into the width and breadth of my lungs, and out again.

On stage, the xx have finished. Fate is calling - it's our turn to play.

....

ABOUT THE AUTHOR

Katherine Dewar was raised surrounded by books, computers and animals. She studied politics and worked in Leeds before emigrating to Aotearoa NZ, where she runs a business and volunteers for the Green Party.

Katherine made up stories using toy creatures before she could wield a pen. When she began writing she was supported by her schools, by the Arvon Foundation and by her endlessly encouraging parents. She has been writing ever since.

Prior to *Ruby and the Blue Sky*, Katherine has had a short story published in the Black Swan collection, *Home*.

MEANWHILE, IN THE REAL WORLD ...

Ruby and the Blue Sky is fiction but climate change is real, rapid and scary as hell. We can still duck the worst of it, and go for a happier ending, if we all act together - fast. The current slow change makes polluting options, like sky-seeding (which is a real world thing), more likely.

If you want to know how we can change hop online, join a local climate action group or try these non-fiction titles:

This changes everything by Naomi Klein
Postcapitalism by Paul Mason
Another world is possible if ... by Susan George
Winning the carbon war by Jeremy Leggett
Fleeing Vesuvius by Gillian Fallon (editor)
The Third Industrial Revolution by Jeremy Rifkin

Thanks to my Green Party Aotearoa whanau for these suggestions. Discover more at www.KatherineDewar.net.

THANKYOU

This novel wouldn't have happened without my inspiring sister Sarah and her persuasive deadlines – thanks sis! Thanks also Mum, Iona and Mark for being insightful early readers, Fiona and Diana for copy-editing help, Janine and Karen for proofing, Paula, Nicola and Glenys for expert guidance in the world of books and to Keely for making my cover look great.

Thank you to everyone who has ever said an encouraging thing to me about anything I have written, especially Claire P, Leonie, Sheena, Rebeccah, Claire I, Jacqui, Savage, Chris, Amanda, Helen, Elaine, Bob, Will, Rachel, Richard, Kate, Jo, Hinerangi, Maia, Casta and Asti, who wrote me my first ever fan letter. Endless gratitude to Dame Fiona Kidman whose wisdom I draw on daily and to both my writing class cohort and my local writing group for fellowship along the way.

And of course thanks to my darling Tony who makes me laugh and sustains me in so many ways.

Kia ora koutou.

A NOTE FROM KATHERINE

Dear reader, if you have enjoyed *Ruby and the Blue Sky* in any way please do share your thoughts on GoodReads or Amazon or anywhere else you like. Reviews are an important way for independently published authors, like me, to be discovered by new readers. If you can post a review you will have my undying gratitude.

If you enjoyed *Ruby and the Blue Sky* I would love to hear from you. Please email me@katherinedewar.net. This is my first published novel and I thrive on feedback.

If you use Twitter please do follow me: @KatherineDewar.

You can find more about this book and share it from Facebook.com/Ruby-and-the-Blue-Sky and at **www.KatherineDewar.net.**